Blue Freedom

BY

SANDRA PEUT

BLUE FREEDOM

ISBN 978-0-9555283-5-4

First published in Great Britain in 2010 by Rose & Crown Books
www.roseandcrownbooks.com (Sunpenny Publishing)

MORE BOOKS FROM ROSE & CROWN:
Embracing Change, by Debbie Roome
A Flight Delayed, by KC Lemmer
Redemption on the Red River, by Cheryl R. Cain (coming soon)
Heart of the Hobo, by Shae O'Brien (coming soon)

MORE BOOKS FROM SUNPENNY PUBLISHING:
Dance of Eagles, by JS Holloway
Going Astray, by Christine Moore
My Sea is Wide, by Rowland Evans
The Mountains Between, by Julie McGowan
Just One More Summer, by Julie McGowan

Dedication

This novel is dedicated to all those who have longed to find true freedom in their lives.

Thanks

As with any project, the writing of *Blue Freedom* has involved many steps: writing, then shelving; writing some more, editing, and then more shelving!

Thanks must firstly go to all my ever-patient and long-suffering friends and family for believing that somehow, someday, I would finally FINISH! This group of course includes our informal "Writers' Group" of girlfriends, who delighted in plotting hilarious endings to my unfinished manuscript; and my father, Peter Findlay, who spurred me on by making a bet about who could finish their project first to a marketable standard. Dad, I think you won by a whisker!

Special mention must go to my cousin Adele, who went "above and beyond" in her editing efforts. Thanks also to ex-diving master Lloyd Brooks, for his very useful information about diving and being lost at sea.

I am very grateful to Jo Holloway, my editor and publisher, of Rose & Crown Books, for taking a chance on me and seeing the potential in my raw talent. I've really appreciated your insight, encouragement, and sense of humour.

But there are two main people who particularly deserve my gratitude: my husband Craig, for his constant support (especially in looking after our four energetic children while I wrote) and for believing in my dreams; and to my Creator, who gave me an active imagination, a love of words, and a desire to communicate His heart to others.

Prologue

Somewhere in the Pacific Ocean

He never should have swum off alone. What had at first appeared to be a shallow indentation in the coral-encrusted rock had turned out to be a cave. The diver had spent almost twenty minutes exploring the cavern and its colourful marine life—but when he emerged, the rest of the group was gone.

Checking his diving watch again, he fought against the rising panic. Everything he had learnt in his years of scuba diving flashed through his mind. *Stay calm and breathe normally. Stay in the same place and wait to be rescued. Never swim away from your diving partners.*

He'd been completely stupid. But the inside of the cave was so fascinating, and he'd wanted to take a closer look so he could describe it to his fiancée. With her writer's creative appreciation of all things unique and beautiful, she would love it.

Now he wondered if he would ever see her again.

He'd still had some oxygen left in his tanks, but had discarded them, along with the weights in his diving belt, after he surfaced. There was no sense in trying to tread water or swim with all that weight on his back. And even without the oxygen, he had little hope of reaching land, over ten kilometres away.

He would just have to swim. And pray.

The alarm had surely been sounded by now. His rescuers had probably already begun the search.

Chapter 1

Brisbane, Australia

4) The Blame Game
The final, and perhaps most damaging, form of self-sabotage is that of blaming ourselves. "We all recognise we're our own worst critic," says psychologist Dr Sarah Green. "The problem is that external messages—such as those from media advertising, and even from family and friends—can serve to reinforce our own negative thought patterns."

The key, according to Dr Green, is deciding to be kinder to yourself. "By making small, positive changes to the way you think and speak, it can be possible to stop negative self-blaming patterns."

Learning to change old habits and eliminate these four areas of self-sabotage can help you move on into the successful and confident future you deserve.

"There! Finally finished!" Bella Whitman typed the last few words with a flourish, before moving her neck around in slow circles in a vain attempt to work out some of the knots. "Typing gives me cramps," she complained, lifting her arms up to the ceiling in a languorous stretch.

"Well, writing *is* your chosen profession," Krista—her housemate—reminded her as she padded past the kitchen table to the refrigerator. "You just have to put up with the occupational hazards that go along with it," she mumbled around a bite of apple.

"You can talk!" Bella retorted, leaning back in the chair, her eyes closed. She lifted up the tangled mass of her chestnut curls, allowing the air to cool her neck. "Sticking people with needles every day sounds pretty hazardous to me."

Krista reached over and playfully tugged her friend's hair. "It's called *phlebotomy,* for your information. And at least it's a job with a steady income." The end of her reply faded as she walked through to the lounge. Bella smiled. Krista was no doubt watching her favourite afternoon soap on TV. Like clockwork.

Bella sighed wearily as she began gathering up her paperwork, now strewn across the table's surface. She enjoyed being a freelance writer—loved the freedom, the challenges, the chance to express her creativity. But the constant pressure of deadlines and lack of secure income took their toll.

"What I need is a holiday," she murmured, rubbing her blurry eyes. Her last holiday had been a couple of years ago, right before—

Bella squeezed her eyes tightly shut, trying in vain to block out the memories of Andrew. His smile, those chocolate brown eyes, the way he would look at her just before they kissed ...

But then he was gone, disappearing so suddenly, leaving Bella alone and crying on a Pacific island beach. Wondering why the men in her life were always taken from her prematurely—asking the heavens what she'd done to make God so angry.

As Bella started making dinner in an effort to distract her thoughts, she realised she was still asking those same questions now, a couple of years on. Memories swirled about her as she sliced an onion. She couldn't be sure if her tears were from the fumes or her depressing thoughts.

With a sigh, she put down the knife decisively. "I need a change," she announced to the kitchen walls. "They say a change is as good as a holiday—don't they?"

"Are you talking to yourself again?" Krista's head popped around the edge of the door. "Writers," she mumbled to herself, shaking her blonde head in mock frustration as she came all the way into the room.

Bella ignored the comment, choosing to focus on the diced onions now frying in a pan.

"I just saw a new magazine advertised on the TV," Krista casually mentioned, sneaking a carrot slice from the cutting board. "It's called *Healthy Lifestyle*, and it's published right here in Brisbane."

Bella lifted her head and looked at her friend. "A new magazine? That might help." Work had always been a source of welcome reprieve.

"Help what? And haven't you conquered enough magazines already?" Krista asked, chomping on the carrot. "Never satisfied ... it must be a writer thing," she flung over her shoulder, returning to the TV.

Bella smiled to herself as she emptied some tuna into the pan. She would make some enquiries tomorrow.

Two days later

A sharp rap on the open office door interrupted Ethan Gray's busy focus. He sighed impatiently, lifting his eyes from his weekly planner to glare at the unwanted intruder. "Make it snappy!" he barked.

The usually self-confident office assistant visibly shrank before the editor's obvious irritation. "Umm ... Gemma's asked me to tell you that because of the big fitness-wear fashion shoot next week, we've had to reschedule October's planning meeting to this morning. Nine-thirty." She hesitated. "Is that okay with you?"

Ethan checked his planner, noting his 9:30 am appointment with a freelancer—Bella Whitman. "Shouldn't be a problem," he replied without looking up. "There's nothing here that can't be put off."

The woman turned with a relieved smile, and started to walk out through the doorway. "Susan," Ethan called, halting her in her tracks. The editor's voice was like granite, hard and brittle. "I expect to be given more than fifteen minute's notice of any future schedule changes. Understand?"

Susan stammered her assent before hurrying from the room. She almost tripped on her ridiculously high heels in her haste.

Ethan smirked as he observed her discomfort. Women! They were only good for one thing.

Chapter 2

With a screech of brakes and a sharp jolt the train pulled into Central Station. Pneumatic doors wheezed open as Bella hurriedly grabbed her shoulder bag, water bottle and coat. Although the blazing sun promised a warm spring day, she never could trust those air-conditioned office buildings.

The rush of commuters streaming from the train caught Bella up in its midst, carrying her out onto the platform and up the escalators to the street level.

She waited with the crowd for the traffic lights to change. It was a gorgeous day. The cloudless sky, as yet untinged by city smog, reminded her of the cornflowers in her grandmother's garden. A slight breeze played with wisps of her hair that had strayed from the high chignon. With a sigh of annoyance at her unruly curls, Bella attempted to tuck the errant hair behind her ears as she crossed the street. She was beginning to feel anything but professional, and the interview was less than an hour away.

Bella continued down Edward Street, which fell steeply towards the city. A few minutes later, with her feet already beginning to ache from the high heeled sandals she'd carefully chosen to match her ivory suit, she found herself at a small café and tumbled into the nearest seat.

She caught her breath while waiting for the waiter to bring her order of a skinny cappuccino and blueberry

muffin.

muffin. She had just under an hour before her interview with Ethan Gray, editor-in-chief of *Healthy Lifestyle*. Strangely, her stomach twisted in knots just thinking about it. Bella was normally confident and self-assured—or, at least, she managed to convey that impression to those around her.

Perhaps it was because she seriously wanted to make a good impression and obtain some new avenues of work. Life seemed so ... so *unfulfilling* at the moment, and she didn't quite know why.

Actually, she had a fair idea, but Bella had always shied away from being too brutally honest with herself. Now though, the sentiments crowded in ...

It had to have something to do with Andrew, she thought, stirring sugar into the frothing cup the waiter set before her. She'd never felt the same since he had gone; she was stuck in limbo, a prisoner of her past.

Her eyes flitted around the café, scanning desperately in an attempt to distract her from the painful images threatening to invade.

A man two tables over caught her eye, mainly because he was obviously wishing he was somewhere else. His toe tapped restlessly, causing the waves of his windswept blonde hair to bob in time to the rhythm. He sighed, checked his watch, then looked over to the door.

Their eyes met for just a moment, Bella noting that his were an oceanic shade of blue. She thought she detected the hint of a smile on his lips before he rose and walked out onto the street.

He must have been waiting for someone, she thought, an unexpected twinge of envy causing her to frown. It had been a long time since she'd had a coffee date or dinner with a man. Too long.

Bella remembered the last time only too well: kissing Andrew goodbye at the pier, making dinner plans for later that evening at their hotel restaurant ...

"I'll be back in four hours," he'd reassured her. "Sure you don't want to come?"

Bella wrinkled her nose. "You know how I hate sharks."

"Well, I'm sure you'll be able to find something to amuse yourself with." Andrew's brown eyes twinkled.

"I don't know," she pretended to pout. "There's hardly anything to do here—only swimming, or going to the gym, maybe a massage in the day spa." She grinned, giving him a playful swat on the shoulder as he turned to go. "I'll miss you," she called after him.

Andrew looked back at her with his dark eyes, blew her a kiss ...

And that was the last time she ever saw him.

The loud cry of a hungry toddler at the next table rudely jerked Bella out from beneath the dark clouds of past memories. A glance at her watch sent her into a mad panic. *Nine twenty-five!* She drained the last of her now lukewarm coffee, stuffed the untouched muffin into her bag, and raced down the footpath towards the imposing office building that housed *Healthy Lifestyle.*

Too late, Bella realised she had left without paying for her snack! Her cheeks flamed with embarrassment as she determined to return and pay her bill. But not now ... it would have to wait until after the interview.

It was 9:35 am by the time she stepped out of the elevator at the 10th floor suite of offices. She felt hot and frazzled, not at all like the organised, professional image she had hoped to project.

"Excuse me ..." Bella approached an efficient-looking secretary behind a marble-topped counter. The woman, identified as Susan by her gold name badge, seemed perfectly suited to the opulent surroundings. Her blonde hair was swept up in a classic French roll, and her tailored suit cried out 'expensive'.

Susan looked up from beneath long eyelashes, examining Bella as though she was an unwelcome insect.

Bella rushed on: "I have a nine-thirty appointment with the editor, Mr Gray. I'm a little late."

'Miss Perfect' gave her a decidedly blank stare.

"Umm ... there should be a record somewhere." Bella self-consciously smoothed her hair down with one hand. "I confirmed the appointment just yesterday. My name's

Bella Whitman ... if that helps ...” Her voice trailed off. She doubted if anything short of her being a celebrity, or a Pulitzer Prize winner, would get her past this woman.

The receptionist was clicking through screens on her computer. A light suddenly went on in the skillfully made-up eyes, and her whole manner instantly changed.

“Of course, Ms Whitman,” she purred. “You *were* booked in to see Mr Gray this morning.” Bella let out a breath she didn’t even know she was holding.

“However,” the woman paused for effect, her gold pen pointed at Bella from her manicured fingers, “Mr Gray has had to attend a rescheduled meeting this morning. Last minute, you understand. He must not have been able to reach you.” She shrugged, almost as if to blame Bella for being out of contact. “He now won’t be available until after lunch. I suggest you make a new appointment for another day.” Her tone softened slightly at Bella’s disappointed expression. “He *is* a very busy man, you understand.”

Bella was more than disappointed. She was frustrated, even a little angry. This was the last thing she needed right now. But she wasn’t going to give up this easily.

“Could I make a new appointment for later today?” she asked, attempting to keep the tense edge from her tone.

The secretary’s voice was almost sympathetic. “I suppose you could wait here if you have the time. Mr Gray sometimes has a few minutes to spare between meetings, and he usually walks through here to his office.”

Bella gave her a sceptical smile.

“Maybe—just maybe—you might be able to catch him this morning.” Her small attempt at being helpful seemed to leave Susan feeling exhausted, and she merely nodded at Bella’s thanks.

With a sigh, Bella settled down onto the black leather couch opposite the counter, glad that she had brought some articles to work on. She wasn’t very hopeful about her chances, but maybe she could grab the editor at lunch. The man had to eat sometime, didn’t he?

Ethan Gray looked at his watch for the fifth time, barely

suppressing his growing irritation. While planning meetings were vital in running a publication, the other editorial staff completely lacked focus. They would much prefer to discuss wishy-washy topics like the quality of the graphics, than real issues such as the summer holiday feature.

He had managed to keep them vaguely on track, addressing eighty per cent of the matters on the meeting agenda. But when he noticed Gemma, the fashion editor, filling in assistant editor Chloe on her upcoming wedding plans, he lost all patience.

"Okay, everybody!" he barked—a little too harshly, perhaps, but they needed to show some respect. "That's it for today," he continued over the rustle of papers being gathered together. "We'll have a follow-up meeting on Friday. Check your e-mail for the time."

One-thirty! Ethan fumed silently as he strode from the room, oblivious to the annoyed glances shared between his co-workers. You would think they had nothing else to do but gossip all day!

He dumped his organiser and notes on his desk, and nodded to Susan on his way out. "Lunch. Back in an hour."

"Mr Gray!" she called after him, pausing at his audible sigh of frustration. "Uh ... there's someone here to see you. Ms Whitman—your nine-thirty appointment."

Ethan's lips had already begun to form a negative reply, when he noticed the attractive woman seated on the reception couch. Wisps of chestnut curls framed her oval face, with creamy skin, a soft blush, and bright blue eyes that looked up at him expectantly—all counterpointed by an elegantly tailored ivory skirt-suit covering a body that curved in all the right places.

"Ethan Gray," he smiled, cranking up the charm as he extended his hand. "How would you like to join me for lunch?"

Chapter 3

Before she knew it, Bella found herself whisked out of the office building and seated at The Blue Perch, a nearby upmarket restaurant specialising in seafood and Mediterranean fare. She was still wondering why Ethan hadn't notified her about her appointment's cancellation—she did have her mobile phone with her, after all—but he didn't mention it.

Apart from this omission, he was the perfect gentleman—opening the door for her, and seating her in style at their table. That, and the fact that his brown eyes never left her face, was decidedly unsettling.

"So what got you into writing, Bella?" Ethan asked after they had ordered. "I'm familiar with all the bare details from your résumé, but I want to hear about the *real* Bella." He leaned forward, gazing at her intently—a little too intently, Bella thought.

Flushing slightly, she took a steadying breath and tried to focus on the question.

"It's something I've always wanted to do," she began slowly, fiddling with her water glass. "Ever since I can remember, I've been writing. Poems, short stories, journalling ... Just the sight of a blank page or computer screen excites me with its possibilities." Bella stopped, embarrassed at her candour. The editor didn't want to hear all the details of her passion.

But when she dared to sneak a glance at him under

lowered lashes, he seemed totally absorbed. If she didn't know better, she could have sworn he was interested in other, more personal possibilities beyond their business relationship.

Ethan gazed at her earnestly, his low voice encouraging Bella to go on. Smiling a little self-consciously, she continued: "I started off doing advertising and PR in Melbourne, getting in on the ground floor of copywriting. I enjoyed the work, but it still lacked that creative spark I was looking for. So after four years, I made a leap of faith to move to Queensland and write freelance." She paused, silently contemplating the huge understatement.

"That's quite a move," Ethan acknowledged, "and you've certainly had some success." He cleared his throat slightly, signalling an unspoken shift from personal to business matters. "What do you think you could bring to *Healthy Lifestyle*?"

Bella hesitated, looking down at the linguini marinara that had just been placed before her. She really wanted this job—needed more work to bury herself in, as a distraction from too much internal reflection. Not that it had ever really helped.

"Well," she began, taking a deep breath, "I've had a broad base of experience writing health and fitness articles, mainly for magazines with a similar focus to *Healthy Lifestyle*. I'm pedantic about thorough, fact-based research, and I've never yet missed a deadline. I'm big on teamwork, which I feel is essential as it's a foundation of both the advertising and publication industries."

Bella relaxed slightly, gaining confidence as she noted Ethan's slight nods of approval. "I have a special interest in alternative therapies and herbal medicine, which are hot topics—" She halted mid-sentence at the sudden cooling of Ethan's expression.

He lost no time in clearing up her startled confusion, his disapproval evident in each clipped word. "I don't think your style is what we're looking for. At *Healthy Lifestyle*, we only publish articles with a more mainstream, medically-based approach. We do *not* advocate treatments based on circumstantial reports or historic folklore."

He finished one of his oysters, looking over at Bella as he wiped his mouth with a napkin. A distinct chill had replaced the warmth of just a moment ago.

Bella sat silently for a moment, stunned. What had brought this on? She had obviously pressed some buttons here. Had Ethan, or perhaps one of his family, been taken in by some quack? All she knew was, she didn't deserve this.

He went on. "I took you for a more educated woman than that, Bella. I can't imagine you would deliberately choose to mislead your readers." He went back to his oysters, communicating an end to the conversation.

Bella could take no more. Her pent-up frustration that had been rising for some weeks had now found an outlet.

"I'm sorry you feel that way," she began, her voice seeming to rise in volume with each word, "but if you had looked at the market research for your demographic, you would know that alternative medicine is a rapidly growing area of interest, with a need for authoritative, factual information!"

Bella stopped momentarily, feeling herself losing control, her face turning red. "It's a pity you're missing out on a broader readership because of narrow-minded opinions."

She stood up, ignoring her untouched linguini and the open stares of the other diners, and was stooping to pick up her bag when Ethan stopped her with a firm hand on her arm.

"Sit down, Bella. Uh—maybe I was a bit Draconian." His forced smile betrayed the effort the admission had cost him.

Bella remained standing, her stony expression unaffected by Ethan's about-face.

"Look, we got off on the wrong foot. Why don't we get together for dinner—when we've both cooled off—and discuss the option of you doing some work for us at *Healthy*—"

"That won't be necessary!" Bella snapped quietly, painfully aware of the scene she was creating. She grabbed her coat and handbag and turned swiftly, but the large tote's leather strap caught on her chair. Her first steps pulled it over with a crash.

Bella's face was now flaming with embarrassment as well as anger as she hurried out the restaurant door and away from fifty pairs of curious eyes.

"Oh, God," she groaned as she half-jogged down the street, trying to get as far away from the humiliating scene as possible. "I've really made a fool of myself this time. What am I gonna do now?"

A flashing reflection in a store window caught her attention—a neon coffee cup sign. *The coffee shop bill!* This day was just getting better and better!

Bella dragged herself across the street and quickly paid the money she owed. Her body—and aching head—was crying out for caffeine, so she ordered another cappuccino and slumped into a chair.

She was still berating herself when the coffee arrived. This had been a stupid idea—it wasn't as if she really needed the extra work. She hadn't even followed the golden rule of evaluating a publication's style and target market, but had just jumped in—uncomfortable high heels and all.

Bella kicked off the offending shoes and sighed. She allowed her mind to drift back over the morning as the caffeine did its work. The only highlight in a frustrating day had been that short, shared smile—really only a glance—with the handsome blonde stranger before her cancelled appointment with Ethan. She could still picture his blue-green eyes, as clear and open as the editor's were dark and shadowed ...

Bella blinked the thoughts away and finished the last of her coffee. The only thing that made her feel better at a time like this was some serious retail therapy.

Ethan made no effort to go after Bella as she stormed out of the restaurant, choosing instead to sit back and enjoy the departing rear view. "Women!" he muttered to himself, nodding politely to several staring diners before going back to his meal.

Women needed to be put in their place, to be told who was boss in the relationship. Or the workplace. Well, same thing, really. Ethan had never held reservations about office dalliances—had even welcomed them—as long as the woman could handle getting fired if it went sour.

He finished the last of his oysters with relish, wondering silently how Bella would react when he made his move.

Chapter 4

The train ride home seemed especially long this afternoon; or maybe it was because she felt so drained. Bella eyed the pile of shopping bags beside her on the seat. She couldn't believe she'd done it again. First, the striking red dress had caught her attention, then the designer jeans ... But the giddy pleasure of the purchases had already passed.

Why did she do these things? Inside, she knew that shopping and overwork wouldn't make anything go away, that they were actually adding to her stress levels. But she didn't know how else to cope.

Sometimes Bella felt as if she was being tossed about like a tiny boat in a storm. It reminded her of a time she was travelling with her family as a child, crossing the Bass Strait from Melbourne to Tasmania during a bout of wild weather. Being thrown about, stumbling, seasick.

Other images flooded in from her childhood. Of a simpler, more innocent time. Going to church. Sunday School songs. *The rains came down as the floods came up ... but the house on the rock stood firm.*

"Mummy, I love Jesus, and Jesus loves me ..."

"Ferny Grove, Ferny Grove Station. All passengers please detrain. This is the end of the line."

Bella woke up with a jolt. She grabbed all her bags automatically, almost dropping them as she stumbled to

her feet

her feet. Still in a daze, she waited in the crush of other passengers to disembark, before beginning the short walk to her house.

Her head was swirling with clouds from the past. Long ago the storms in her life had washed away any last vestige of that young, innocent child, with her simple faith. And now, as an adult, Bella too often felt as if she'd lost her way, so helpless there was nothing she could do but pray.

Except she rarely even did that any more, didn't know what to say.

Who knew if God was really up there, listening? All she knew was that she sure could do with some help.

Bella wearily unlocked the front door and trudged through the narrow entryway into the living room, dumping her bags on the couch. The house was oppressively hot and silent, with the weather being unusually warm for early spring. She opened all the windows and doors, keeping an eye out for Samara, Krista's white chinchilla cat.

Once she was feeling a little cooler, Bella settled down beside the phone for her daily ritual of checking the answering machine messages. Perhaps a magazine editor had called to commission her for a series of articles, giving her something else to focus on instead of lost opportunities at *Healthy Lifestyle.*

There were no messages from editors. A couple of Krista's tennis club friends had called, and so had a frustrated-sounding telemarketer. Then the gentle voice of Bella's mother, Jennifer Whitman, came over the small speaker.

"Bella, darling, just phoning to say hello and see how you're doing. I'll be going out for a while, but give me a call after dinner. I love you."

Bella smiled softly—she loved her mum. She made a mental note to phone her later, and then pressed the machine's button to listen to the last message.

"Hi, Bella. Ethan here." Bella screwed up her nose and hit pause—she was tempted to just delete the message. The man sounded as arrogant and overbearing over the phone as he did in real life.

Her curiosity overran her good sense, and she hit the button again.

"I apologise for our little *misunderstanding*"—he spoke the word as though the problem was all on her side—"at lunch. Why don't you join me for dinner at Mount Coot-tha's Summit Restaurant at eight o'clock? I have a proposal that may interest you. See you then."

Bella felt her earlier anger rising once more. "Proposal?" she almost choked. Ethan obviously disliked her writing style and philosophy, yet he was still trying to offer her work—probably all the boring little jobs that the staff writers couldn't be bothered doing. Well, she was better than that!

She hit the delete button with more force than was necessary.

"The nerve of that man," she fumed to Samara. "First, he charms me by taking me out to lunch, then patronises me for my forward-looking views. And *now* he's talking about proposals!"

She shook her head in disgust, deciding that she needed a good, long run to clear her head.

Bella was just heading out the door, clad in her work-out gear and running shoes, when Krista's purple hatchback pulled into the driveway.

"Hey, Bella," she called out, arms laden with her tennis clothes and work papers. "Ryan and I are going out to watch a movie. You wanna come?"

Ryan was Krista's boyfriend of six months. He was a great guy, but Bella didn't want to intrude on the love-birds.

"No, I probably won't be back in time. I might be going out later, though," she mentioned casually, purely to avoid Krista's nagging that she should get out more. There was a kernel of truth to the statement—she *might* go to dinner—but deep down she knew it would take a miracle for her to voluntarily see Ethan again.

"Have fun!" she flung over her shoulder, jogging down the driveway and out onto the tree-lined street. This was just what she needed. She delighted in the steady cadence of her feet hitting the path. A nice long run would help her sort everything out.

But by the time Bella returned an hour later, red-faced and breathing heavily, she knew that things were anything but sorted out. Her mind had raced as fast as her feet, with no single thought taking form.

She was totally confused. On the one hand, she wanted to work for *Healthy Lifestyle*, would seize with both hands the new challenges and opportunities it presented. On the other hand, she couldn't stand to work for someone like Ethan Gray. The man was too self-assured for his own good. Even worse, he made her so mad!

She most certainly would *not* give the obnoxious editor the pleasure of ordering her around again at dinner!

The evening crawled by slowly. Bella had a shower, made herself a snack, checked the evening's television shows—boring—and glanced at her watch twenty times.

The stillness of the empty house was overpowering. Without realising it, she found her eyes straying to her
* bedroom door and her mind rifling through her wardrobe. Maybe there was still time ...

"That's it!" she exclaimed suddenly in defeat. "Okay, I'll go."

Bella raced around the house like a wild thing, and was out the door in just over fifteen minutes. Gunning her small red sedan, she headed towards a beautiful meal, an unpredictable editor, and a mysterious proposal.

* This should be 'riffling' I think, so re-reading the sentence here.

Chapter 5

Ethan arrived at the Summit Restaurant just before 8 o'clock, dressed in business-like black trousers and white dress shirt. The only difference to what he wore every day to the office was the absence of a tie. He felt strangely underdressed. Still, he didn't want to scare Bella off with the 'power-trip' image.

A mirthless chuckle rose from deep in his throat. At last, by some stroke of good fortune, things were starting to fall into place. After some planning this afternoon, he'd decided that Bella would be very useful to him. She just didn't know it yet.

He turned slightly in his seat to scan the restaurant. Bella was just coming through the entrance, looking slightly harried, yet the total image of her was dazzling. Her shining dark hair curled softly about her shoulders, setting off the stunning, strapless red dress and silver heels.

She walked slowly towards him, her face a mixture of curiosity, anticipation, and dread. Ethan smiled to himself. He must be getting to her. Perfect.

"Hi," she greeted timidly as he seated her at their table, a hesitant smile betraying her wariness.

Ethan mentally kicked himself for being too harsh at lunch. His temper had always gotten the best of him; could even ruin his carefully-laid plans if he didn't contain it better. He reined himself in and turned on the charm.

"Good evening, Bella," he smiled, sitting down opposite her. "You're looking lovely this evening." He eyed her appreciatively.

Bella seemed uncomfortable with his admiring assessment. "Thanks," she murmured, subconsciously twisting a chestnut curl around her index finger.

He had noticed the same nervous action over lunch. Good. If she was on edge, perhaps she would more easily agree to his plan. He chuckled quietly.

"Excuse me?" Bella looked up from the menu she had been studying, her blue eyes questioning.

"Uh ... nothing." Ethan shook himself mentally. He had to hold his cards closer to his chest, or the evening would not be successful. He decided to launch in right now, instead of waiting until after dinner, to ensure he didn't lose her again during the first course.

"Bella," he began, smiling confidently, "I've been looking closer at your résumé, and was interested to note that you had written a feature on Queensland's top health resorts." He paused, collecting his thoughts. Bella was giving him her full attention, her brows drawn together in concentration.

"*Healthy Lifestyle* is doing an upcoming feature on health resorts and spas of South-East Asia and the Pacific. With your previous experience, I think you would be perfect for the job." He watched her closely, waiting for her reaction.

There was none.

Bella was obviously too overwhelmed with his offer to speak. She started to open her mouth, thought better of it, and snapped it shut again.

Ethan knew his obvious amusement wasn't helping, but she did look comical.

Bella found her voice then, hurriedly excusing herself. Ethan worried that she might be leaving, but saw her head towards the ladies' room instead.

He picked up his menu and stared at it. He had expected some sort of surprise, or even opposition, but not this. She had probably never had such a big break in her career before, he mused. But it had less to do with her writing experience—or looks—than she might have thought.

Though she was gone, Bella's perfume still lingered in the air. With her beautiful face and appealing figure, Ethan conceded that it maybe did have *some*thing to do with her appearance, before returning to the menu.

Bella stood in front of the ladies' room mirror, her head spinning. She was so embarrassed at her reaction to Ethan's offer that she didn't know how she could leave the room and face him again.

To say she was shocked would be an understatement. And to think that she'd assumed he was going to give her some menial writing work—and that she almost didn't come tonight!

Glancing at her pale face in the mirror, Bella noticed with dismay how the fabric of her red dress clung to her curves. She had wanted to wear her new purchase, but hadn't meant to appear like she was trying to seduce the man, rather than talk business!

She paced past the toilet stalls and then back to the mirror. Her eyes grew wider as the enormity of the project began to sink in.

All she knew were two things: one, this was clearly the opportunity of a lifetime, one that would cement her position in writing circles; and two, she definitely did *not* want to work with Ethan Gray.

Bella finally managed to make it back to their table several minutes later, lamely apologising for her absence (due to a headache, she claimed).

The rest of the evening went by in a blur. She couldn't remember what she ate, or even if she ate at all. All that stood out were the details of her assignment—if she accepted it. She would be flying to Noumea, via Sydney, in a week's time, and from there travel to four other resorts in the Pacific Islands and Thailand. The whole thing seemed like a dream—except she didn't know if she would ever wake up.

"One question: why me?" she asked as Ethan paused to take a bite of his meal. "Surely you have staff writers who would jump at this assignment?"

He studied her over the glow of candlelight. "You forget: I've seen your CV. You're obviously well qualified for the job, and your previous experience is perfect for this project."

Bella's face clearly communicated her doubt—doubt that was quickly turning into suspicion.

"I do have a confession, though," Ethan began.

Here it comes ...

"Our other travel writer pulled out, and you were the only person available on such short notice. But," he hastened to assure her, "I'm fully confident of your abilities."

Listening to him now, and as he carried the conversation over dessert, Bella thought that it would be easy to forget Ethan's performance earlier. The charisma she had seen when they first met was back in full force. However, she did notice it slip every so often during the evening, a somewhat Jekyll-and-Hyde character revealing itself.

Like the arrogant way he simply assumed that she would take on the assignment. She hadn't said a word about accepting it, and yet he was talking as if it was all settled, even asking her if she had a current passport.

Suddenly it all became too much for Bella. The shock of such a huge assignment landing in her lap, the headache—a real one, now—starting to pound behind her eyes, the possibilities, the locations, all crashed in on her at once.

She pushed her chair back and stood unsteadily, stopping Ethan mid-sentence.

"Are you alright?" he asked, a glimmer of concern showing in his brown eyes.

"Just a splitting headache. I'll be fine—really," Bella asserted, grabbing her small handbag. "Why don't I phone you tomorrow and let you know what I've decided?"

Ethan looked taken aback, confirming his automatic presumption that she would be doing the feature.

Bella had no patience to discuss—or argue—the issue further, so she turned and made her way out on shaky legs. This time it wasn't just the heels, she thought wryly.

Bella lay in bed an hour later, eyes wide open. She knew that any attempt at sleep was futile, no matter how many sheep she chose to count.

"Asia and the South Pacific," she breathed. "But why me?"

True, she had written a similar article previously, but it was on a much smaller scale, and wasn't commissioned. She had sent query letters to several magazines and newspapers to get it published.

But she almost hadn't completed it in the face of the life-shattering tragedy that had occurred just weeks before the magazine's deadline.

The last time she had been to the South Pacific islands—Vanuatu, specifically—was with Andrew. And that was the last time she had seen him alive.

The realisation sunk in, dropped down through her stunned excitement, and settled somewhere in her chest, hard and cold.

"How could I even consider going back there?" she whispered, a lone tear slipping down her cheek and onto the pillow. It would be too painful digging up all the past memories, going back to the places they had been together.

She shook her head as if to confirm her decision. "There's no way I can go. But ..."

Memories of a long-ago Sunday School lesson drew her back in time. Bella clearly recalled the story of Gideon—how he had been hiding in a well, but was commanded by an angel to gather an army and fight those he feared so much.

The story had made a big impact on her nine-year-old mind. She was facing a bully two grades above her, and could relate to Gideon's cowardice. Yet he had confronted his fears—and won.

Bella was ashamed to admit to herself that she had never faced her fears before. Had, in fact, run in the opposite direction with her tail between her legs. If it had been up to her, and not Gideon, the enemy would have overrun the place while she remained huddling in the well.

She sighed raggedly, turning on the bed to find a more comfortable position. Did mental indecision *have* to make you feel like you'd been run over by a truck?

And now she was back at the proverbial square one. She could swallow her fear and do the feature—take a great opportunity for her career but have a terrible time emotionally—or she could say no, and then always wonder what would have happened if she had said yes.

A few more hours of tossing and turning elapsed before Bella finally made her decision: she would be like Gideon. She would go.

In two minutes she was fast asleep.

Chapter 6

The phone rang. And rang. And rang. The jingle reverberated in Bella's head like a clanging bell. She groaned loudly, opening one eye to look at her bedside alarm clock. *Ten-thirty!*

She leaped out of bed and shuffled quickly to the phone out on the kitchen wall. She must have accidentally turned off the answering machine yesterday afternoon. Giving herself a quick mental telling off, she picked up the receiver.

"Good morning, Bella here." The croaky greeting did not befit a good morning, but old habits died hard.

Jennifer Whitman's sunny voice brightened the room. "Good morning, darling. Did I wake you?" The innocent question held the hint of a tease.

"Mum, you know I'm usually an early riser," Bella protested. "I've just been wrestling with some ... decisions." In frustration, she ran her fingers through her hair, dismayed to find it full of tangles. She'd forgotten to braid it before sleeping—again!

Never one to beat around the bush, she blurted, "I've been offered a feature on Pacific and South-East Asian health resorts—and I've decided to do it. It's a great opportunity, Mum, and I know I'll have to go to Vanuatu again and dig up the past, but I'm being like Gideon." She paused for breath, her head spinning. She was rambling, a sure sign she was feeling stressed.

"Bella, darling," Jennifer's voice was concerned. "Are you okay? Do you want to talk about it?"

Bella took a deep breath and smiled around the growing tension beneath her temples. She could always count on her mum. From her typical teenage angst with growing up in rural Victoria, to her struggling early working life in Melbourne, the premature death of her dad from cancer, followed by the even more unexpected death of Andrew—her mum was with her through it all.

Jennifer Whitman had left a promising career as a theatre nurse to focus on raising her two children, and they had thrived under her love, gentle care, and wisdom. These were all evident now as she quietly waited for her daughter to begin.

Bella briefly shared the events of the past few days, recounting all the important details—the new *Healthy Lifestyle* publication, its awful editor, her upcoming assignment—and leaving out the unimportant ones—like her struggles to find fulfilment and direction. And her continuing grief.

Jennifer's honed ability to read between the lines meant she discerned the situation correctly. "So you're concerned about going back to where Andrew died, and you don't know if it's worth the pain?" she probed gently.

"Yes," Bella whispered, sliding her back down the wall to a hunched sitting position on the cold floor.

"You know Who can help you with it, don't you?"

Jennifer's tone was mild, but it stirred a defensive reaction in Bella.

"Mum, you know I don't want to talk about that," she said, annoyed that the topic had been brought up. She respected her mum's belief in God, but that didn't mean Bella too had to embrace it.

"Okay, darling," Jennifer soothed, backing off. "I didn't phone to lecture you. But remember, I'm always here to listen if you have any more difficulties like this."

Bella nodded, forgetting that her mum couldn't see her response.

"Actually," Jennifer continued, "I called to remind you

that Todd, Carly, and Jasper will arrive tomorrow, and—" She stopped at Bella's sharp intake of breath. "I realise it's been a busy time for you, darling, and it's totally understandable for you to forget."

Bella loved how her mother covered for her.

"Thanks, Mum," she said, her eyes scanning the messy living room and all the cleaning she faced before they arrived. "It did slip my mind. I'll give Todd a call on his mobile to touch base with them."

Bella ended the phone call with busy lists adding to the pounding pressure in her head. There were clothes to wash, beds to be made, floors and the bathroom to clean, they'd need extra groceries ...

She was excited that her older brother, his wife and their one-year-old were coming to visit—she usually only saw them once a year since she had moved away from Victoria to Queensland. But the thought of getting the whole house ready as well as preparing for her trip next week was more than she—or her headache—could handle.

By the time she had showered, dressed, and had breakfast, it was nearing lunchtime. Bella knew she was dragging her feet, purposely putting off phoning Ethan with her acceptance of the job. After last night—that unbusinesslike red dress, his arrogant presumptions, that discomforting way he looked at her—she didn't want to see or speak to him for a long, long time. Well, as long as possible, at least. He would now be her editor, after all. And Bella was determined that the relationship remain on a solely professional level. No more going out to lunch. No more cosy 'business' dates for dinner. Ethan had to be shown that she was not interested.

Bella's thoughts had free reign to romp about her mind as she hurriedly straightened the living room, washed the breakfast dishes, and vacuumed the floors. She was just thinking she should put on a load of washing when Krista breezed in through the front door.

"Hi, Bella," she called out from the kitchen. "I'm on an early lunch break. Do we need any more groceries?" The end of her question was muffled as she buried her head

in the refrigerator,

in the refrigerator, no doubt noting its sadly depleted shelves.

Bella walked in from the laundry, drying her hands on her faded jeans. Her hair was falling out of its ponytail, and her face felt flushed and hot.

"We need everything," she informed Krista's back. "Todd and Carly are coming tomorrow—and there's so much work to do!" she wailed.

Krista turned from her inspection of the pantry supplies and shot an amused glance at Bella. "Well, from the looks of you, the cleaning must be almost done." She grinned mischievously, neatly sidestepping the dishcloth as it sailed past her head.

Her smile quickly disappeared as she saw Bella's tense face. "What's wrong?"

Krista held up her hand quickly, to stop the stream of Bella's list of cleaning that still remained. "Actually, there's not that much to be done," she said calmly. "I've already made the beds up, and I'm ducking out for some groceries now."

Bella's open mouth and wide eyes voiced her question.

"I wrote the date in my diary weeks ago," Krista explained. "Hey—I always thought you were the organised one."

"Normally I am," Bella sighed, running a hand over her face as she slumped into the nearest kitchen chair. "But I haven't been feeling very normal lately. I've just been letting things get on top of me, and now that I've got this health resort assignment overseas, it's—"

Krista cut her off with a squeal. "What? You haven't told me! Tell me everything! *Now!*"

Bella chuckled at Krista's enthusiasm, and briefly explained what she would be doing for the next few weeks. "I know it sounds fun on the surface," she said with a hint of a whine, "but there's a pretty hectic schedule, and I'll have to produce several feature articles including photos, plus sidebars." For some reason, she didn't mention the main problem of having to revisit the place of Andrew's death. She and Krista normally shared all their secrets—

but as she had said, this wasn't normal.

Bella looked up from studying her fingernails to notice Krista's previously excited expression was replaced by a sceptical one—and was that envy she detected?

"Wait a minute—you're not jealous, are you?" Bella asked incredulously. Krista squirmed. "You would *not* want to work with this editor, trust me. And sure, it'll be nice scenery, but there's still those articles to write." She sighed, feeling burdened by it all.

Krista was obviously unconvinced. "That's what they *all* say. You'll be swanning around with the natives and drinking cocktails by the pool. I'm sure all that work will be *exhausting.*" She turned to dry the washed dishes on the draining rack, but not before Bella caught a hint of a smile.

"I really am happy for you, Bella," she said over the clatter of the plates she was stacking, "even though I'd love to tag along. Just make sure you bring me back a souvenir." She paused to think, then grinned slyly. "A tall, handsome Polynesian would suit me just fine."

Bella's laughter followed her flatmate as she walked out the door to shop, and return to work.

Chapter 7

Jay Hinkley was angry. With Sasha, and both of their parents, but mostly he was mad at himself. So now he was leaving.

He should have known better than to rely on his feelings and jump into something without thinking it through properly, praying about it. And when was the last time he'd asked for God's guidance in anything? Especially for this—one of the most important decisions of all.

He pulled out his suitcase from under the bed, blew off the layer of dust that had accumulated since his last trip, and started to pack. Feeling like he was on auto-pilot, he mindlessly grabbed piles of clothes from the wardrobe and drawers and dropped them into the case, not caring what he packed. Or where he went. Alaska would be fine, although a bit chilly for this time of year. Maybe an equatorial jungle somewhere ...

Thoughts and emotions tumbled about his mind like clothes in a dryer. Jay knew that running away probably wasn't the best solution, but he desperately needed some space to work out his priorities, his mind and heart. His love for adventure had been great for his career, but jumping in without thought wasn't always the best strategy when it came to relationships.

Jay ran his hands through his hair in frustration. Deep down, he somehow knew that everything would come together for him some day—but he sure was getting sick of waiting.

In an attempt to distract himself and to cool down a bit, he flopped down in the office chair in front of his computer and opened his email account. Plenty of spam, some photography e-newsletters, this month's freelance classifieds ... Jay opened the attachment, doubting that there would be any work that would interest him at the moment. Unless it was on the other side of the globe, of course.

A small ad jumped out at him: *Urgently required: photographer to shoot for lifestyle mag. Several Pacific Islands and Phuket. Incl accom and travel. Start Sept 13.*

That was in just four days. Excellent!

Without another thought, Jay sent off an email in reply, intending to follow up with a phone call in the morning.

"Thanks, God," he murmured, feeling a little calmer now. "You knew I needed to get away for awhile, spend some more time with You."

He glanced over to the bulging suitcase on his bed, his earlier frustration now turning to resolve.

He would take this contract, if it was still available. And he would get away from the expectations, the smothering, the presumption that he'd be settling down.

For now, Jay needed to be free.

"Todd!" Bella squealed, running into her brother's outstretched arms. "It's so great to see you guys!" She buried her face in his soft cotton shirt, drawing from his comforting strength.

"You too, Baby Sister," Todd teased. He gave her curls a playful tug as she turned to Carly and Jasper, both looking like they had just woken up. "How are you doing?" Bella asked, enfolding them both in a big hug.

"We just thought we'd pop in for breakfast," Carly quipped through a yawn. "It only took twenty hours."

"And well worth the trip," Bella laughingly responded. She ushered them inside, luggage and all. "Just dump your stuff here and we'll sort it out after breakfast."

The trio straggled behind her as she headed to the kitchen. "Krista's already gone to work," Bella said as she took some fruit and milk from the fridge, "but you can catch up with her later this afternoon—*after* you've all had a sleep," she said pointedly, grinning at their half-closed eyes as Todd and Carly slumped at the table. Jasper was already in dreamland, snuggled into his mum's shoulder.

Bella's heart tugged as she looked at them all, exhausted from the trip up just to see her. She couldn't ask for a better brother and sister-in-law. They had weathered some tough times over the years—their father's death when Todd was just 15 and she 13, their mother's breast cancer, and then Andrew's death. The support within their tight-knit family had been invaluable, had kept them all—especially her—afloat through the years of heartache.

There was something about Todd and Carly, Bella mused as she cut up some strawberries and apples and sliced the bread for toast. They had a great marriage, strong and loving—one just like she would want one day. But there was something else, a sense of stability, security ... *peace*.

The toaster popped up loudly, stirring the half-asleep travellers at the kitchen table. Bella brushed her thoughts away with the crumbs on the bench top.

What is wrong with me? she asked herself as she took the food over to the table and sat down. A heavy weariness was beginning to blanket her like a thick, dark cloak, weighing her down inside and out. She had to start getting more sleep—or something. But what?

Her head jerked up as Todd said a quiet blessing over the meal. She couldn't escape from this religious thing, even in her own home!

"You're pretty quiet this morning, Bella," Todd observed, apparently oblivious to Bella's discomfort. "Anything wrong?"

Bella felt Carly's concerned brown eyes on her, and coloured slightly. "I'm fine," she lied, staring down at her cooling toast. "I've just been really busy and tired lately, plus I've got a big overseas writing job next week to prepare for."

Todd and Carly's eyes lit up with interest as Bella gave them the details of her assignment and where she'd be going. She inwardly sighed with relief that the conversation had been deflected away from her emotional state. As much as she loved them both, Bella didn't want their pity—or their advice.

Why hasn't she called?

Ethan looked at his watch for the tenth time that morning, noting that it was almost time for lunch. "She had better come through for me," he fumed silently. "I've got a lot riding on this."

He would have to locate someone else if it didn't work out with Bella. But there *had* to be someone else. There was no way he was taking the rap for this if it all fell down.

The intercom at Ethan's left elbow came to life, startling him to alertness. "There's a caller for you on line one, Mr Gray. It's international." Ethan ignored the overt curiosity in Susan's voice. He was in no mood to facilitate her penchant for office gossip.

He pushed the button that cut his secretary off, and picked up the phone's receiver. "Ethan Gray," he answered curtly.

"Mr Gray. How are the plans?" The Asian-accented voice was cold and business-like.

"I've made some definite progress, but I'm waiting for a few details to fall into place." Ethan would never admit that a major component was even now on thin ice. He had to maintain control. Everything hinged on control.

"I'll be over there on the twenty-first, as we discussed," he continued. "Phone me same time next week, and we'll finalise all the particulars."

Ethan hung up abruptly, a bitter taste in his mouth. He hated dealing with this guy. He ran a hand over his face, pushing down the anger. As much as it grated on him, he needed the man—he was the best in the business.

And to Ethan, the best was all that mattered.

Todd rolled over sleepily and blinked up at the ceiling. It took a moment for him to realise where he was. His half-open eyes took in the framed seaside prints on the pale blue walls, the vase of fresh flowers sitting on the dressing table, their suitcases by the door.

Next to him on the queen-sized bed, Carly was still sleeping soundly, her blonde hair fanned about her head on the pillow. Little Jasper snuggled in the crook of her arm. Todd's blue eyes softened as he leaned over and brushed a wisp of hair from her face. Carly was beautiful, and even more so when asleep.

The digital alarm clock on the bedside table flicked over another minute, catching Todd's eye. It was already two o'clock. They had been sleeping for over five hours. His stomach was growling in protest at missing lunch.

Todd hauled himself out of bed, ran his fingers through his wavy brown hair in a half-hearted attempt to look presentable, and headed for the kitchen.

Bella was perched on a stool beside the phone, her tension evident by the whiteness of her knuckles as they gripped the receiver.

"No, please don't disturb him. I'll just leave a message." She took a deep breath, her index finger becoming hopelessly entangled in a long curl. Her eyes were staring down at the floor in obvious concentration. Todd leaned quietly against the door jamb, not wanting to intrude.

"Please let him know I've decided to do the health resort feature." She paused, a look of frustration flitting over her face. "Yes, Bella Whitman. W-h-i-t-m-a-n. Could you also ask him to email all the details to me?"

Bella told her the email address, then repeated it for good measure. "Thanks, Susan," she said. "Yes, Ethan has my number if he needs to contact me. Goodbye." She replaced the receiver a little more firmly than necessary, the "click" punctuating her loud sigh of annoyance. "That woman—" Bella looked up, and jumped when she saw Todd, his long legs crossed as he leaned against the door frame.

"Todd! You scared me!"

"Sorry, Sis," he grinned, strolling over to rest his arm

on her shoulder. "I thought five hours was plenty long enough for a nap. Besides," he said, walking over to the fridge, "it's way past lunch." He opened the door and bent down to better view the fridge's contents, pleased to find ample supplies of cold sliced meat, cheese, and salad vegetables.

"Oh, is it lunch time already?" Bella looked around distractedly, her mind obviously elsewhere.

Todd grabbed her by the arm and pulled her over to the table. "Why don't you sit here and relax while I make some sandwiches."

Bella resisted at first. "No, I'm the hostess—and a terrible one at that," she murmured, rubbing her tired eyes.

"When the hostess is under stress, she needs to take a rest." Todd grinned at his weak attempt at poetry.

The humour was obviously lost on Bella. She laid her head down on her folded arms and closed her eyes. "I don't know what's wrong with me," she yawned. "I'm sure I used to have twice the stamina. Must be old age," she concluded wryly.

Todd paused from his sandwich preparations to study his sister. "It could be that everything's getting you down," he quietly commented. "If you don't deal with one problem before another hits, then it all just piles up."

Bella hadn't moved from her slumped position at the table. He hoped she was listening.

"Maybe you need to open yourself up to getting whole on the inside," he continued gently as he moved over to the table and sat down beside her. "You can't do it alone, Bella. As humans, we naturally tend to hold onto things, including our hurt and pain." He slipped an arm around her shoulders. "It's only when you open up to God and ask Him to take it all away that the healing can begin."

Todd stopped, certain he had heard a small sniff from the circle of Bella's arms. "Are you alright?" He felt her shaking shoulders beneath his arm, pulled her a little closer. She was obviously facing some difficult issues at the moment.

It took Bella almost a minute to answer. "I'm so confused," she sobbed. "My whole life's changed in the last couple of years. Sometimes I just feel like I can't go on," she finished brokenly.

"There's only one Person who can heal you inside, Bella." Todd's voice was soft. "Sure, Mum and Carly and I can support you, but we can't fix things like Jesus can." Bella lifted up her tear-stained face. There was a glimmer of hope in her brimming eyes. "Have you thought about that lately?" Todd asked.

Bella rummaged in her jeans pocket for a tissue and blew her nose soundly. She shook her head, her curls bobbing side-to-side, her expression defensive. "I just don't think I'm ready for that yet," she said, fiddling with a button on her shirt. "I'm not prepared to give up control of myself for something I don't fully understand."

Todd opened his mouth to give her a piece of his mind—gently, of course—but then thought better of it. He wanted to tell her that faith was about trusting in God even when you didn't fully understand Him. He wanted to say that by giving up her old self, and accepting Jesus' gift of forgiveness and grace, she would gain peace and love, and eternity. That she would never know true healing and happiness and fulfilment until she opened her life to God.

He said none of those things. Now wasn't the right time.

"I'll be praying for you, Sis," he said. He gave her shoulders another squeeze as he got up to continue with the sandwiches.

"Please do," Bella whispered, almost inaudibly. "God knows I need it."

Chapter 8

The jet slid soundlessly through the air, high above the fluffy blanket of clouds below. It had taken off from Sydney's International Airport ten minutes earlier, and Bella settled in for the two-and-a-half hour flight to Noumea, New Caledonia. She squirmed into a semi-comfortable position on the seat, thankful that there was no one sitting next to her, so she could spread out—but mostly so she wouldn't have to make conversation. With her mind still spinning from the rush of the past few days, stringing intelligent sentences together would be even more difficult than trying to relax in the cramped economy-class seats.

Todd had not spoken to her further about their conversation on the day he had arrived, but she often felt his blue eyes studying her. Bella found she had to turn away from his concerned scrutiny. It was almost as if he could look right through her sanguine charade to her burdened soul.

Her main distraction from further internal reflection was Jasper. His first birthday had been just two weeks earlier, and he made new discoveries every day—from his first toddling steps, to pulling the long-suffering Samara's hair and tasting the soil from the indoor plants.

Despite her hectic schedule, Bella was determined to give Carly and Todd some quality 'together time', so

Jasper accompanied her wherever she went. Trips to the supermarket had never been so difficult! There was no such thing as ducking into a store for a few minutes. The whole routine of the stroller and nappy bag, snacks and sleep times and nappy changes, was becoming all too familiar.

She was always remembering some extra item or another that she would need for the trip—a spare memory card and batteries for her camera, a new swimsuit, and an extra USB memory stick for the laptop ... And Jasper was only too happy to assist her, with plenty of drooling and chuckles.

Three days before Bella left for her trip, Todd and Carly drove into the city to do some shopping, and Jasper was down for a nap. Bella took the opportunity to dig her camera out of the spare bedroom cupboard where it was stored. It had been some time since she'd been required to take photographs to accompany her articles. Bella was almost afraid she might have forgotten the art. She held the digital Minolta SLR up to her eye, fiddling with the f-stops and focus. She smiled as it all came back to her, her hands moving automatically, effortlessly. Pity life couldn't be like that.

Bella sighed and stood up slowly from her crouched position. She rubbed a hand over her tired eyes. It would be nice to take a nap, like Jasper, but there was still a lot to be done before her trip.

Stifling a mid-afternoon yawn, she walked out into the kitchen and picked up a printout of the itinerary she had received several days ago. She would be spending two days each at five different resorts—one day to gather information on the health spa, and the other to explore the region's attractions and absorb the culture.

The list of locations read like a tourist's dream: Noumea (New Caledonia), Vila (Vanuatu), Lautoka (Fiji), Bali (Indonesia), and Phuket (Thailand). Bella smiled to herself as she tried to imagine the sights, sounds and smells that would greet her. And the heat. She wrinkled her nose at the thought of the stifling equatorial humidity. Better not pack that long-sleeved jacket, she made a mental note to herself.

Susan, the *Healthy Lifestyle* secretary, had proven her worth when it came to handling all the travel arrangements and little details of the trip. Bella was surprised at her efficiency. The woman could obviously be quite organised when she wanted to be.

There was no further contact with Ethan Gray, which Bella found slightly disturbing. Surely, as the editor, he would want to clarify the details of the feature and be available to answer any questions she had? But Susan had been the one to pass on all the information, frequently citing the ubiquitous, "Mr Gray's *very* busy."

Too busy to run the magazine? Bella wondered irritably.

It wasn't just his unavailability to discuss the feature that frustrated her. Bella's pride also smarted after his obvious attraction to her rapidly turned to apparent rejection. At least, that was how she interpreted the silence from *Healthy Lifestyle*'s editor. It only served to confirm her early impression of the self-serving editor, turning on the charm only when it suited his purposes.

Bella's phone rang then, and she snatched up the receiver in an attempt to not disturb the sleeping Jasper. "Hello?"

"Bella, Ethan Gray here." *Speak of the devil!*

He launched right in, obviously no need—or time—for pleasantries. "Susan and I have been looking over the itinerary, and we both agree it's pretty tight. There's not a lot of time for you to write the feature as well as take photos, so we've contracted a travel photographer to help you out."

Bella's stress levels began to ebb just a little. "That's great! I *was* a little concerned about the time factor," she admitted.

"We've booked his flights and accommodation in tandem with yours, so you'll be travelling together."

Bella started to felt a twinge of apprehension. "So we'll be spending the whole two weeks together?" She could just imagine a portly older gentleman puffing along behind her as she explored the islands. Or even worse, an arrogant younger guy like Ethan. “I hope he’s nice,” she mused aloud.

“I’m sure he’ll be fine,” the editor dismissed. “Susan’s already emailed through his phone number so you can discuss any details before the trip. Oh, and his name’s Hinkley.”

“Okay. Thanks—I think,” Bella found herself speaking to the disconnected dial tone.

She sighed as she checked her email for Hinkley’s number, and dialled it right away. Best to get all the unpleasantness out of the way for one day.

An energetic and youthful-sounding male voice answered after just one ring. “Hi, Jay here.”

Bella found herself a little taken aback. This certainly didn’t sound like a portly old man.

“Umm—hi. I’m Bella Whitman. I understand that we’ll be doing a feature together for *Healthy Lifestyle* magazine on Asian and Pacific Island health resorts and spas?”

There was silence on the other end of the line.

“The editor, Ethan Gray, *did* tell you we’d be working together, didn’t he?”

“No. He didn’t.” There was an undercurrent of tension in his voice. “As far as I knew, I’d be taking a selection of shots for the magazine’s editorial team to match with some articles later.”

Bella sighed impatiently. “Well, it must have been a last-minute change. I wish they’d communicate with us a bit more.”

“So do I.” Jay sounded more than a little frustrated now. “If I’d known I was going to be saddled with a writer, I doubt I would’ve taken the job.”

Bella felt her pulse quicken. *Why, the nerve!*

“I’m not too happy about being ‘saddled’ either,” she retorted, “but we’re just going to have to make the best of it.”

“This is not the way I work,” Jay maintained. “I’m an adventure travel and wildlife photographer, not a babysitter.”

Bella only just managed to restrain her fraying temper. “Have it your way!” she bit out. “We may have to travel on the same planes and stay at the same hotels, but we'll definitely be going our separate ways the rest of the time."

"Agreed."

"Fine." Bella replaced the receiver in a forceful huff.

The less she saw of Jay Hinkley, the better.

Why did she seem to be surrounded by overbearing men these days? she wondered as she hurried towards Jasper's hungry wail.

"Excuse me, ma'am. Would you like chicken or beef?" The airline attendant's question shook Bella from her reflections. After choosing the chicken schnitzel and vegetables that looked as tired as she felt, Bella half-heartedly picked at the meal, her mind elsewhere. She mentally rehearsed her schedule for the next few weeks, going over potential angles for each story and creative ways to present the features and culture of the islands.

Her planning served as a welcome distraction from the tense introspection of the past weeks—not to mention her conflicts with Ethan and Jay. She could now look forward to over two weeks of a frenetic pace interspersed with pure indulgence—after all, she had to sample each resort's specialties to fully report on them, didn't she?

Bella smiled around the last bite of her leathery chicken. Things were definitely looking up.

Chapter 9

Krista struggled to unlock the front door with wet hands and dripping uniform. “Coming, coming!” she called to the insistent person on the other end of the jangling telephone. She dumped her bag and snatched up the receiver, silently wondering who would be ringing at this time of the day. Bella would usually be writing on her laptop at her favourite coffee shop by this time, and Krista would be at work. If she hadn’t needed to grab her umbrella sitting forgotten by the front door—again—the house would have been empty.

“Hello,” she answered breathlessly.

An Asian-sounding voice responded. “Is Ms Whitman there?”

“N—” Krista started, then stopped herself. “May I ask who’s calling?” She wasn’t normally suspicious by nature, but something about the cold, clipped tones gave her the creeps.

The man still had not identified himself, and seemed to have no inclination to do so. Krista’s patience seeped from her with the rain still dripping from her hair and clothes. “I’m sorry, but she’ll be gone for several weeks. You’ll have to call again.”

“She has left?” the man asked, an unvoiced threat in the question. “Excellent.”

He hung up, leaving Krista to shake her damp head

in puzzlement. What did it mean? She couldn't place why, but the mysterious call had unsettled her, made her concerned for Bella's safety.

"Bella!" she breathed, her mind jumping into action. Her fingers automatically dialled her flatmate's mobile phone number. Krista waited impatiently as it rang two, three, four times—only to be greeted by a pre-recorded female voice: "The mobile phone you are calling is switched off or out of range. Please call—".

Krista hung up in frustration, her mind ticking over rapidly. Bella would still be on the plane, somewhere over the South Pacific. How could she reach her, beg her to be careful? Warn her?

The jet touched down in Noumea on an unseasonably warm spring afternoon. The tropical humidity hit Bella as she reached the plane's open door and descended the stairs onto the blazing tarmac. Along with the assorted bunch of passengers, ranging from loudly chattering tourists to businessmen and all those in between, Bella was ushered into the main building to claim her baggage and head through customs. Her senses were assaulted by the bright colours of the islanders' clothing, the sound of throngs of people talking at once, the feel of a slight breeze wafting through the open windows and doors. The life around her exuded vivid energy combined with the laid-back islander style. Bella found herself responding to the mood, even beginning to relax a little.

Half an hour and a precariously fast taxi ride later, Bella checked into her first resort, the Noumea Internationale. It embodied the eclectic mix of French heritage and tropical flavours she had seen mirrored all around her in the drive from the airport. The hotel's lobby was huge, featuring numerous palms, a fish-filled pond and waterfall, and clusters of colonial French-inspired tables and chairs dotted throughout the room.

Despite the beauty and opulence, Bella found herself swallowing a lump in her throat. So many elements of her surroundings reminded her of the places she had last visited with Andrew—right down to the palm-and-pond-filled lobby and the tropical décor. She managed to shove the melancholy thoughts aside while she checked in, tried to ignore the interested glances of the smiling porter in the elevator, and made her way to room 53 on the third floor.

She felt herself deflate as she left her bags inside the door and flopped down on the king-sized bed. Try as she might to feel excited—to take in the luxurious furnishings, the sparkling white *en suite* complete with spa bath, the azure ocean beckoning from somewhere outside her balcony—Bella felt tears of emotional and physical exhaustion pricking her eyes.

She knew she should be going over her planning notes for the feature, organising her schedule for the next two days, identifying herself to the appropriate hotel staff, maybe even squeezing in a quick interview ... But too little sleep, her reluctance to leave her brother and his family behind in Brisbane, and a mix of uncertainty and expectation about her first writing job of this size, all combined to leave her feeling like a wrung-out dishrag. Or maybe a month-old balloon that had lost its air. Or was it a pair of underpants with the elastic gone?

Bella stifled an hysterical giggle. Even when she was exhausted, her writer's mind was busily constructing corny metaphors to describe her worn-out state.

At least she wasn't thinking about Andrew.

With a determined toss of her humidity-frizzed curls, Bella pushed up from the bed with more energy than she felt. She dragged her suitcase over to the huge built-in wardrobe. The task of unpacking the few summery clothes she had managed to squeeze in amongst her notes, camera and lenses, and laptop, would not take long. Even though she would only be in each place for a short time, Bella refused to live out of a suitcase.

Two minutes later she stood back and surveyed the few shelves and hangers holding her light skirts and tops, a few pairs of shorts, one good dress, and a swimsuit. They took up only a fraction of the wardrobe's space. Bella smiled as she thought of the extensive markets and handmade clothes she'd heard about. Maybe she would be able to squeeze in the time—and suitcase space—to get a couple of sarongs and extra swimsuits.

Her mood had brightened considerably—thoughts of shopping usually did that for her—so she decided to get out of her hotel room and explore a bit. A beautiful tropical island was no place to mope about, no matter how heavy the burden of suppressed sorrow that dragged around her neck.

As Bella changed into a summery floral skirt and fitted aqua blue singlet top, she wondered if Jay Hinkley had checked into the hotel yet. She had seen no one on the plane trip over, or in the hotel lobby, who looked like a possible travel and wildlife photographer. An overbearing, outspoken, and entirely-too-independent photographer, she mentally added.

Jay hadn't contacted her since their first terse phone conversation, and that was just fine with her. She admitted to herself that they would need to meet soon—today—to discuss plans for the feature. But she wasn't exactly looking forward to it.

Pushing thoughts of the photographer aside, Bella headed towards the elevators. She even caught herself whistling a few bars from a popular song on the radio as she descended towards the lobby. The bright sunshine, fragrant breeze, and rolling ocean visible through the full-length entrance windows all combined to unearth an optimism that had lain dormant for so long. And when you were feeling sociable, what better place to go than the open-air bar?

Bella stopped at the information desk to ask for directions. The woman, a middle-aged Noumean native, identified by her name tag as 'Grace', looked up from her computer screen and studied Bella's face for a moment. "Ms Whitman from Room 53, is it?" she asked, obviously recalling Bella's face from her check-in an hour earlier.

Bella nodded, wondering what her name had to do with getting to the bar.

"A couple of messages just arrived for you," Grace said, her red-lipstick smile brightening the room as she handed over two folded slips of paper. "Oh—and the lagoon bar is just outside the left exit."

Bella thanked her and read the first message. It was from Jay: *Meet me in the lobby at 5:30pm.*

Finally, she huffed silently. She had been feeling cautiously uncertain about her first meeting with the photographer, but her natural curiosity was starting to exert itself. Would he be as blunt in person as he was on the phone? Could they even work together? What would he look like?

Bella frowned to herself as she crumpled his message and tossed it into a nearby bin. Even if Jay was an Adonis, she doubted that would make the task of working with him any easier.

Glancing at the second message, Bella saw it was from Krista, probably just wishing her a good trip or something. Without reading further, she stuffed the note into the side pocket of her skirt. She had thirty minutes before her meeting with Jay, and she was anxious to do some serious exploring—and relaxing.

A glorious display of fading golden rays and pink-tinged clouds met Bella as she exited the lobby and strolled towards the lagoon. Clusters of towering palms circled the crystal water that seemed to call to her, beckoning her to dive into its cooling depths and join the dozen other swimmers. "I should have changed into my swimsuit," Bella murmured to herself, lifting her hair up from her sweaty neck.

The innocent movement seemed to attract quite a bit of attention from several men seated at the bar. Colouring slightly, Bella moved around to the far end of the bar and caught the barman's eye. Her diet cola couldn't arrive soon enough. It gave her a focus for her eyes and hands, anything to avoid the frequent appreciative glances directed towards her.

One of the men, a blonde surfer-type, was seated a short distance away from the others, just over a metre to her left. He was staring down into his drink, seemingly absorbed by the rapid ascent of bubbles through the dark liquid. Bella couldn't help sneaking glances at him from beneath lowered lashes. He looked as though he could have been plucked from one of Australia's surf beaches, was maybe even island-hopping to chase the best waves. Completing the look was his surfing label shirt and casual shorts, topped off with tousled, sun-bleached hair.

As Bella took another long sip of her drink, she noticed that something about him seemed familiar, as if she'd seen him somewhere before. His appearance, the way he glanced at his watch ...

That was it! The café, before her appointment with Ethan. She remembered looking at him that day and thinking it had been far too long since she'd had coffee or dinner with another man. And now here she was, seated near him at a resort bar in Noumea. She almost smiled at the coincidence, before recalling her mother's words: "God doesn't make coincidences, He guides us."

Bella frowned to herself at the intrusion to her thoughts, and reached for the bowl of nuts in between her and the 'surfer'. She didn't know if it was hunger or tiredness, but somehow her elbow connected with her almost-full glass, sending it crashing to the ground.

"Oh, no!" she half-groaned and exclaimed as she surveyed the damage. The flowers on her skirt were now a dirty brown, and sticky droplets covered her legs. She looked up and realised with horror that she had also showered the stranger next to her with cola. He was wiping at his shorts with a wad of red paper napkins.

"I—I'm sorry," she managed, her face mirroring the colour of the napkins.

He looked up at her, and Bella caught her breath in spite of her embarrassment. Just as she remembered from that brief glance at the café, his eyes were blue, with a sea-like tint of green so bright that she took a second look.

"Accidents happen." His voice was casual, as if women spilled their drinks on him regularly. Bella took the stack of napkins he offered to her and began dabbing at her soggy skirt, thankful for an excuse to look away.

When she had removed most of the moisture, she passed her wet pile of red paper to the barman, apologising profusely. He smiled and reached over to take her

glass,

glass, which the surfer had set on the bar.

Bella glanced over at him as he sat on the stool next to her. He was checking his watch again. "I'm sorry, but I've gotta run—an appointment." He grinned apologetically. "It was nice bumping into you."

Bella giggled at the pun, before realising that she, too, had to go. "Are you here for work?" she asked, as he paid the barman and turned to leave.

"Yes—unfortunately." That smile again.

Bella found herself wishing that they had more time for conversation. "Okay—bye." She watched him stroll away along the path to the hotel lobby.

Gathering her shoulder bag, she sighed in annoyance at Jay Hinkley and his ill-timed meeting.

A man had been studying the young couple at the bar, taking care to remain hidden behind some overhanging palm fronds. With a grunt of frustration, he lifted a tanned hand to brush at the water that constantly dripped from his dark hair into his eyes. He had to remain focussed, could not lose sight of her.

Shivering slightly, he moved slowly through the warm water. He hated swimming—almost as much as he hated arrogant Westerners. But it was all part of the job.

He'd had worse assignments. At least staying in a five-star Noumean hotel wasn't bad.

His dark eyes had never strayed from the laughing woman and her companion. "She wouldn't be smiling so much if she knew she was 'insurance'," he muttered.

Some children jumped into the pool then, yelling and splashing each other. The man slipped further back into the shadows, while continuing to concentrate on his task—watching Bella Whitman.

Chapter 10

Bella found herself dragging her feet as she neared the entrance to the lobby. While she knew how to stand up for herself in a conflict, she wasn't one to go and seek it out.

Standing in the reception area, she quickly scanned the spacious room. There was no one there save for a trio of holidaymakers checking in at the desk, and a man seated on a couch with his back to her. He looked just like the man she'd spilt her drink on at the bar. Bella's cheeks grew warm at the memory. His appointment must also have been with someone here in the lobby.

Thankful that he was facing the other way and couldn't see her, Bella sank down onto the nearest couch for what she suspected would be a long wait. Not only had Jay been argumentative and outspoken so far, she fumed silently, but now he was rudely late.

She waited another five minutes, then dialled his mobile phone number—with no success. Trust a man to be either too disorganised or in such a hurry that he forgot to set up international roaming with his phone company.

Bella was just about to leave when the blonde man from the bar stood up, looked around, and started walking over. "Hi, again! Were you waiting for someone too?"

"Yes," she frowned, and checked her watch yet again; "I was supposed to meet a guy here, but he's almost ten minutes late."

"What's his name?"

"Jay Hinkley." Bella thought she saw his eyes narrow slightly, prompting her to ask, "You wouldn't happen to know him, would you?"

"I do, actually." The corners of his mouth lifted in a wry smile. "I'm sure he's not meaning to be impolite. Maybe he just got held up."

"Maybe." Bella felt doubtful. She was beginning to think that working with a photographer was only going to waste her time, not save it.

"If you like, I'll keep a look-out for him and tell him to get in touch with you again."

"That would be great, thanks. How did you say you knew him?"

There was a distinct glint in his eyes. "Oh, we're friends from way back. Anyway, I'd better run. There might be time for a quick surf before it gets too dark."

"Okay. Thanks." Bella found herself watching him walk away for the second time in twenty minutes. What was it about this guy that made her heart rate spike every time he smiled or looked at her with those oceanic eyes?

Apart from the fact that he was handsome, friendly, and—Bella stopped herself with a small shake of her head. *What am I doing?* she asked herself as she rode the elevator back up to her room. She was here to work, not start a holiday romance.

Especially when she hadn't gotten over her last relationship yet.

Bella had just opened her door and dropped her bag on the bed when her room phone rang.

"Good evening, Miss Whitman. Grace here, from the reception desk. There's another message waiting here for you."

Probably Jay Hinkley wanting to set another meeting time. "Thanks, Grace. Please read it to me."

"A Mr Jay Hinkley has asked if you could meet him for dinner in our main restaurant at seven pm."

"Thank you, Grace. Bye." Bella replaced the receiver and flopped down onto the bed. Not even a word of apology over missing their earlier appointment, she thought crossly, closing her eyes.

She seemed to grow more frustrated with Jay at every turn. Well, at least there was time for a short nap before their next meeting at dinner …

Ethan sat alone in his stylish inner-city apartment, his hunched form as unmoving as a shadowed statue in the darkened living room. Normally, he would be out having dinner, spending time with his group of high-flying friends. But he didn't feel like company tonight—he needed to be alone to think. And to try and find a way out of this mess.

He never should have attempted this deal. It was far too risky, even with his connections. And if it landed him in prison, what use to him would the millions be then?

He rubbed a shaky hand over his tired face, feeling far older than his thirty-five years. He had half a mind to phone his overseas contact and call the whole thing off …

But Ethan knew he was in far too deep.

The phone rang just then, causing his tightly-strung nerves to jump. He leaned over to pick up the portable handset from the coffee table, wondering who would be calling him at home.

The voice on the other end of the line filled Ethan's heart with dread.

"Is everything running to schedule?" his Thai contact, known to him only as Sanouk, asked.

"Uh … y-yes," Ethan stammered, hating himself for the show of weakness. He recovered quickly, determined to get the ball back in his own court. "And how about things on your end?" Ethan asked, forcing himself to match the caller's steely tone, though his insides felt like jelly.

"We have the shipment ready," Sanouk was saying, "exactly to how we agreed. Now everything is up to you."

The ominous pause confirmed Ethan's fears. They knew. He didn't know how, but somehow they had found out he was having second thoughts, that he was ready any minute to turn and run.

"Oh, I thought you should know," Sanouk continued, his voice now deceptively casual. "I have someone watching a certain woman—for her protection, of course. I believe her name is Bella Whitman."

Click.

Ethan stared in anger at the phone clutched in his hand. He wanted to throw it across the room into the opposite wall, as if the action could somehow be transferred to the man far away.

He stood up and began pacing a trail between the coffee table and the balcony door. There was no way out now—he was trapped. If he didn't follow through with this deal, Bella—over in Noumea by now, and totally oblivious to the situation she was in—would pay.

Even worse, his carefully-constructed plans could all come crashing down.

Bella rolled over on the bed, smiling sleepily. A nap had been just what she needed. Now to think about getting ready for—

Seven-twenty!

She bolted off the bed and into the shower in almost one movement. So much for being annoyed at Jay for missing their appointment in the lobby—she was almost as bad!

Bella had the quickest shower of her life, threw on a cool and casual cotton dress and pair of flats—no need to dress up for a casual work meeting—and was in the elevator in fifteen minutes. *Phew!*

Bella cringed to herself as she walked into the restaurant, forty minutes late. Jay was bound to be even more prickly than he was on the phone.

She stood in the entryway for a few moments, politely declining the offer of a table by the maître d'. Where *was* that guy? If only she knew what he looked like.

Over in a quiet corner, she spied the blonde man from the bar sitting alone at a table for two. He looked up then, beckoning her over with a grin and a wave.

"We meet again," he chuckled.

Bella found herself smiling despite the pit of anxiety in

her stomach over being so late. “We seem to be doing this lately,” she agreed, trying not to notice how the corners of his eyes crinkled when he laughed. “I’m sorry, but I can’t stay to chat. I’m really late for another meeting with Jay Hinkley. Have you seen him this afternoon?”

“Ah. I do have a confession to make.”

Bella felt a prick of suspicion. A confession? Maybe this guy *had* been too good to be true.

“We haven’t been introduced.”

“Oh.” She couldn’t keep the relief out of her voice as she took his outstretched hand. “I’m Bella Whitman.”

“I know.”

“How?” Bella asked, feeling her eyebrows rising in surprise. Jay must have mentioned her name.

“I’m Jay Hinkley.”

“What?!” She dropped his hand, subconsciously wiping her palm on the skirt of her dress. “Are you serious?” Her initial surprise was quickly turning to embarrassment—and a good dose of annoyance.

Cheeks burning, she glared at Jay. He was trying to look serious, but not quite managing. “Why didn’t you tell me who you were in the lobby this afternoon?” Despite trying to be civil—if only for the sake of their future working relationship—Bella couldn’t keep the edge out of her tone.

A smile was playing at the corners of his mouth. “To be honest, I thought you would’ve worked it out yourself. But you still seemed embarrassed over spilling your drink on me, plus pretty annoyed over me supposedly being late.” He looked down to fiddle with the menu on the table. “Maybe I just wanted our working partnership to start off under calmer, more controlled circumstances.”

“Am I looking calm and controlled now?” Bella’s voice oozed sarcasm. “I think you were just having fun at my expense.” If only she hadn’t have been so gullible, she silently chided herself. Must have been the jet-lag ...

“No, I wouldn’t do that!” Jay held up his hands in mock protest. “Well,” he admitted cheekily, “maybe just a little. Seriously, why don’t you sit down, see if we can start over?”

Against her better judgement, Bella took her hand off her hip and dropped into the seat opposite Jay. "I hope you take photos as well as you gab, mate," she needled as she began to peruse the menu.

"Better," he countered.

"Well then, prove it." She could feel a chuckle begin to rise in her throat in spite of herself.

"Okay." He put his menu aside, his set jaw belying the playful glint in his eyes. "Come out with me for a drive tomorrow morning. There's this great place in the hills, with beautiful views all across the island. I'll show you some shots, and you can tell me about your plans for writing the feature."

Bella felt he was almost daring her to accept—quite a turnaround, after they'd agreed on the phone to have nothing to do with each other. "Well, okay—but I've got to get into some interviews tomorrow, so it'd better be quick."

"Don't worry," Jay said, summoning over the waiter to take their order. "It most definitely will be."

His comment confused and needled at her as they ate their entrées in relative silence. Bella's appetite had deserted her, and she was determined to get out of there and up to her room as soon as possible. After making a weak attempt at the food on her plate, she quickly excused herself.

Jay gave her a polite smile, said, "See you in the morning," and went back to devouring his meal. She didn't know how on earth he could eat, with the tension so thick between them.

Bella fumed quietly to herself as she walked back to her room. She wondered how she would manage to get through the next two weeks working with Jay Hinkley.

Why did it have to be that the first man she'd been attracted to in two years—since Andrew—had to be so exasperating?

Bella woke not long after dawn, even though she had stayed up planning her feature the night before. She couldn't quite fathom the sense of anticipation that had begun to bubble inside her. What was it she was expecting—another argument with the infuriating Jay?

Yet even while she showered and dressed her mind strayed continually, and most annoyingly, to the handsome photographer.

She stood in front of the open wardrobe, eyes staring blankly at the clothes as her thoughts whirled and sped like butterflies in a field of flowers. Where was he taking her? Would she need to wear special clothing, boots for hiking? Why had she agreed to go with him in the first place, when she should be working on her writing?

Bella firmly closed the wardrobe door on her racing thoughts, after choosing casual three-quarter shorts and a pale pink top. She slipped on a pair of sandals and headed towards the lifts and breakfast. “I'm not going anywhere that requires sturdier footwear,” she addressed her reflection in the lift's mirror, her stomach grumbling in agreement.

Jay was sitting by a window in the large dining room, the remains of a croissant and coffee on the table. The aquamarine eyes lit in greeting as Bella entered the room. She gave a small, impersonal wave—they hardly knew each other, after all—and joined the line at the breakfast buffet.

The mouth-watering array of tropical fruits and traditional dishes, combined with the typical Western fare, sent her stomach growling like a lawn mower. No one else in the line—a love-struck honeymooning couple in front and a young family with three hyperactive children behind—seemed to notice. Bella hurried away with her flushed face and gurgling belly to find a table.

She thought Jay would have left by now, but he was still sitting there, a second cup of coffee and some handwritten notes sitting on the table. Part of her wanted to turn away and find a seat at the opposite end of the room. But the other, less-rational part—the one that was sending her mind and heart racing—forced her to walk towards him and sit down.

“Good morning, Bella. Did you sleep well?” he asked politely. The eyes peering over his raised coffee cup were

bluer than she remembered,

bluer than she remembered, his manner more relaxed. And that smile ...

Bella popped a piece of melon in her mouth and tried to recall his question. “Fine, th—” Her reply was cut off by a choke and splutter as the melon lodged in her throat. She recovered quickly, wiping her red face with a napkin, and looked up to find Jay regarding her with a concerned expression.

“Are you alright?” he asked, his twitching mouth and twinkling eyes betraying his amusement.

“Fine, thanks,” Bella repeated through her embarrassment, this time without coughing.

She hurried through breakfast, leaving half of it on her plate. She had to get away from this man—he made her nervous and frustrated in all-too-rapid turns.

Jay was apparently oblivious to her discomfort, making relaxed, impersonal small talk about the climate, culture, and people of the islands. Remembering their argument at dinner last night, Bella crossly decided that he was starting to sound like a talking guidebook. Well, at least that would save her doing some research, she thought, as she downed the last of her orange juice.

Jay took her cue, and they stood up together. “Meet you in the lobby in twenty minutes?” he asked, all business-like.

Bella kept her mind in neutral as she rode the lift back to her room to get her camera and hat. She had no intention of getting distracted on this trip. The reason she was here, she reminded herself sharply, was to write a feature—and hopefully to work through her demons concerning Andrew’s death.

Thankfully, Jay merely saw her as a work colleague, someone he was stuck with. She gave a small, inward sigh of relief.

A holiday fling would be totally out of the question.

When Bella entered the lobby fifteen minutes later, Jay was already waiting, dressed in casual shirt and shorts. Sure enough, he wore hiking boots. He raised his eyebrows slightly when he looked down at Bella’s sandals, but said nothing about it. Bella smiled to herself. He was either too much of a gentleman (unlikely!) to suggest she go and change, or he had just made a last-minute adjustment to their excursion plans.

Let him change his plans, she thought rebelliously as they climbed into Jay's hire car in the hotel parking lot. Since her clashes with both Ethan and Jay, she was finding herself on the defensive around men.

The short trip up Mount Humboldt was rich with views of white beaches and lush rainforest. Bella spent most of the journey staring out of the window at the scenery rushing by, since Jay remained quiet. He was either not a morning person, was concentrating terribly hard on driving, or had something on his mind. Bella eventually concluded that it must be the latter, since he'd been fine at breakfast earlier on, and appeared to be handling the car with ease.

They turned off onto a side road and began winding steadily upward through dense foliage. As she caught glimpses of the city and ocean below through breaks in the forest, Bella wondered what could be bothering Jay so much. In the short time she had known him—a fact that she often had to remind herself in view of his increasing appeal—Jay had been relaxed, with plenty to say during their few exchanges. Certainly not withdrawn or reserved, as he seemed now.

Something about the small frown wrinkling his tanned forehead, and the distant look in his eyes, tugged at a chord deep inside Bella. He appeared to be struggling with sorrow, or perhaps wrestling with a major decision—two things she had become frighteningly familiar with in her twenty-five years. Without even being conscious of it, she began to feel a sense of empathy.

Suddenly drawing to a halt, Jay turned towards Bella, an expectant expression banishing the shadows on his face. "Wake up, Sunshine!" he grinned, making as if to poke her with the car key.

Bella almost jumped through the ceiling of the car. "Hey!" she protested, giving his arm a jab with a well-placed elbow. She didn't wait for his reaction, scrambling out of the car—and into paradise.

Bella stopped short, her eyes wide open. Everything else around her faded into the background, brushed aside by the majestic view that swept towards the shimmering horizon. Here the mountain dropped steeply away, its sides densely covered with a thick blanket of verdant foliage whose folds ran down, down, down to the fringe of the island—white beaches and buildings that reflected the dazzling sun. Like a multi-faceted Ceylon sapphire, the azure sea beyond was almost blinding in its brilliance.

Bella barely noticed when Jay came and stood a short distance behind her, his camera hanging around his neck.

"I just love God's creation," he breathed, his hushed voice almost reverent. "It's sights like these that inspire me to capture them on film, to show people a glimpse of what heaven must be like."

Bella reluctantly turned from the view to look at Jay, vaguely aware of a slight stirring of annoyance deep inside. Something about his words reminded her of Mum and Todd. Surely he couldn't be ...!

She pushed her questions aside, determined to enjoy the day. Just because Jay spoke about 'God's creation' and heaven, it didn't mean he was a Christian.

But despite her reasoning, Bella couldn't escape the niggling suspicions that had arisen in her mind.

Even far away across the seas, she couldn't escape!

Jay found himself uncomfortably aware of Bella's nearness as he stood behind her. Despite their clashes, she still fascinated him: her friendly-yet-cautious manner, the way her blue eyes flashed when she was mad. Which, come to think of it, seemed to be quite frequently since they'd met ...

Yet at other times, he had noticed the pain behind those eyes. It had tugged at the masculine part of him that wanted to rescue; to fix things. To soothe the hurt away.

His response scared him.

Jay tore his thoughts away and forced himself to look

out over the horizon, sizing up some good panoramic shots. He had to forget about the firecracker writer, and focus instead on his work. His life already had too many complications.

Besides, he had no right to be spending so much time with another woman.

He walked over to the right, closer to where the mountain dropped away. Looking down over the edge of the precipice brought an ironic smile to his lips. Funny how often lately he felt he was perched on the edge of a cliff, unable to go back and unwilling to go forward.

If Bella only knew the hurricane inside him at the moment, she would run the other way.

Jay turned back to where she stood, only to find she was indeed moving in the other direction, her gaze captivated by the flittering of a black Meliphage honeyeater, a rare bird on the island. Without realising it, she was straying terribly close to the brink of the mountain—too close.

"Bella!"

Jay looked on in horror, unable to move fast enough to prevent the inevitable. Bella twisted around towards him, a smile on her face, just as her sandals slipped on a patch of loose dirt and stones.

Her mouth opened in a soundless scream, her eyes wide with terror, as she fell.

Chapter 11

Jay lunged towards Bella, but he was too late, and only just managed to stop himself from following her over the edge of the cliff. Lying flat on his stomach, he frantically scanned the forested rock face far below, but there was no sign of her. His stomach lurched at the mental image of Bella sailing over the precipice to a terrible death; but he knew he couldn't entertain such thoughts—he *must* keep a level head. If she was alive down there, he had to reach her.

A slight movement in a scraggly columnar pine fifteen feet down and to the left caught his eye. Through the dark green foliage, he could just make out a flash of pale pink fabric. *Bella!*

On auto-pilot, Jay raced over to the car, hesitating as he saw Bella's mobile phone beside her bag on the passenger seat. He could call the hotel, get them to contact the emergency services ... but knowing that any outside help would probably arrive too late, Jay decided to attempt to rescue her himself.

He thanked God for all the rock climbing and abseiling practice at the yearly youth camps he'd attended as a teenager—and that he always carried a rope with him to help get the best angle in precarious mountain or treetop photos. Grabbing it, he raced back to the mountain's edge. Securing the rope to a sturdy gum oak five feet back, he tested the strength of the knot, then started to lower himself down over the side.

Jay prayed all the way down. He didn't know how long the pine would hold Bella. Or even if she was still alive.

Bella was caught in a thick blanket of fog, its cool tendrils wafting all about her ... feeling light as air, totally weightless. *Is this what it's like to fly?*

A voice was calling out to her, struggling to reach her through the mist.

Bella! Bella!

The haze began to lift slightly. She opened her eyes, but what she saw almost made her pass out again. She was wedged against the base of a small conifer, facedown over a dizzying thousand-foot drop.

Bella's first instinct was to scream and struggle, but the swaying of the fragile tree convinced her otherwise. She was frantically trying to figure out what to do next, when she saw movement somewhere to the right, out of the corner of her eye.

She didn't dare turn her head—anything could cause her to slip—and she didn't want to get her hopes up about a fast rescue. As far as she knew, attempting daring mountain retrievals wasn't in a photographer's job description. She would just have to wait until an emergency crew arrived from Noumea. Bella resigned herself to an extended wait.

She had just mentally composed her last will and testament, and was starting on her memoirs, when Jay appeared at her right elbow.

"Next time you go bungee-jumping, try not to forget the cord, okay?" he cracked, a grin belying his strain.

Bella attempted a weak smile, then lowered her brows into a glare. "Will you stop joking around and get me out of here?" she demanded.

She knew she was in no position to be demanding—was completely at Jay's mercy, in fact—and that only made her feel worse.

"Yes, ma'am!" Jay snapped to attention, working quickly to stabilise Bella and disentangle her from the tree.

As they prepared to climb up to safety, Bella reached over and stroked one of the conifer's branches. "Thanks, little tree," she said. "If it wasn't for you, I'd be right down at the bottom by now." She shuddered, trying not to look down to the jagged rocks and dense forest below.

"God must have planted that tree there just for you," Jay remarked casually as he tested the rope's strength to support them.

"Yeah, whatever," Bella mumbled. She was in no mood for a religious discussion. The most she could manage right now was, "Help, God!" He would just have to be happy with that.

Jay returned to the summit later that afternoon. He had wanted to stay with Bella—to prevent her from getting into any further life-threatening situations—but she had shooed him away. She was fine, apparently. The thought of her feature deadline was all it had taken to get her over the shock of this morning's accident.

Naturally, she'd refused to go to the hospital for a check-up. The woman was so stubborn! Jay shook his head with a mixture of bewilderment and frustration, pausing to adjust the focus on his camera lens.

Taking photos always relaxed him. That was probably why he'd become a photographer. Whenever he was angry, or feeling down, or facing a difficult decision, he found that getting in touch with nature through photography seemed to make things easier to handle.

He sure could do with some calming now, he thought wryly, snapping a blue goshawk in mid-flight. He was facing a crossroads in his life, with each choice leading down an entirely different path.

And if things seemed difficult before, they were even more so now. This trip to get away from everything, to analyse his options and make a decision, had only offered him one thing:

Bella.

And man, did she complicate things!

Jay stood up from his crouching position and wiped at a trickle of sweat on his forehead. It was hot out in the glare of the mid-afternoon sun. He had wanted to stay and get some sunset shots over the bay, but that was a couple of hours away yet.

He was still concerned about Bella. Before he left her after lunch, he'd warned her about the possibility of a concussion, or strained muscles—even whiplash from the jarring action as the tree broke her fall. Unfortunately, she was too focussed on the job at hand to listen to him. So he would just have to stick close by and keep an eye on her, whether she wanted him to or not.

And, to his surprise, he hoped she did.

"That's great. A little more to the left. Ahhh ... yes, that's it. Perfect!"

Bella was beginning to thoroughly enjoy this assignment. She had now investigated a variety of services the hotel's day spa offered, including the mineral bath, full body masque, and aromatherapy facial. Now she was letting a masseur knead the tension from her aching muscles. Jay had said they might be sore, and he was right. She wouldn't admit it to him, though; she had no intention of being on the receiving end of a smug 'I told you so'.

The massage, accompanied by recorded background sounds of flowing water and rainforest birds, was supposed to relax the body and mind, but Bella used the opportunity to mentally run through her checklist of the resort's features for her article. Apart from the day spa there was a gym, a huge lagoon swimming pool, and of course the healthy spa cuisine.

Her late lunch in the dining room had been delicious, but she remembered finding it difficult to focus on the food. A young Asian man was sitting several tables away from hers in the empty post-lunch room, apparently intent on reading his newspaper and sipping his fifth cup of coffee. Bella counted them as the waiter kept coming back and refilling his cup. The man either had a serious caffeine addiction, or that was an incredibly riveting newspaper. Or ...

She'd caught him looking at her several times, and

they weren't the usual admiring male glances she was used to. His dark eyes held a malevolent coldness that made her shudder despite the tropical warmth. He gave her the creeps. It felt almost as though ...

No, of course not! It couldn't be that, Bella chided herself as she concentrated on the smoked salmon and salad on her plate. *Why would he be watching me? I'm just a free-lance writer, a nobody.*

Bella had hurried to finish the rest of her meal and head back to the safety of the day spa. Descending in the lift, she made a mental note to have dinner sent up to her room tonight. She would be busy typing up her article—and she definitely didn't want to chance running into that particular man again if she could help it.

Krista sprayed on a light spritz of her favourite vanilla perfume, and then stepped back to better view herself in the full-length wardrobe mirror. She was wearing dark denim jeans, sky-high heels and a sparkly top, a combination she hoped would impress Ryan on their date tonight.

They were meeting in the city for dinner and a movie, and Krista was glad to be out of the house for another night. The place was so quiet with Bella gone, and even Samara, the cat, seemed to be pining away for her favourite housemate.

"Traitor," Krista muttered as a white ball of fluff slunk past her doorway to settle itself in Bella's bedroom. Still, she didn't really blame the animal. If anyone paid her as little attention as she'd paid Samara lately, she would look elsewhere, too.

She turned off the radio that had been blaring loudly, grabbed her bag and keys, and started for the door. Her hand was already on the door knob when the phone shrilled in the stillness.

Krista sighed impatiently. She'd be late—as usual—if she stopped to answer it. She half-decided to let the answering machine do its job, but then stopped and turned back to the kitchen. It could be Ryan, calling to say he had to work late again ...

Krista snatched up the receiver on what surely must be the last ring.

"Hello," she answered breathlessly. She expected Ryan to start speaking straight away, but there was only silence. "Hello? Is that you, Ryan? ... Bella? If this is some prank call, I'll—"

"Yes—Bella." The voice was muffled, menacing. Krista felt her muscles tense. "Bella could be in great danger. You should warn her."

Chapter 12

The next morning Bella woke much earlier than she would have liked. The ultra-bright sunlight shining into her eyes, combined with what sounded like a bird riot outside the window, just might have had something to do with it. She did have a lot of work to do, wrapping up the New Caledonia section of the feature, but another hour of sleep would have been nice.

She stretched sleepily and then sat up, her hand touching a piece of paper sitting on the bed next to her. A small smile lifted the corners of her mouth as she picked it up and reread it—a note from Jay that had been delivered with her dinner. He was still concerned about the possible after-effects of her accident, and joked that she needed a full-time bodyguard to protect her against herself.

"Hmm ... Jay as a bodyguard wouldn't be too bad," Bella murmured. She caught herself, cutting off the thoughts before they could take shape. *What was she doing?* A pang of guilt tugged at her insides. She almost felt as if she were betraying Andrew—if not him in person, then his memory.

Especially since tonight she would be flying to the island where they'd last been together.

Bella tugged a hand through her sleep-matted curls, deep in thought. She knew there had to come a time when she could finally leave Andrew in the past, remembering him as a wonderful friend and lover, but nothing more.

The problem was, she didn't know how.

Maybe another relationship is what I need.

The idea, previously unthinkable, now seemed almost tantalising. Especially if it involved Jay.

Yet the more she tried to convince herself that this would solve the ache inside, the louder Todd's words sounded in her heart.

"There's only one person who can heal you inside, Bella. God."

She brought her hand down hard on the light bed cover, cutting off the thought. "Then where is this God when I need him?" she grumbled, swinging her pyjama-clad legs out onto the floor.

Inexplicably, a quiet stillness began to steal into her heart, seeming to brighten the sunshine-filled room.

Bella began to get herself ready for her last day in New Caledonia, never questioning the almost foreign peace as she showered and dressed, but enjoying it all the same. It almost felt as if God had heard her grudging 'cry for help', and had shown her a small taste of what He could provide.

But Bella's mind was centred only on all the loose ends she had to tie up before she left for Vanuatu late that afternoon.

Humming a nameless tune, she took her clothes out of the wardrobe and started to repack them in her suitcase. As she was folding the skirt she had worn on the day she arrived, she felt a crumpled piece of paper in its pocket. It was Krista's message to her that had sat forgotten for two days.

Hope you had a good flight. Received strange phone call. Please be careful—you may be in danger.

Bella took a deep breath. Her heart started beating faster as she remembered the man watching her in the dining room yesterday. Could there somehow be a connection?

She didn't want to take any chances. Her movements hurried now, she threw the last of her clothes and toiletries into the suitcase and zipped it up.

The telephone on the bedside table rang just as she

was putting her bags beside the door. The piercing sound startled her, and she dropped the large suitcase on her bare foot.

"Oww!" Bella managed to hop over to the phone before it stopped ringing. She wasn't expecting any calls. Her pain only heightened her annoyance at the intrusion.

"Hello," she answered, around a grimace.

"Hi, Bella. It's Jay."

She found herself smiling at the sound of his voice, despite her throbbing foot.

"I was just calling to see if you'd like to have breakfast together. It might be a good idea if we discuss any last shots you need before we leave Noumea."

Bella's smile dropped. That was Jay, always focussed on work, nothing more.

"Okay, breakfast would be good." She tried to sound nonchalant.

Part of her wanted to see Jay again—even if he did make her so mad at times. Almost before she could stop herself, Bella found herself asking him to accompany her for the day to look at some of the island's main attractions. "I think we'd need at least a couple of photos for that section," she finished, almost feeling as if she was asking for a date.

Jay didn't hesitate. "No problem. Okay, see you soon."

Bella noticed her flushed cheeks as she checked her hair and makeup one last time. She frowned at her reflection. Hadn't she told herself that a holiday fling was totally out of the question? If it wasn't for the fact that she felt an uneasy need for Jay to act as a bodyguard today, then it would have been better to just have breakfast together and then spend the rest of the day by herself.

Well, she'd made the plans now. And she had to admit, the thought of spending the whole day with those blue-green eyes was pretty appealing.

Chomanan Prem lounged back on his bed, enjoying the luxurious surroundings. He could definitely get used to this, though he knew for now it was short-lived. In just a couple of weeks, he would be chasing some petty crook through the back alleys of Bangkok, or getting rid of some stupid operator who tried to double-cross his boss.

He was very good at his job, thorough yet efficient. That was why he was the boss's chief enforcer. Still, Prem felt he deserved a little more respect, and rather better treatment all round. So he was determined to enjoy these easy two weeks.

Stifling a yawn, he checked his watch, then reached over to grab his mobile phone from beside the lamp. It was time for the first of his twice-daily reports. Naturally, Prem avoided using the hotel phone for these business calls. He didn't want anybody to be able to trace the number through the hotel's records.

Prem dialled, and waited a little impatiently for the boss to pick up. He had a job to do. From what he had gathered from listening to Bella's telephone conversation earlier—by way of a hidden listening device—he could be following her all over the island today.

"Hello." The voice was rough and muffled. The boss must have had a hard night.

"Khun," he began respectfully, "you remember the 'complication' I told you about yesterday? Well, it's still here. He's following her around everywhere. You want me to get rid of him?" Prem smirked, fondling the Beretta hidden under his jacket, stuck into the back of his trousers.

"Slow down," the boss growled. "I've just learnt that he's actually a last-minute contract photographer hired by Gray for his magazine."

"So do you want me to keep tabs on him as well, then?" Prem asked.

There was silence on the other end of the line, with the boss probably thinking through his next move.

"I want you to send Gray a message to show that we have complete control here. That he must follow through with our instructions to the letter."

Prem grinned, knowing what was coming.

"Send Gray a warning through this photographer, Jay Hinkley. Be creative—use your imagination."

Prem loved this part of the job. He could be *very* creative when he put his mind to it.

"After lunch should be the best time," the boss was saying, "before they leave for Vanuatu this evening."

Prem frowned with irritation. "Of course."

He ended the call and threw the phone on the bed. What right did the boss have to tell him how to do his job? He was the expert. He'd done this often enough, and his timing was usually right. And anyway, he happened to know that the air tickets had been re-booked; his targets were on the late flight out tonight.

It would be difficult to corner the guy alone in his room during the day. After lunch? No—he would wait for the cover of darkness.

The photographer would never know what hit him.

Jay got ready to go down for breakfast, his movements slow and thoughtful. Part of him was looking forward to spending the day with Bella, but his more rational side was warning him to back off. Hadn't he come on this trip to get away from everything and everyone? To pray for direction?

The shower's hot water jet helped to ease the tension from his muscles, but it couldn't do the same for his mind. He dried off and dressed hurriedly, noting the time on the bedside clock. Bella would be waiting.

As Jay scratched through his suitcase for a clean shirt, his hand felt something hard and square—a jeweller's ring box. He cringed inwardly, unable to stop himself from opening it. The delicate sapphire and diamond creation sparkled in the morning sunlight. *Just like Sasha had sparkled for him, once.*

Jay snapped the box shut and threw it back into the suitcase. He went down to breakfast with a heavy mind and heart.

Finishing her entrée at dinner that evening, Bella forced herself to focus on the end of Jay's story. She didn't want to mar her memories of this day by brooding.

They'd had fun exploring some of Noumea's main

tourist attractions: the Tjibaou Cultural Centre, the Place des Cocotiers and Olry Square in the heart of the city, and the market at the Baie de la Moselle. Bella had been fascinated by the melting pot of cultures and nationalities. Kanaks, Vietnamese, Javanese, Tahitians, and the ever-present Western tourists swirled about them in the marketplace, providing a mosaic of colours and languages. She was determined to come again for an extended visit.

Jay had been quiet as they ate lunch at a beachside café on Anse Vata Bay. Bella noticed he had been avoiding her eyes all morning, talking to a spot over her left shoulder. It was almost as if he had something to hide. She found herself searching his face for any trace of guilt as he gazed out over the bay. Unfortunately, she hadn't inherited her mother's perception along with the blue eyes and dark hair.

Whatever was bothering Jay, she hoped it didn't involve her. She didn't think she had done anything wrong, unless spending time with a fellow Australian could be considered a crime. Unless he already had a girlfriend back home ...

Now she looked across the table at Jay and offered a small smile. He was regaling her with the story of a previous escapade in South America, trekking through the Andes in search of the elusive condor. His photos, taken at the summits of perilous mountain peaks, had been snapped up by publications as diverse as National Geographic and the New York Times.

Bella truly was glad he had survived to tell the story. From the sounds of things, her rescue yesterday was tame in comparison.

But despite Jay's light-hearted conversation, Bella found her thoughts drifting to Vanuatu—their next destination—and to her last dinner with Andrew the night before he'd disappeared. Was she strong enough yet to go back there, and face the past?

Turning back to her shrimp cocktail, she wondered if she had done the right thing in convincing Jay to allow her to reschedule their flight to after dinner. All it had done was prolong the inevitable.

Bella sighed and lifted her head just as Jay concluded his story. He sat back with a grin on his face, obviously expecting some kind of response.

"Uh—awesome," she stammered, racking her brains for something intelligent to say. Her watch provided a welcome diversion. "Look at the time!" she blurted, standing up. "We've got to be at the airport in forty minutes!"

Jay also jumped to his feet, taking charge. "I'll pay for dinner, and you go grab your bags. I'll meet you in the lobby in five minutes."

As she rode the elevator up to her room, Bella couldn't help thinking they made a good team. *A professional, work team*, she reminded herself. And nothing more.

Chapter 13

Jay stood in line waiting to pay for dinner, beginning to doubt the wisdom of having taken on this assignment. He hadn't expected things to unfold this way at all.

Just months ago—or was it a lifetime?—he'd had his whole life mapped out. He thought he was ready to settle down, and even focus on the more stable work of portrait and commercial photography. The more he'd thought about it, though, the more confined he'd felt. The need for freedom, spontaneity, and adventure still beckoned. So Jay had followed.

But he knew this trip was just a short-lived chance for breathing space. There were still expectations and responsibilities. He felt the weight of them constantly, knew he would have to return and face them all.

Working with Bella had helped him to blank out the looming decisions, if just for the moment. He'd forgotten what it felt like to be free—but with her, he had remembered. And he didn't want to let it—or, to his growing surprise, *her*—go.

After paying for their meal, Jay raced up to his room, grabbed his bag, then headed to the lobby to wait for Bella. When she still hadn't come down ten minutes later, he hurried up to her room.

Bella answered his knock on her door with a harried expression.

"I thought you'd be ready by now," Jay teased, but

then stopped when her face crumpled.

"I can't find my laptop anywhere!"

She may have been packed earlier on, but now her room resembled the aftermath of a bomb strike.

"It's not that small," Jay offered. "It shouldn't be too hard to find."

Bella turned her frustration on him. "Stop being so calm! I *never* lose things! It's been stolen! *All of my work* is on that computer, including the articles for this feature!" She punctuated the sentence by throwing the pillows off the bed, presumably to look under them. When one hit his leg, Jay knew they were being aimed at him.

"What about a memory stick?" he asked, moving closer to the door and away from the whirlwind of flying articles. "Surely you would have backed up your work?"

Bella turned suddenly towards him, causing Jay to cringe slightly. She had just picked up the table lamp, and he didn't want to be on the receiving end.

"You're a genius!" she laughed. Jay breathed a small sigh of relief. "Normally I keep my memory sticks with the laptop, but this time I packed them in my suitcase so they'd be safer." She bent down and began scratching through her previously packed clothes. "I guess I just forgot."

"Well, we'd better not forget to catch that plane on time, especially since this is the last flight tonight," Jay reminded. He scooped up a pile of Bella's clothes and shoved them into her half-open suitcase, averting his eyes from some of the more delicate, lacier items. "We can report the theft at the desk on the way out; they need to know they have a thief working their corridors."

It was all too easy to break into the man's hotel room. The security here was a joke. Prem let himself in, and quietly surveyed the darkened room. He had seen Bella and her photographer friend finish dinner just twenty minutes ago, before going their separate ways. He should have just enough time to accomplish his task before leaving to shadow Bella as she took her flight to Vanuatu. Alone.

Prem smiled as he gripped the heavy crowbar.

Somehow, he doubted that the photographer would make the flight with a couple of broken knees.

The bathroom door was closed, with a thin strip of light showing underneath. Prem walked towards it, making no attempt to muffle his heavy footsteps. He wanted the guy to be good and scared when he got to him.

He wrenched the sliding door open in one violent motion. The empty bathroom stared back at him mockingly. Prem cursed. He must have missed the guy when he left. Hinkley was probably already with Bella.

He turned to leave; perhaps he could still surprise them both in Bella's room. He was sick of being subtle. It was time for some real action. Bargaining chip or not, the woman deserved some of it, too.

Prem stopped with his hand on the door handle, scanning the room one last time to make sure he hadn't missed anything. He spied a wastebasket tucked in beside the small writing desk. You never knew what useful information you could discover from people's rubbish.

Prem smoothed out the few pieces of crumpled paper on the desk. A travel brochure, an entry ticket to the Tjibaou Cultural Centre, a draft handwritten letter that began with the words, "Dear Sasha." He skimmed the letter, then shoved it into his pocket. It could perhaps serve as some blackmail leverage if required later on.

Prem frowned to himself as he left the room and hurried down the hall. He would have to finish this business in Vanuatu.

Krista was becoming frantic. It was two days since she had sent her warning message, but she still hadn't heard from Bella. That phone call last night had only made things worse. She was a basket case at dinner, worrying about Bella constantly. Ryan suggested several scenarios, but none of them sounded reasonable to Krista's anxious mind.

She didn't know how she'd got through her work at the hospital today, with her head obviously elsewhere. Any chance she got, she phoned Bella's mobile, always with the same result. The silly girl must have forgotten to set

up international roaming,

up international roaming with her phone company before she left!

Even Samara sensed her worried mood. The cat had rubbed itself around Krista's legs as she fixed dinner, and was now ensconced on her lap, purring consolingly.

"Thanks, buddy." Krista scratched Samara behind her furry ears, and was rewarded with a louder rumble of purrs. "You knew I needed cheering up."

She settled back on the sofa, looking up to the ceiling as if for inspiration from above. "Now, what are we going to do about our housemate? Something fishy is going on—" Krista was sure Samara's ears pricked up at the mention of her favourite meal "—and we have to do something about it."

Samara rumbled her assent, snuggling deeper into Krista's trackpants-clad legs. "Well, you're not much help," her owner scolded gently. "I was looking for a suggestion. The problem is," she sighed, "how do you warn someone thousands of miles away, who seemingly doesn't want to be contacted?"

Bella relaxed into her seat on the last flight to Vila, Vanuatu's capital. Her heart rate had only just returned to normal following their mad dash to the airport. After the drama over her missing laptop, they had been lucky to make it onto the plane just minutes before take-off.

They had also been unable to get seats together due to the last-minute flight change, but Bella didn't mind a bit. As much as she enjoyed Jay's company, she was happy for the chance to be alone, to think over everything that had happened during the last few days. Her head should have been spinning—it wasn't every day that she visited an island resort, met a handsome guy, fell over a cliff, and had her computer stolen—but she felt unusually calm.

Maybe it had something to do with that peace she had felt this morning. Or more likely, her cynical mind objected, it was a result of the massages and beauty treatments she'd been receiving. This was certainly a relaxing work assignment—that is, when she wasn't almost killing herself, or being watched by strange men.

The plane had levelled off, and was now jetting through the sky over the dark Pacific. As the seatbelt sign flicked off, Bella was almost tempted to seek out some company and take the now-empty seat next to Jay (perhaps a passenger hadn't turned up after all?), but something held her back.

Painful memories had a funny habit of resurfacing at the worst of times, as much as she tried to block them out of her mind. After two years, she was finally heading back to Vanuatu—the place where Andrew had died.

Or rather, where he had disappeared.

The investigation had concluded that he had died, although a body was never found. There wasn't even a proper funeral, only a memorial service. It made it so hard for Bella to let go and move on.

Even though her rational, grown-up mind knew that Andrew truly was dead, the part of her that still believed in magic and fairytales was not convinced. What if he was living on a deserted island? What if he had been concussed, rescued, and was now suffering from amnesia and living under a different name? The possibilities were endless, and they prevented Bella from putting his memory—and love—to rest.

She looked up and over at Jay, sitting two rows in front and to the right. His blonde head was bowed as he pored over a magazine. The warm feeling his image inspired frightened Bella. She didn't know how to respond.

And even after these few days together, she knew so little about him. Jay still seemed like a stranger, yet at the same time, he felt like a friend. What she knew for certain was that he had already helped to begin the process of healing her heart.

Chapter 14

Ethan looked terrible, and now other people were beginning to notice it as well. He didn't know how many questions he'd received about his health, or whether he was sleeping well. When they probed he just laughed it off, blaming the stress of running the magazine.

Bloodshot eyes stared back at him in the bathroom mirror, dark smudges beneath complementing them nicely. Combined with Ethan's pale face, the effect only served to remind him of a joke he had heard as a kid: "What's black, white, and red all over?"

"Not a newspaper," he murmured tiredly. "Me."

Yes, it was stress he was suffering from, but the magazine wasn't to blame. If only that was all he had to worry about. He was due to fly out in five days and finalise the deal, and just the thought of it left him nauseous.

He was supposed to be feeling excited by now. Ten million would set him up for life! But he hadn't counted on complications—the biggest of them being Bella.

They were keeping a close watch on her. He could handle that. So far he had kept his end of the agreement.

The problem was, now they were turning up the heat. Had even stolen her laptop. He could still hear Sanouk's sneering tone as he informed him on the phone last night. Apparently, they were making sure that Ethan hadn't told her anything—protecting themselves against a double-cross.

Idiots! How did they think she could work without a computer?

Ethan stopped mid-way through dressing, his mind racing. Could Sanouk be planning to hijack the ship-ment after the deal had been made? No—surely not. The tension was just making him paranoid, he decided as he returned to getting dressed.

He would have to toughen up if he was going to mix it with the big guns in this business. Somehow he would need to learn to handle the pressure better, prevent any repeats of that moment of weakness a couple of days ago when he'd phoned Bella's flatmate. He'd panicked ...

Straightening his collar as he walked out his door for work, Ethan decided that he wouldn't let things get to him again. Especially since this deal would be all over in a matter of days.

Then he would be either rich, in jail, or dead.

(sorry, couldn't correct erroneously) ✓

"You've really done it this time." The voice was angry, threatening. "Didn't I give you specific instructions to get him after lunch?"

Prem knew without asking that he had fallen sharply out of the boss's good graces. Despite his near-perfect track record, it only took one mistake.

"I humbly apologise, Khun," he managed, around the bad taste in his mouth. He hated apologising.

"I want Gray shown who's in charge here as soon as possible!" *Was that hissing sound the bad phone connec-tion, or the boss's voice?* "This is your last chance ... and you know what comes next ... after you've blown your last chance."

Prem idly flicked at a piece of lint on his jacket. He was the best in the business. Who was the boss going to get to replace him? He was merely full of idle threats.

"When I get to Vila—" he began.

"—And you missed your flight, too!"

Prem's anxiety heightened a little. The boss's voice was livid.

"I want you on the next flight to Vila. This time, finish what you were supposed to do in the first place." The phone clicked in his ear.

Prem frowned at the ambiguity of that last statement. Was he supposed to finish warning the photographer off, or finish him altogether?

He slipped the mobile phone into his trouser pocket and stared out through the window at the velvet New Caledonian sky. Maybe he would leave the decision until he confronted Hinkley, and then see how it worked out.

He did enjoy finishing things.

The plane touched down in Vila beneath a sparkling night sky, but as he disembarked Jay felt drained. Living out of a suitcase for these past days, combined with an even longer period of mental indecision, left him longing for a hot shower and soft bed.

They were booked into Vanuatu Royal Sands, an impressive beachfront resort surrounded by two acres of tropical rainforest.

"So this is home for the next few days," he remarked as the taxi driver handed their bags over to the porter at the imposing front entrance.

"Nice home," Bella agreed, walking beside him.

Jay thought the receptionist appeared unusually bright for one working the night shift. "How may I help you?" she purred, her white teeth dazzling against dark Polynesian skin.

Bella stepped forward. "I have a reservation for Bella Whitman."

The receptionist tapped away on her computer keyboard for a moment, then handed over a set of keys. "Room 30." She smiled at them both. "The porter will take your luggage up to your room. Enjoy your stay at Vanuatu Royal Sands."

Jay watched Bella blush to the roots of her hair.

"Uh—I also have a room booked, under Jay Hinkley."

The woman recovered quickly. "Of course—I apologise. I believe your room is directly next door, sir." A few more keyboard strokes, and Jay was in possession of the keys for room 31.

Bella was looking more limp by the minute. "Thanks for helping out there," she smiled weakly as they rode the lift to the third floor.

"No problem. Still," he teased, "it might have been interesting."

Bella shot him her 'look'—a cross between disapproval and disbelief. "I'll ignore that." She sagged against the lift wall like a wilting flower.

"You need some sleep, missy." Jay's voice was soft. "Get a good night's rest, and I'll meet you bright and early in the dining room for breakfast."

The opening of the elevator doors masked Bella's quiet groan. "I'm really going to need some serious massages tomorrow." She shot Jay a lopsided grin over her shoulder as he followed her down the carpeted hall. "This job is *sooo* hard. I might even have to face an extra facial or body scrub."

Jay reached room 31 and gave her a small push towards her own door. "You can't be tired enough," he observed dryly. "There's still plenty of cheek left in you."

He unlocked his door and then turned towards Bella. She was still standing there, staring dumbly down at the keys in her hand.

"You put it in the lock and turn it," he gently teased.

"I know." She looked up at him, her eyes softening. "I just wanted to thank you for being a good sport about all this, especially since you aren't used to working so closely with a writer." She hesitated. "You're a really great guy. Thanks."

She entered her room without looking back, leaving Jay staring at the closed door. Things were *definitely* becoming complicated. If he wasn't mistaken—and he was sure it was more than just his male ego dreaming—Bella was beginning to have feelings for him. It was in the way she looked at him, or occasionally touched his arm while she spoke, or leaned in close across the table at dinner. A myriad of things all added up, and the weight of it was beginning to give him a mother of a headache.

Jay sighed heavily and closed his door. The last thing

he wanted to do was break Bella's heart. Or Sasha's.

Bella shuffled over the polished wooden floor to the bed, completely exhausted. She had almost made it when her heavy feet tripped on the woven bedside rug. In an instant she pitched forward onto the mattress, the feather pillow muffling her yelp.

"That's a health and safety hazard," she grumbled, rolling over to stare up at the white ceiling. "And speaking of hazards—I'll be in big trouble if I don't phone Krista and tell her how I'm doing." Certain that her night-owl friend would still be up, even considering the time difference, she reached over to the bedside phone.

Bella smiled to herself as she waited for Krista to answer. "No doubt she'll ask me if I've found a muscular Polynesian hunk yet. Still ... I *do* have a man tagging along. Polynesian—no. Hunk—definitely."

She ended her monologue, afraid of being caught talking to herself again. Krista already considered her to be 'artistically eccentric', but this would just confirm it.

She would be answering the phone any time now.

The connection rang out, leaving Bella to stare quizzically at the handset. Krista always diverted the home phone to her mobile if she was going out or expecting a call. And knowing her, she would have been hoping Bella would phone—any chance to catch up on the 'exotic life of a freelancer', as she had said to Bella at the airport just a few days ago.

Bella frowned. She hoped Krista was alright. Despite her competence in the health profession, Bella could not look past her blonde friend's ditzy nature. Even Samara knew where her food security lay—ownership meant little to an animal.

As Bella sank back into the bed her weary mind started to worry about what might have happened to her housemate. She could have been on her way home and had a breakdown on a dark road ... or she could be lying sick in bed. Worse still, whoever made that 'strange' phone call may have discovered that Krista had tried to warn her—and something terrible could have happened to her!

Even Bella's over-creative mind checked her on that last one. After all, she had no proof that anything underhanded had occurred—except for a mysterious phone call and a potential stalker.

Bella grinned in spite of her worry. With the way she was jumping to conclusions and looking for a mystery behind every bush, maybe she should switch to writing thrillers.

With a sigh, she got up and undressed for bed. Hopefully she'd be able to contact Krista tomorrow—and her mum, and Todd, and everyone else she had forgotten about during the past few crazy days.

Jay was sleeping soundly, his body relaxed on the plush king-sized bed. He was oblivious to everything around him—the night sounds wafting through the open window, a late check-in shuffling down the hall.

But what was that scratching sound? It was becoming louder, more insistent, intruding into his slumber.

Jay's eyes snapped open, his body suddenly alert. Adrenaline surged through his veins as a shadow beside the window began to move. Gradually it increased in size and depth: a fluid, inky mass.

His heart began to pound as the shape took form. It couldn't be—! A gigantic, muscular tentacle slithered through the window, followed by another and another. Eight grasping limbs surged towards him, paralysing him with fear.

They were less than a metre away now. Jay's doom seemed imminent. He was filling his lungs with air to yell for help, when the owner of the tentacles showed itself.

Jay squeezed his eyes shut and then quickly snapped them open again in horror. Was that Sasha's face leering down at him, her clutching arms about to squeeze the life out of him?

They were slithering up to his neck now, tightening, wrapping, crushing. Jay's lungs burned. Vainly he struggled to loosen the death grip, but his arms too were bound.

He felt himself slipping away ... sliding into swirling blackness ...

"Oh, God! Help me!"

Jay shot up from the bed, his body covered in sweat. His chest was heaving with exertion, taking in great gulps of air.

Air! It felt so good to breathe again ...

He sank down on the bed and rubbed a shaky hand over his face. It was just a nightmare. He hadn't had one in years, and never like this.

Maybe God was trying to tell him something. His conscience was certainly doing a pretty good job. The more Jay thought about it, the more obvious it became. His daytime guilt had seeped into his night-time dreams.

And this was the result.

He knew he couldn't ignore it any longer. Tomorrow, he had to tell Bella. It could risk their growing friendship, but he felt he had no choice.

There was no way he wanted to have another dream like that again.

Chapter 15

Eww! Yuck!" Krista reached into her mouth and unceremoniously removed a white cat hair. She glanced at the studious-looking man beside her, and gave him what she hoped was a pacifying smile. "It's my cat, Samara," she explained, trying to ignore his glare of disapproval. "She leaves her hair everywhere!" She wiped her hand on her shirt. "I hope she'll be okay with my boyfriend while I'm away—he's really not a cat person. How about you?"

Her co-traveller responded by picking up his magazine and moving to a vacant seat in the next row.

Krista wasn't put out in the slightest, a trait that often got her into trouble with oversensitive hospital patients. She reached for her mobile phone to remind Ryan to buy more cat food—but then remembered that she had turned it off before take-off, as they had been instructed. Now she would have to wait and call Ryan from the airport at Vila.

Krista smiled as she imagined her boyfriend's reaction to her request. It would do him some good to leave his work at a reasonable hour for once to feed her pet. He was verging on becoming a workaholic—something Krista herself had never had to worry about.

Already bored with the in-flight movie—her tastes ran counter to the science fiction offering—Krista rummaged in her bag for a magazine. She'd picked up a copy of

Healthy Lifestyle before take-off, curious to check out the publication that had given Bella such a great break. Her hands closed around a piece of paper—the work itinerary Bella had copied for her. According to the schedule, Krista noted, her friend would be beginning her first full day researching the spa at the Vanuatu Royal Sands resort. It sounded very ... regal.

She wondered how many criminals could seriously blend into such an environment without attracting suspicion—if someone was actually following Bella, that is. Still, something strange was definitely going on, and it was up to her, Krista, to alert her friend. She just hoped she was in time.

Bella was fed up with waiting for Jay. It was well past eight, the time they had always met for breakfast, and he still hadn't shown up. Her stomach was beginning to protest so loudly, she had half a mind to go and eat by herself.

As a last resort she walked over to the information desk. Maybe he had been asking there about her earlier, and she had missed him.

"Excuse me." She cleared her throat of its morning croakiness. "I was wondering if a man has asked about me? We were supposed to meet here twenty minutes ago. Oh ... my name's Bella Whitman." She never could get her brain to work properly in the mornings.

The female desk clerk's puzzled expression spoke volumes. Bella tried again. "I was supposed to meet someone—blonde hair, tanned, late twenties ..."

"I'll just check if there are any messages left for you. What was his name?"

"Jay Hinkley." Bella smiled to herself as she recalled their first meeting, and how Jay had pretended to be someone else. She'd been pretty mad, but had obviously forgiven him by now ...

Something brushed her shoulder, and she reached up a hand to swat at the pesky bug. What she found, however, were two rather large fingers, belonging to ...

"Morning, Bella."

She swung around, still holding the fingers, to find they were connected to a smiling Jay.

"There you are!" she exclaimed. Bella became aware that she was still holding his hand, and quickly jerked hers away. Jay appeared to be enjoying it a little too much for her liking. "I've been waiting here for ages," she said huffily, trying to regain her composure.

"Sorry," he apologised. "I had a bit of a rough night, and slept in." He smiled innocently back at her scowling expression, and held the dining room door open for her. "By the way, weren't we supposed to meet in here? ... I've been waiting for a while too," he grinned, enjoying his moment.

Bella smacked her forehead in disgust. "Of course! My mind's like a sieve!"

"Well, I hope it's not as much of a sieve as your pockets," Jay needled. "You must have a suitcase full of traditional island clothing and souvenirs by now."

Bella barely heard him behind her as she made a beeline for the breakfast buffet. She hadn't eaten since their early dinner in Noumea last night, and she was starving.

Jay beat her to a table. His eyes registered surprise at the volume of food piled on her plate. "I guess that takes care of lunch as well."

"I probably won't even have time for lunch today," she retorted, biting into a thick slice of pineapple.

Jay dusted off the croissant flakes from around his mouth. "That'll give me a chance to check out the island for some good shots." He grinned cheekily over at Bella, who was now devouring a bowl of fruit salad and yoghurt. "So, have you planned a hard day of massages and facials?"

She finished her mouthful. "I'll ignore that comment."

"Well, at least someone has to work around here."

Bella gave him a playful glare, her gaze travelling downward to his crumpled shirt. Hadn't he been wearing that yesterday?

"There's a laundry service here at the resort, or there should be a laundromat close by," she said pointedly, a grin tugging at the corners of her mouth.

Jay looked down at his shirt with a sheepish expression. "Yeah, I guess I do need to pay them a call. Doing laundry has never been high on my list of priorities. But," he smiled slyly, "I guess I'd better lift my game now that I'm in the company of Miss Bella Whitman."

Bella's poorly aimed grape sailed over his head. An unbidden thought popped into her mind as she grabbed another for a second shot.

She might enjoy seeing Jay Hinkley domesticated.

"How's that baby grandson of mine doing?" Jennifer Whitman asked. Her affection for her only grandchild brightened her words.

"He's fine, Mum. Still getting into everything." Todd smiled over at his son, who, having seemed to understand the comment, toddled straight towards the nearest houseplant. Jasper chortled loudly, obviously delighted at the thought of playing with the pebbles around the base of the plant.

Todd chose to ignore the movement. They were running out of places to stash the plants up out of reach of little hands. Besides, if it wasn't the pebbles or pot soil, then Jasper would just find another way to get himself dirty.

"Carly manages to keep him out of trouble most of the time," Todd continued, idly coiling the phone cord around one finger.

"How's she been doing?"

"She's been feeling a little tired lately, and even sometimes a bit nauseous. It's nothing serious, though," he hastened to assuage his mother's concern, "but she has a doctor's appointment tomorrow."

Todd lowered his voice to a conspiratorial whisper, purely for effect. Carly had gone to pick up a few groceries for dinner, so only he and Jasper were in the house. "I think she might be pregnant again, Mum. She assures me she couldn't be, but the symptoms are the same as when she had Jasper."

Todd could picture his mother's face-splitting grin on the other end of the line.

"That's great, honey! Of course, it's not certain yet, but you be sure and let me know the minute you find out."

Her voice sobered. "Have you heard from Bella lately?"

Todd was sure he detected an undercurrent of anxiety in her voice.

He concentrated on keeping his tone casual. "No, I haven't, but I'm sure she's really busy with all that travel and writing. It's only for another week, and then she'll no doubt be back to her usual routine of ringing you every day," he teased.

"She's not *that* tied to my apron strings, you rascal. Still," Jennifer sighed, "it has been almost a week and a half since she last called ..."

Todd was gentle but firm. "You worry too much, Mum. Remember what you were like at that age? Would you have kept close contact with your parents if you were overseas?"

"I—I suppose not." She sounded weary, resigned. "I just can't shake the feeling that something's not quite right. And she told me herself that she'd find it pretty traumatic to go back to where Andrew died." She paused. Todd waited quietly, certain she would come to the right conclusion eventually.

"I really should stop worrying so much and pray some more, shouldn't I?"

His mum sounded so much like a child confessing a misdemeanour that Todd had to smile. "You hit the nail right on the head. We all should pray more, Mum. And if it gives you any comfort, I'm sure she's having a great time. Knowing Bella," he said, remembering their conversation before she left, "she'll be throwing herself into her work so she won't have to face her feelings. But she might even end up finding herself over there ... and hopefully, maybe even find God."

Although this was only the second resort she had visited, Bella was already becoming comfortable with the routine. First she interviewed the spa's manager for a description of the treatments offered and the experience provided for customers. Then she checked out a few of their specialities. She especially enjoyed the full-body massages. With the emotional stress she'd been under lately, Bella felt she deserved the pampering.

She was coming to realise that this was a dream assignment, and not just for the spa treatments or island locations. The chance to get away from it all and experience a piece of luxury, meeting new people—okay, one person in particular—was a godsend.

There was that word again—God. Bella squeezed her eyes shut as the beautician wiped a seaweed masque from her face. The subject of God seemed to be popping into her mind at the most inconvenient times. Maybe it was because she suspected Jay was a Christian, so whenever she thought of him, the subject of spirituality naturally followed.

Bella had to admit that she'd been feeling calmer inside lately. She hadn't even found herself dwelling on Andrew much, even though she was now in Vanuatu. It couldn't just be from the distraction Jay provided, since there was nothing remotely romantic between them.

At least, she didn't think there was.

A short time later, Bella was relaxing on a plush leather couch in the spa's waiting room. Her hot rock massage wasn't due for twenty minutes, so she took advantage of the time to scrawl a few more notes. She was really missing her laptop. The resort contained a fully-equipped conference room, along with computer facilities, but it wasn't the same. Jay had even offered her the use of his laptop, but she'd declined, knowing he would need it frequently to download the images from his camera. Unfortunately, she would just have to wait to buy another one when she got home.

Home. Bella didn't want to think about that. It represented going back to predictability, to her old routine, even her old way of thinking. Something imperceptible inside her was beginning to change. She couldn't pinpoint it, didn't even know if she wanted to.

Just like she didn't want to think about leaving Jay.

Jay slumped down onto a wooden bench next to Port Vila's bustling market. He stared down at the camera held in his hands, oblivious to the sights and sounds all around him. He was trying to work out why he'd bothered to bring his camera with him today, as he was definitely not in the mood for taking photos. That required creativity, passion ... and right now, all he felt was emptiness, uncertainty.

Jay knew all along that he would have to tell Bella eventually. It would have been a lot easier sooner, when he wasn't so ... he struggled for the right word. His head denied it, but his heart already recognised the facts.

He was beginning to fall for Bella.

This was the reason he had delayed telling her his secret, something that wouldn't have been such a big deal right at the start. Now it *was* a big deal, and Jay stood to lose a *great* deal if she hated him for it.

"Why, God?" His whispered voice rose to the cloudless sky through the heavy scent of brewed coffee, fruit, and frangipanis. "Why does life have to be so hard? Why couldn't I have met Bella back in Australia before all this mess, before I"—he swallowed past the lump in his throat—"became attached to someone else?"

Jay shook his head sadly, his fingers mindlessly fiddling with the camera focus. Whoever said, 'life wasn't meant to be easy' sure got it right.

But then, his conscience piped up, *they probably didn't have God to trust in and help them through problems ... not that you've been trusting Him in this!*

Jay sat up straighter, the realisation hitting him hard. It was true—he hadn't been praying for God to guide him in this situation; had thought he could manage on his own. He had strangely reasoned that since he and Bella were really only friends, and he wasn't looking for a romantic relationship, then it wasn't something he needed to seek God about.

God, help! he cried out inwardly, once more lifting his face to the sky. *I'm sorry I left You out of this and tried to cope in my own strength. I've ... I've made a mess of things now. Please guide me.*

The peace that usually came when he spoke with God—that sense of connection with his Creator—was absent. In its place, though, was a quiet, urgent thought—almost a command. *Tell her tonight.*

Jay should have felt panicked, but he didn't. Instead, verses that he had learned as a child flooded into his mind. *I know the plans I have for you ... My ways are higher than your ways ... commit your ways to God, and He will give you the desires of your heart.*

Opening eyes that had been tightly screwed shut just moments before, Jay breathed in a deep, cleansing gulp of air. The marketplace leapt into focus in its full vibrancy of life. It was funny, but talking to God always made things seem clearer, fresher. Newer.

Jay lifted his camera then and started busily snapping the images around him. It was settled in his heart, and gradually, his mind.

He would tell Bella tonight. Whatever the consequences.

Chapter 16

Bella finished her research just before dinner. The sun was already beginning its descent into the ocean, turning the sky outside the lobby windows into an artist's masterpiece of orange, pink and gold.

She hurried down the white stone path through the resort's landscaped gardens, towards the rolling waves just beyond the greenery. Something inside her felt a desperate need to be near the ocean, connect with nature. Perhaps find the peace there she'd been craving. Passing the last sentinel-like palm and out onto an expanse of white sand, she saw that the beach was almost deserted.

Bella sank down onto the sand, letting the cooling breeze caress her face and hair. Her eyes were drawn to the waves, their tips washed with pink. They were small and playful now, but on the day Andrew had disappeared they had been angry and dark. Just like the pain that had been brewing way down inside ...

As though a long-festering wound had been ripped open, something broke deep within her. Bella dropped her face into her hands, allowing the hot, pent-up emotions to gush out at last, her shoulders shaking violently as the sun slipped down into the sea.

Angry sobs finally gave way to healing tears. After all this time, she finally felt herself letting go of the past, and the guilt, and the 'what ifs'.

Long minutes later, Bella stood up stiffly and lifted her

face to the starry sky. As she made her way back down the path to the resort she felt lighter somehow, stronger, ready to embrace the future—whatever came her way.

Bella made it up to her room without running into Jay—a good thing, considering the swollen eyes and red nose the lift mirror reflected back at her.

As she approached room 30, she noticed a white piece of paper taped onto her door. The hurriedly scrawled note contained just three words: *Surprise inside—guess!*

Bella took an involuntary step backwards. Out of nowhere, explosive scenes from action movies she'd viewed sprung into her mind. Could there be a bomb inside, an intruder waiting to surprise her?

She quickly moved towards Jay's door, hoping he'd be there. Just what she needed—a man to spring any trap that might have been set!

It didn't occur to her that her plan might be putting Jay in danger. All she knew was that she felt drained—physically and emotionally—and she just wanted to get into her room. In one piece, preferably.

Her hand was pulling back to knock on Jay's door, when she stopped. *Surprises ... hmm.* It could be Jay pulling a prank. Unlikely, but possible.

With a determined toss of her curls, Bella turned back to her own door. She was just being silly, paranoid.

And if not—if there was a reason for her worry—she would find out in two seconds ...

With a grunt of disgust, Prem flung his coat onto the bed and loosened his tie. He hadn't been prepared for the warmth of Vanuatu in springtime. Since it was further south than Bangkok, he had expected it to be cooler. Still, to stay in character meant he needed to dress in a full suit. Like a businessman, the boss had insisted.

Ha! he thought bitterly as he crossed over to the balcony. At the rate he was going, he would never rise higher than a glorified hit-man.

Prem frowned to himself as he stuck his hands in his trouser pockets. The letter from the photographer's room crinkled between his fingers, drawing him back to the task at hand. He'd found it quite an interesting read.

Apparently this Jay Hinkley had been having second thoughts about some woman, Sasha. It made Prem thankful that he himself had not had the misfortune of relationship entanglements. As far as he was concerned, it wasn't worth his time.

Time ... something it appeared he was running out of on this job. He flopped back on the bed and studied the muted ivory ceiling, deciding that he was tired of this business. The sooner this Hinkley guy was out of the way, the better. And there was no better time to strike than tonight. The woman's schedule meant they would both be at this hotel for another two days, so there would be no missing him this time. He would have everything planned out, would consider every detail.

Prem shuddered as he recalled his previous botched attempt. It had not only wounded his pride, but also his reputation. And that was the most important thing to him; was really all he had.

With a burst of determined energy, Prem sat up and began unpacking his guns and other tools. He'd sort out Hinkley, and then continue to watch Bella—if she didn't take fright and fly back to Australia, that is. Hopefully, before the week was over he'd be back in Bangkok.

Bella turned the handle and pushed her door open in one swift motion, hoping to have the element of surprise on her side. It was a bit silly really, considering whoever was inside would be expecting her.

But the person waiting on the bed definitely wasn't anyone Bella could have expected.

"Krista!" she squealed, as much out of relief than happy surprise. "What are you doing here? How did you get in?"

Krista's enthusiastic bear hug muffled her questions. "Oh, I just showed them my driver's license and told them we were housemates. We *do* share the same address, you know." She flopped back onto the bed, eyeing the room appreciatively.

A prick of alarm alerted Bella. If Krista had been allowed entry to her room so easily, what could a professional criminal accomplish? She pushed the thought to the back of her mind as she struggled to catch on to her friend's prattle. How had she switched from talking about sharing the same address to cat hair in her mouth on the plane?

"This really boring-looking man was sitting next to me," Krista demonstrated his thick glasses with her hands, "—and I freaked him out!" she laughed gleefully, her smile dimming a little when Bella failed to respond.

She walked over to stand directly in front of Bella, interrupting her reverie. "I was talking about the flight over. Uh ... earth to Bella?" Krista stood toe-to-toe with her now, waving her hand in front of Bella's face.

Bella started. "Oh! Umm—sorry. I was just thinking how some pretty strange things have been happening on this trip." She looked at Krista, feeling that her sudden appearance was one of the strangest things of all.

"That's why I came, to warn you!" Krista grabbed both of Bella's hands, worry crinkling a line between her wide blue eyes. "I've been trying to call you for days! Did you get my message in Noumea? And then there was that terrible phone call! Why has your mobile phone been switched off?"

Bella managed a laugh, her head spinning. "Slow down!" She dragged Krista across to the bed and pushed her down into a sitting position. "Now, start from the beginning—SLOWLY."

She hid a smile at Krista's impatient expression. 'Slow' wasn't in her housemate's vocabulary, especially when it came to talking.

"Well," Krista began, clearly making an effort, "I sent a message to you at your hotel in Noumea, letting you know that some strange person had phoned and was asking about you."

Bella nodded, remembering the note she had foolishly stuffed in her pocket and forgotten for two days.

"So you got the message ... but why didn't you phone me? Weren't you worried—or even curious about the details?" Krista appeared to be a little confused at her friend's apparent indifference.

Bella was actually wondering why she hadn't followed up on the warning. "I've just been flat out doing the feature," she responded, knowing full well that it was more her distraction with Jay than anything else. "It's probably nothing, anyway."

Her attempt to convince Krista—and herself—sounded weak, even to her biased ears.

"But that's not all!" Krista's voice rose in near-panic. "The other night, a man phoned and warned me that you were in danger! I've been so worried about you!"

Bella was touched by the unshed tears glistening in her friend's eyes. Right now, though, she had to focus on calming Krista down.

"As you can see, I'm fine." She stood up and twirled around for effect. "Maybe it's someone just pulling a twisted prank." She sat down next to Krista and wrapped an arm around her slumped shoulders.

Krista dabbed at her eyes with the back of her hand, hopelessly smudging her mascara. Bella stifled a laugh at her panda-eyed friend. The tears were over her, after all.

"We're surrounded by people here, and hotel staff," Bella reassured her. "It's probably even safer than at home." She faced Krista with a serious expression. "Do we have a security guard patrolling outside our house every night?"

Krista gave a watery smile at Bella's attempt at humour. "No, I suppose not," she sighed. "I'm such a worry-wort. But that's because I've had such a good teacher." She stood and walked quickly over to the window.

Bella wondered why she moved away so fast. "Who?" she asked innocently.

"You of course, 'Mother Hen'!" Krista was laughing now.

Bella reached for a projectile—a large embroidered pillow—and marvelled at how rapidly Krista's moods changed from storm clouds to sunshine.

Chapter 17

Bella had never eaten so much in her life. She, Krista and Jay had been at the hotel restaurant for two hours, eating, talking, and laughing—in that order. She had wondered how Krista and Jay would get along—considering her early descriptions to her flatmate of the 'arrogant photographer'—but she needn't have worried.

Jay had initially been in a subdued and reflective mood, but Krista soon had him swapping tales of their adventures punctuated by regular bursts of laughter.

Bella glanced up at Jay, who was busily devouring his mud cake dessert as he entertained Krista. She was beginning to feel a tiny bit annoyed with the two of them—or was it just a reflection of how she felt towards herself? Usually she wasn't given to jealousy, and had no right to be now. Jay and she were nothing more than workmates, after all.

Are you sure that's all he means to you? her inner voice prodded.

She looked across at his laughing features, those blue, blue eyes so filled with life. No, she wasn't sure. But she was beginning to realise that her emotions weren't to be trusted where Jay was concerned.

"Bella, I have a question."

She jumped as the blood rushed to her face. Could he somehow sense what she was thinking? That would be too embarrassing!

Jay was grinning at Krista, so he wouldn't have noticed her discomfort. He turned back to Bella, a puzzled expression on his tanned face.

Calm down, Bella, and just listen to the question. And don't get so caught up in those eyes!

"Is there an unwritten rule that everyone who lives in your house has to have a name ending with the letter 'a'?" Jay's brow furrowed in mock bewilderment. Krista looked like she was trying not to choke on her cheesecake.

"Umm—what do you mean?" Bella wondered what he was getting at.

"Well, there's Bell*a*, and Krist*a*. And I just found out that the cat's name is Samar*a*." He grinned lopsidedly as he looked into Bella's eyes, sending her heart rate up a few notches.

"So we'd have to call you *Jaya*!" Krista laughed uproariously at her own joke, sending a piece of cheesecake sailing towards an unsuspecting gentleman diner as she flicked her spoon in a flourish.

Bella ignored her flatmate's antics, holding Jay's gaze, and wondering if he was thinking the same thing as her. Through her little wordplay, Krista had innocently implied that Jay would be moving into their house with his new 'name'.

The more Bella thought about it, the more the idea grew in appeal.

Reluctantly, she broke their eye contact and pretended to be intensely interested in the remains of her chocolate mousse. In reality, she wanted a chance to think, to process the dawning revelation.

Could there really be a chance for them to be together?

This isn't getting any easier!

Jay absentmindedly scraped the mud cake crumbs together on his plate. He was procrastinating, trying to draw the night out as long as possible. Every minute that ticked by brought him closer to 'the discussion'.

The way Bella was looking at him tonight made him

feel even more of a heel than he already did. He didn't want to hurt her—would do anything to spare her pain—but knew that it would happen anyway.

Krista was chirping away between them, not seeming to mind that neither of them appeared to be listening. Jay smiled in spite of himself. Krista had been a welcome distraction this evening, her light banter lifting his spirit. She was bright, funny, and attractive. But she paled next to Bella's inner and outer beauty.

Jay chewed and swallowed the last chocolate crumb and put his spoon down decisively. It was now or never. He owed it to Bella—and himself.

Krista just then took a breath between sentences. Jay seized the opportunity and plunged in.

"Bella, would it be okay if I talked with you after dinner? It'll only take a moment." He wouldn't win any acting awards with his feigned nonchalance, but it was the best he could manage.

Bella looked up quickly, a cloud of concern flitting across her face.

"Uh—sure." Her voice was quiet, uncertain. She glanced over at Krista, who for once wasn't saying anything at all.

Krista appeared to be analysing the interaction between her two dinner companions as she dabbed at the corners of her mouth with a napkin. "I've got some serious exploring to do," she announced, giving Bella a none-too-subtle wink. "I hear this place has a great spa and sauna, so I should be occupied for a couple of hours at least."

She stood up hurriedly and surveyed them both, unsuccessfully trying to hide a knowing grin. "I'll pay for dinner. You two have fun together. And Bella," she threw over her shoulder, "I won't wait up."

Jay shook his head slightly and rolled his eyes, eliciting a subdued giggle out of Bella. At least she was still able to laugh. But that wouldn't last for long ...

Prem leaned against the wall and blew out a pent-up breath. He couldn't remember being nervous on the job since his early days. But then, the stakes had never been as high to him personally. He had to do this right, eliminate the problem. Prove to his boss that he was still the best.

He shifted his weight from one foot to the other and stared across the darkened room. Only a pale glow of moonlight filtered through the muslin curtains. Shadows of furniture were barely discernible in the darkness.

Prem grinned as he gripped the cool steel of the crowbar, felt the reassuring weight of the Beretta beneath his jacket. The conditions were perfect.

He activated the light on his watch dial, noting the time. Hopefully Hinkley would be returning from dinner soon. Prem could already feel the rising excitement he always experienced before a job. The rush it gave him, the sense of power at seeing someone beg for his life ... it had been too long.

This time, he was ready.

They had been walking along the beach for only a few minutes when Bella stopped and touched Jay on the arm. "What did you want to talk about?"

She was clearly trying to remain relaxed, but worry still constricted her voice.

Jay paused for a moment to ask for some heavenly help. As he gazed out at the dark ocean, he could feel Bella's eyes on him, waiting and wondering. But he had learnt his lesson earlier today. There was no way he was going to blunder into this without God's guidance.

He took a breath before launching in. "Bella, we've been friends for, well, almost four whole days now." He smiled at the reality of it. Could it really have been just four days? "So I figure it's time that we got to know each other a little better than just on the surface."

Bella was nodding, so he must have been doing okay so far.

"I'd like to get to know you more as a person, instead of just a work colleague."

Bella sighed with obvious relief. She must have thought that this was just going to be a 'getting-to-know-you' conversation, instead of something more serious. "I agree. You're quickly becoming a special friend to me—" Jay winced inside "—and I think we should talk more about our individual directions, and our goals ... all the important stuff." She spontaneously reached for his hand. "This is so lacking in most friendships."

Jay heard the smile in her voice as he stared at the sand beneath his feet. Maybe his approach had been too subtle. "I'll go first." He took a deep breath and plunged in.

"For me, this trip has been part working holiday, and part escape. You've probably noticed that I've been a little withdrawn at times."

Bella nodded her head vigorously.

She didn't have to agree *that* much, he thought! "Well, that's because I've had a few issues to work through, some decisions to make. And the biggest one has had to do with my future marriage partner."

Bella's eyes were as big as saucers. She couldn't think he was meaning to propose to her, could she?

Jay rushed on. "Back in Australia, I've been in a long-term relationship with a woman, Sasha. Before I left, I was on the verge of asking her to marry me."

Bella dropped his hand abruptly—not a good sign.

"But even after buying the ring, I wasn't fully comfortable with the idea. Something wasn't right, so I got away to think." He stared out at the ocean, mostly to avoid looking at Bella. "I was planning to phone Sasha tonight to call things off, but decided I'd tell you first," he finished quietly.

Bella spun away and walked a few steps across the sand. Jay knew she would need time to process the revelation, but he wished she would respond. Anything was better than silence.

"Just when were you intending to tell me about this?" Bella stalked back towards him, her temper making her steps unsteady.

"Umm—now?" Jay looked down at his feet scuffing in the sand. He'd hoped she wouldn't take it quite this hard.

"But *why* now?" she shot back, her blue eyes charged

with sparks. "Why not in six months' time, or two years? Why not never?" She punctuated each sentence with a finger forcefully poked into his chest. Jay started backing away. He hadn't been prepared for Bella's unrestrained anger.

"I thought friendships were based on openness and honesty—at least they are where I come from. So I'll be honest with you—the reason why I'm so mad is that I haven't had a good run in the relationship stakes. In particular, my fiancé drowned two years ago—right here in Vanuatu, somewhere in the ocean off this beach." Her last words dissolved into a sob.

Jay's heart plummeted. How could he have been so insensitive? Maybe he should have probed into her background a little before he dropped the 'big one'. He'd never realised her own tragedy could be so ... *huge.*

He reached out for her, wanting to cradle her against him, soothe the pain away. But Bella wasn't in the mood for comfort.

"How *could* you?" She emphasised her accusation with a two-handed push on his chest, sending him stumbling backwards over the sand. "How could you be so deceitful, and—and *lie* to me?"

She turned and started half-walking, half-running up the beach, her gasping breaths audible over the rolling of the waves. When she was fifty metres away, she stopped and turned back towards him. "What if I had fallen for you?—Which I *haven't!*" And she continued at her previous pace, as though she couldn't get away from him fast enough.

Jay watched her go, torn between running after her and giving her some space. He'd thought she might react badly, but—well, he hadn't expected this!

With a heavy sigh, he started to trudge back to the hotel, feeling lower than a dung beetle. No, even lower than pond scum.

God, that didn't exactly go very well, did it?

A small voice sounded in his heart. *But you did the right thing. Now you can pray that Bella will let Me heal her pain.*

Jay did that as he stood under the star-studded sky, giving the whole situation—and Bella—over to Christ. He resolved in his heart to always be honest with her, if their friendship continued, and to be aware of the consequences of every action.

Because tonight, he deserved everything he got.

Chapter 18

After just a few minutes of sobbing and running, Bella's lungs, throat and eyes started to burn. She slowed her steps to a panting, plodding walk.

She knew she was overreacting. What Jay had told her wasn't completely earth-shattering, as confessions went. It was just that he should have been open from the start, told her before ... before she ...

With a deep sigh, she released her frustration and sorrow out into the salty night air. Yes, he should have told her before she started to care for him, before it meant something to her that he had been already committed to someone else. Why had he held back?

Helpless to stop it, Bella felt the anger rise once more, pushing up past the familiar lump of pain in her chest. Jay had no right to deceive her like that, to betray her ... And she'd dared to hope he had feelings for her! If he had *really* cared about her, he should have stayed away.

She kicked a convenient shell in frustration, scattering sand up into the velvet sky. If Jay *had* stayed away, then they wouldn't have shared those fun times, the laughter, the scary times ... Bella shivered as she remembered almost falling over the cliff, looking down at her feet dangling far above the trees. If Jay hadn't been there ...

A lone tear slipped down her cheek, only to be whisked away by the brisk salty breeze. She tipped her face up to the heavens, a dark glass ceiling studded with thousands

of tiny lights

of tiny lights. Impenetrable, cold glass.

"Why, God?" she whispered. "Why do all the men I love have to leave me, either through death, or ... deceit?"

In the dark stillness, with the distant rumble of the ocean sounding in her ears, a voice whispered to her on the wind.

I have never left you.

The peace that followed was something Bella was coming to recognise as being from a heavenly source. But her mind was not as easily stilled.

"You may never have left, God," she addressed the stars, "but I wasn't aware of when You came, either."

Jay was exhausted; he had never felt so tired in his life. Emotional stress did that to you. His body felt like it had run two marathons, and his neck muscles were tied up in knots.

The elevator couldn't move fast enough. Jay was thankful there was no one else riding with him—it gave him a chance to think.

To beat yourself up, you mean.

Okay, so he was having a bit of a pity party, even if the situation was his fault ...

He finally reached his room. *Why couldn't Bella have reacted more calmly?* he wondered as he fumbled in his pocket for the key. She had really lost it—her temper, her common-sense—everything!

He had to admit, though, that the revelation about her fiancé drowning explained a large part of her response. Without going through a similar experience, it would be impossible to imagine what Bella had been through—and yet she hid her pain so well.

Jay stopped with his hand on the door handle, his brow furrowed.

Mentally replaying the last few days, he realised that wasn't entirely true. He had seen glimpses of her hurt, evidenced by her over-sensitivity of his occasional contemplative silences ('brooding', she'd called it), the shadow of worry flitting across her face sometimes when she didn't think he was watching.

Bella's emotional pain—and how he figured in her present and future—weighed heavily on Jay as he let himself into the room and then sagged against the closed door. He had some serious thinking—and praying—to do.

Then he had to call Sasha. And that was one phone call he wasn't looking forward to making. He didn't fully know how she'd respond, but surely she must have had some clue when he suddenly took off like he did?

It was just weeks ago that they were having dinner together with her family. Their smiles, knowing glances, questions about any plans the two of them may have had for next year ... And then suddenly he was packing his bags for the South Pacific.

Jay took a step into the still-dark entrance, memories pushed aside as he stopped abruptly. The eerie sense of someone else being in the room with him crept up his spine, danced in the moon-cast shadows on the wall.

Something was definitely wrong.

Ethan was having a terrible day. They were scrambling to meet the afternoon deadline for this month's issue, he had paper piles the height of Mount Everest on his desk, and Susan's voice was beginning to give him a headache.

And the morning was just about to get worse.

He'd had some difficulties organising transport for the shipment through the usual channels—namely, safely getting the contraband through Customs' security checks.

Although he'd managed to work around this for a few previous smaller deals, this particular one was much bigger—and, as he was finding out, much more complex.

So now he would have to go to Plan B. The problem was that this option could turn out to be even more risky. He expected this operator would refuse to be involved, had probably already smelled a rat. But as Ethan was rapidly discovering, his choices were becoming very limited. Now he would have to resort to some serious threats and blackmail—both sure to land him in even more trouble if the authorities ever caught up with him.

Steeling himself, Ethan picked up the phone and dialled.

The crushing blow would have killed Jay if it had hit his head, but his left shoulder took the brunt of it. He staggered into the wooden desk chair, grabbing it as he twisted around to face his attacker.

He was just in time.

The second hit took the leg off the chair. The guy must've had a heavy steel crowbar. Jay ducked sideways, and looked up into the most menacing face he had ever seen.

A pair of dark eyes glittered in the moonlit room, blazing with hatred and fury. Jay had no doubt the man meant to kill him—if not by bludgeoning him to death, then with a gun or some other weapon concealed beneath the voluminous dark coat.

The assailant now had him backed against the writing desk, with no room to move. Jay's eyes darted over to the door. If he could slip past the man and around the bed, then he just might make it.

He lunged with the chair at the black-clad figure, hoping to put him off balance—and not a moment too soon. The man was reaching for something behind his back. If he pulled out a gun, it would all be over.

Jay stepped to the left as he shoved the chair between himself and the man. Now, to get around the bed. Pity it was so large ...

The attacker—deadly gun in hand, its black barrel fitted with a silencer—dove to cut Jay off. Jay braced himself; he could almost feel the bullet tearing through his flesh, sense himself falling towards the wooden floor ... *Help, God!*

He turned to face the inevitable. But where he'd expected to see his attacker standing pointing the gun at him, rage in his eyes, instead the man's face showed confusion and surprise. His right foot slipped from beneath him as it landed on the bedside rug, which scooted across the polished floorboards. A dull thud followed.

Jay looked on in disbelief at the still figure lying beside

the television cabinet, bleeding from a gash in his forehead. Was he dead?

Jay's shock-numbed brain sprang into action. He had to call hotel security, let them know he needed the police and an ambulance. But mostly, he had to protect the girls.

He backed towards the door, noting that his antagonist had not stirred. Still, it wouldn't hurt to somehow try and bar the door from the outside.

His bashing on the door of room 30 was surely loud enough to wake the whole hotel. Krista peered through a crack, her guarded expression changing to wary surprise as she focussed on his face.

"What is it?"

"There's an intruder in my room—call hotel security!" he blurted, trying not to stare past Krista to Bella's slumped form on the bed. She looked like she had been crying—and all because of him, he knew.

Krista was pushing past him. "Can I have a look?" Her excited face could have fooled him into thinking she was headed for the amusement park, instead of taking a peek at a dangerous criminal.

"No!" Jay shoved her back into the room. "Call security! And an ambulance. He's knocked out, but I'd still better keep an eye on him."

Jay bolted back to his room and grabbed the metal door handle, pulling it hard towards him to ensure the door remained closed. Even though the assailant was probably still unconscious, Jay was taking no chances. It would be too easy for his strong attacker to pull the door open from the inside and make his escape.

One minute later, two security guards bustled onto the scene, firing questions at Jay as they scanned the area with expert eyes.

Only after explaining the situation did he step aside from the door. It remained closed—a good sign.

The larger of the two guards silently opened the door a crack, slid his hand around to the light switch, and then quickly pushed the door fully open.

He stood in the entrance for a moment, before turning

back to look at Jay. The expression on his face spoke volumes.

Jay peered past the guard's broad shoulders, his eyes widening.

Where—?

The room was empty.

His attacker had vanished without a trace.

Chapter 19

"I can't believe you fended off that armed intruder with your bare hands!" Krista exclaimed, her face and gestures animated.

Bella sighed and continued to stir her bowl of cold cereal. As much as she loved Krista, her friend's innate cheeriness was starting to get on her nerves.

"Well, what else could I do?" Jay grinned. "It was either him or me."

Actually, Jay was beginning to get on Bella's nerves, too. He could at least *pretend* to be sorry that she wasn't speaking to him. But he didn't seem that concerned, had hardly even noticed. And Krista—well, she talked enough for the two of them.

"Where do you think the man's hiding?" Krista asked as she picked through a bunch of grapes. "He couldn't have gone far—we're on a small island, after all."

Jay's expression sobered. "Well, after he escaped over the balcony he could have left the island last night by boat or plane. Or he might even still be here." He paused to scan the hotel dining room, almost as if he expected to see his opponent seated at the next table. "The police are on the lookout though, so hopefully he'll be captured soon."

Krista's eyes lit up then, and she reached out to grab Jay's arm. *Oh, great!* Bella thought. They were in for another of her flatmate's hare-brained schemes.

Krista's voice rose with excitement. "Why don't we try searching for him? We were going to check out the sights anyway, so it wouldn't hurt to explore a bit more of the island."

Jay appeared doubtful. "I don't know. Why go looking for trouble, when the authorities are already on it? And," he glanced across the table, "I don't think Bella would be too keen on the idea."

Bella tried to maintain her mask of stony silence, despite her surprise at Jay's concern. It was the first time he'd considered her all morning—although, she grudgingly admitted to herself, maybe he was just giving her some space.

However, that didn't change the fact that he'd hurt her last night. He deserved to suffer a little, just as she was suffering.

But that won't make you feel any better, will it?

Bella dismissed the unwelcome thought as she put down her spoon.

"I don't care what you guys do, because I'll be busy all day with research." For some reason, she couldn't quite make herself meet Jay's eyes. She didn't want to look into them and see how he was feeling, how her coldness was affecting him. "So I guess I'll see you both at dinner," she finished quietly, standing to leave.

She gathered up her shoulder bag and a muffin to snack on later, hoping crazily that Jay would try to stop her, ask if she was alright. Instead, he just said, "Okay, then. Have a good day."

"Bye, Bella," Krista added breezily.

Bella stalked away breathing a huffy sigh. Neither of them really cared about her or what she was going through, how she was feeling ...

Let them annoy each other all day, she thought angrily as she rode the elevator up to her room. Because at the moment, she didn't want anything to do with either of them—especially Jay.

Krista almost had to jog to keep up with Jay as they pushed through the crowds in Vila's bustling market place.

"Remind me again why I let you talk me into this?" he grumbled.

"Because it's a good idea, and you know it. If the attacker spots the police looking for him, he'll immediately go into hiding, but we can do it *incognito*." She lifted up her sunglasses to peer at Jay from beneath them. "Hey! Put your sunnies on." She grabbed the glasses from the top of Jay's head and pushed them down onto his nose. "He might have already got a good look at you, so you have to be *extra* careful."

She was beginning to enjoy this. Move over, Nancy Drew!

Jay stopped abruptly, causing Krista to almost collide with his broad back. He stared out at the ocean, its blue waves visible between the market stalls, and sighed. "Can we dispense with the cloak and dagger stuff? Right now, I could be relaxing on the beach—or even better, up in the jungle photographing the native wildlife."

Krista let out her own frustrated sigh. Jay might be very good-looking, but she was beginning to understand how he and Bella were having problems. Men could be so difficult sometimes.

She grabbed Jay's arm and pulled him back into the throng of shoppers. "Have you thought about the fact that until this guy's caught, you could be in danger? For all we know, he's still hunting you."

Jay let out a laugh, a deep, rich sound that reminded Krista of warm sunshine. "I seriously doubt I'm in any danger—like the police said, just in the wrong place at the wrong time. Besides," he grinned, giving her a playful shove, "who would want to kill a humble photographer? Although ... then again, he could be jealous of such a handsome, extremely lovable photographer as myself," he teased, flashing her a lopsided smile.

Krista giggled and shook her head. On second thoughts, perhaps she *could* see what Bella saw in him.

As she strode along beside Jay, her thoughts turned to Ryan. She wondered how he was getting along without her—if he'd even noticed she was gone. Well, at least having to feed Samara would remind him that she wasn't there.

Suppressing a sigh, she quickened her steps to catch up with Jay. There was no point dwelling on her workaholic boyfriend right now, when there was a criminal to catch ...

Patrick McKenzie jumped as the phone trilled beneath the clutter on his desk. He was working late again, his secretary gone home over an hour ago. Swiping away a few of the papers, he warily reached to pick up the receiver. Surely he could afford to relax now. It had been over two years ...

He breathed a wheezing sigh of relief at the voice of the tourist on the other end of the line—just another cashed-up Westerner who wanted to hire a sea-cruiser.

McKenzie finalised the details and then leant back in his chair. He rubbed a hand over his weary face. It wasn't good for his health to work such long hours—would just aggravate his blood pressure, the doctor had told him—but there was nothing worth going home to. Marilyn had left him over a year ago, and now the place seemed empty and cold.

If anything *could* feel cold in Phuket in the spring. He wiped the sweat from his forehead and looked around the office through blood-shot eyes. Yes, he had done well for himself. Ten charter boat companies throughout the Pacific, and now expansion into South-East Asia, had made him a wealthy man. Miserable, sick, and alone—but rich.

McKenzie suddenly slammed a pudgy fist onto the desk, sending more papers flying. Everything would have been perfect if not for that 'incident' a couple of years ago. The stress had sky-rocketed his blood pressure, wrecked his marriage, and put him constantly on edge.

The phone rang again. McKenzie swore, and went back to his paperwork. He would let the phone ring.

If only he could ignore the past as well ...

Brrr, brrr. Brrr, brrr. Jay drummed his fingers impatiently

SORRY!!!

on the bedside table in his room. He'd spent a lot of time thinking and praying about this phone call, and now he just wanted it over and done with.

"Hello," a young woman's voice answered.

Jay only just stopped himself from launching in. It was Sasha's sister. "Hi, Leah. Is Sasha around?" He tried to make his tone light, casual, but the tightness in his throat was making his voice crack.

"She had to run a few errands, but she accidentally left her mobile phone at home. Sorry." Leah hesitated. "Is everything okay? We haven't heard from you in a while."

Jay released a small breath he didn't realise he'd been holding in. It looked like he wouldn't be talking to Sasha today, after all. "I'm fine." He was glad Leah couldn't see his fake smile. "The islands are beautiful. I just thought I'd see how Sasha was doing."

"She's great. She's been enjoying going out for coffee and movies with the young adults' group from your church."

Jay smiled in spite of himself. Sasha was a fairly new Christian—had started coming along with him to church just six months ago—and she really needed to spend time with other Christians. Maybe something good for her had come out of him being away.

"I'm glad to hear she's keeping herself busy," he chuckled. "Tell her not to bother calling me back—I'll phone her sometime tomorrow."

Jay said goodbye and ended the call as he flopped back on the bed. He was feeling awfully tired all of a sudden.

And unfortunately, with his relationship with Sasha still unresolved, he knew he probably wouldn't get a lot of sleep tonight.

"I'm beginning to wish this assignment was over!" Bella lay propped up on her elbows on the bed, trying to organise her notes on the spa in Vila. Without her laptop to keep things neat and tidy, she was finding it difficult. And the two 'distractions' she was travelling with didn't make things any easier.

Krista turned away from doing her hair in the mirror. "I

know you're having a hard time with Jay at the moment," she acknowledged, "but I don't think you *really* mean that."

Bella gave up on her notes and shoved them aside with a sigh. "I guess you're right," she admitted grudgingly. "All the same, I don't think I'll go down for dinner. I've still gotta pack for our flight tonight." She rolled over onto her back and watched Krista out of the corner of one eye. "Didn't you say you were heading back home, now that you're convinced I'm safe from danger?" Bella couldn't keep the sarcasm from her voice.

It was obviously lost on Krista, though, who was busy spritzing perfume and touching up her lipstick. "I've decided to have a bit of a holiday," she smiled into the mirror. "Before I left, I let the hospital know that I could be away for a couple of weeks."

She moved over to the bed and sat down, jostling Bella's body, and her nerves. "We can spend some fun time together exploring paradise—and I can keep you company so you won't have to be alone with Jay."

Trying not to think about last night, Bella managed a smile. "Thanks for your help. But remember, I'll be pretty busy during the days with my research."

"That's okay. There's plenty for me to do by myself while you and Jay are working."

Jay... Bella had been forcing aside thoughts of him all day, but now they flooded through into her consciousness. Part of her wished that things could go back to how they'd been before that walk on the beach, before she knew the truth. But now that seemed like a lifetime ago—as if there was too much of a chasm between them to ever cross; no way to go back to how things had been.

If only ...

A few tears welled up in her eyes and trickled down her cheeks onto the bedspread. Bella quickly wiped them away, not wanting to let Krista see she was so upset, and annoyed at herself for the emotion.

Krista was standing by the door. "You're *sure* you don't want to come down?" She pulled a comical face, attempting to look sad but not quite succeeding. "It'll cheer you up."

Bella doubted that very much. "I'll be fine," she yawned. "I've got a bit of work to catch up on, and then there's that packing." She sat up slowly, feeling like a tired old woman. "Don't be too long. Our plane leaves in a few hours, and you know how long it takes for you to get organised to leave."

"Yes, *mum*," Krista giggled, waltzing out the door.

Bella trudged over to the wardrobe and started to pack her things, crinkling her nose at the scent of Krista's perfume lingering in the room. Unfortunately her friend's air of cheeriness remained, too. And Bella was not in the mood to be cheery.

She pulled her clothes off the hangers, rising frustration fuelling her energy levels. Sometimes Krista made her so mad! She was always so happy, and outgoing, and beautiful. And right now, she was having dinner with Jay, probably fluttering her dark eyelashes and giggling like a schoolgirl.

Bella dumped her semi-folded clothes into her suitcase, along with her unfounded suspicions, and dropped onto the bed. She remembered feeling this way before, years ago in school. Jason Turner, who always sat next to her in class, had one day decided to sit next to Allison Ward instead. Bella had been left hurt and jealous, even a little angry.

But how could she be feeling that way now about Jay? She didn't even like the guy! And if he even *looked* like he was showing an interest in Krista, she would dislike him even more.

Prem sat slumped on the side of his bed, nursing a killer headache. He had lain low all day, suspecting that the police would be on the lookout for a man matching his description. With the bandaged wound on his head, he would be sure to be a suspect, but since his businessman-cover didn't match the profile of a cloaked intruder, he was still hoping to escape detection.

He stood and paced restlessly to the window, staring out into the darkening sky. If he wanted to live, he would need to leave the island tonight. For as sure as the throbbing in his head, the boss would have already sent someone to deal with him—permanently.

Prem almost hadn't phoned with his regular report this morning, but knew the omission would only confirm his guilt. He had tried to sound cocky and convincing, but unfortunately, despite his line of work, he had never been a particularly good liar. The boss now knew he had not succeeded—and incompetence was unforgivable.

For Prem too, failure was not an option. It was a matter of honour, of personal pride. If it cost him everything—even his life—he would finish his task. He would not only eliminate this Hinkley man, but the woman Bella as well.

With his face set in grim resolve, Prem began to pack his few belongings and weapons. He would follow them to their next destination—Fiji—and there he would finish what he came to do.

Chapter 20

McKenzie Charter," McKenzie growled into the phone receiver. He was working late again. With the amount of time he'd spent in his office lately, he was beginning to feel as if the four walls were closing in on him.

Twenty years was a long time to run a business, but he had been successful enough that he could finally retire comfortably. He would go somewhere cool, some place where there were actually distinct seasons instead of simply 'dry' and 'wet'.

Just the thought almost made him smile.

The voice on the other end of the line instantly banished any trace of humour he may have felt.

"Good evening, Mr McKenzie. We spoke previously about you transporting some cargo to Australia at the end of the month."

McKenzie swore under his breath. "I told you I'm not a shipping company. I hire charter boats!"

He was sick of this man and his calls. Although he had only contacted him twice, it was two times too many. There was something about his voice—the oily smoothness, the undercurrent of ice—that made his skin crawl.

"You may regret your decision," the man continued, his tone hard as granite.

"Well, so be it. As far as I'm concerned, the only people wanting to use small charter boats to transport goods

that fast,

that far are drug runners."

That would get him to shut up—or show his hand.

There was a short moment of silence, followed by a loud sigh. "I thought it might come to this."

McKenzie waited, a bead of sweat trickling down his temple.

"Mr *McKenzie*"—the name was turned into a sneer—"do you recall an incident two years ago with your boat company in Vanuatu?"

McKenzie's heart stopped for a moment. The past had finally caught up with him.

"Are you there?" the man barked. "Perhaps you have amnesia? Allow me to jog your memory. Was it just two short years ago that one of your diving boats left a tourist behind in the ocean off Vanuatu? The man disappeared, his body never found. Didn't you pay the others who were on board to keep their mouths shut during the investigation? And at the inquest, didn't you testify—"

"Yes! Stop!" McKenzie shouted, his breath coming in short gasps. The release of the tension that had been building inside him for two years was like a cork shooting out of an exploding wine bottle. But now in its place was a growing dread.

"How did you find out?"

"Let's just say that one of the women on your boat that day is an intimate friend of mine. The question is, *now* will you do it?"

McKenzie wiped a shaking hand over his face, a sense of powerlessness welling up and drowning him inside. "I don't see that I have any choice, do I?"

"You've made a wise decision. I will contact you shortly with the details."

Click.

McKenzie replaced the receiver and dropped his head into his hands. His worst fears had been realised—he had begun to reap a bitter harvest from the deceit sown two years ago.

Now there was no turning back.

Bella squirmed around for the fifth time in two minutes,

trying to find a better position on the uncomfortable seat in the departure area. Jay looked over at her, his eyes twinkling with amusement.

"Are you alright there?"

"I'm fine. I just wish the flight wasn't delayed," she grumbled, forgetting she hadn't intended to speak to Jay. "We've been waiting for almost an hour!"

"Well, what else would you be doing right now, except trying to sleep on a cramped little plane?" Krista joked sarcastically, her foot tapping in impatient rhythm with a fan overhead.

"Sleep would be nice," Bella sighed. "Sleeping in my *own* bed, in my *own* house, with Samara curled up on the floor rug."

"Is someone getting homesick?" Jay asked, leaning forward so that their heads almost touched across the narrow aisle.

No, only heartsick.

Bella quickly sat back in her seat, trying to put as much distance between her and Jay as possible. Despite the fact that he had continued to show he cared—while also giving her some space—Bella still wasn't ready to go back to how things were. And that included being near him.

She had to admit that her self-imposed silence—and sulking—was hurting only one person, and it wasn't either of her travelling companions.

Ever since she was a child, Bella had known she took things to heart, loving—and hurting—so deeply. She didn't release pain easily, clutching it to her chest and wearing it as a badge of honour.

Bella stared down at the pink-painted toenails peeking through her sandals. It was strange, but she seemed to be doing a lot of reflecting about her life on this trip, dragging out her feelings and attitudes from under the carpet of denial, and dusting them off for a better view.

This particular evaluation was long overdue. Bella just hoped it wasn't too late to change her ways ... or her future.

She looked up at Jay, who was lazing back in his

chair, one leg propped up on the other knee. He looked so relaxed and carefree, despite the inner turmoil and decisions he'd said awaited him back home.

How did he handle it so well? Bella wondered. She made a mental note to ask him when they got to Fiji—and could perhaps be alone—how he managed to remain so peaceful.

She closed her eyes and took a deep breath, psyching herself up to offer an apology for her behaviour today.

But when she looked over at Jay, he was leaping out of his chair.

"Hey! Stop!" He dashed around the row of seats and sprinted towards the nearest exit.

Running away, already almost at the door, was a dark-haired, olive-skinned man dressed in a business suit.

"Where's he going?" Bella was totally confused. Could the businessman have grabbed Jay's backpack?

Krista scrambled out of her seat. "I don't know, but I'm gonna check it out."

Bella remained sitting with their bags, unable to ignore the knot of apprehension tightening in her stomach.

Prem swore under his breath as he sprinted towards the airport exit. His feet pounded noisily on the tiles, but not as loudly as the thundering of his heart. He couldn't believe he'd been so careless as to book a ticket for the same flight as his targets. Maybe his head injury had affected him more than he'd thought.

Prem's head swivelled around as he reached the open door. He could feel the cool night air on his clammy skin, could almost smell the scent of freedom above his overpowering fear.

Hinkley was quickly gaining on him, was now only thirty metres away. A security guard lumbered forward at the edge of Prem's vision. He could feel the net closing in, the noose tightening around his neck.

Even time in jail would be akin to a death sentence. The boss had contacts everywhere, especially in prisons. Prem would be as good as dead.

But he would rather die trying to make his escape, as

a free man. With honour.

Without hesitation, Prem reached round and whipped the Berretta from under his jacket. He didn't even have to think about aiming. Expert marksmanship—killing—was to him as natural as breathing.

The photographer skidded in his tracks at the sight of the weapon pointed in his direction. As Prem squeezed the trigger, Hinkley leaped to the side.

The action was too little, too late.

Prem spun around and raced away from his pursuers, disappearing into the darkness. But not before he saw Hinkley crumple onto the tiled floor, a crimson stain spreading across his shoulder.

Prem smiled as he made his escape. He had completed his assignment just in time.

Jay had never felt so much pain. The intensity of the searing fire in his shoulder took him by surprise. It consumed everything around him, flooded his senses, until he was barely aware of the cold tiles under him, something warm and sticky oozing from beneath his fingers, muffled voices shouting ... And someone groaning.

A figure intruded into the fog. There was a hand on his arm, a sob. Jay forced his eyes to remain open, squinting at the harsh terminal lights. Faces swum above him, eyes filled with horror and concern: a security guard, Krista. Bella, her eyes brimming with tears.

Somehow through the confusion, one conscious thought emerged. Jay was sure he had evaded a direct hit, had dodged to the left at the last moment. Hopefully, it was just a graze ...

He really didn't need this. With trying to sort things out with Bella, and make plans to soon return to Australia and renegotiate his future—not to mention taking shots for the magazine feature—he was far too busy to waste time recuperating.

Jay felt a lifting motion and groaned again as paramedics hustled him out to the ambulance on a stretcher. But surely he wouldn't need an ambulance if it was just a scratch?

He opened his mouth to protest, but stopped short as Bella bent over him again. She was crying in earnest now, no doubt tears of fear and concern. Love? Jay couldn't quite tell, but felt a faint flicker of hope.

If something good was able to come out of this, Jay hoped it would be for Bella to open her eyes—and, once he'd had a chance to end things properly with Sasha—her heart.

That was way too close.

Prem sank back into his seat on the flight to Bangkok. He couldn't believe how near he'd come to actually getting caught this time. And not even by a cop, but an unskilled civilian!

The thought flashed through his mind that he would have to start concealing his face again, as he had in his earlier days. He had hated the amateurish appearance of balaclavas, and he'd never taken the time to perfect some good disguises. The thing was, none of his victims had ever lived to identify him.

Until recently.

A satisfied smile briefly lifted his tired features. Tonight he had dealt with his last victim. From the blood he'd witnessed spreading over Hinkley's chest, he too wouldn't be identifying the shooter in this lifetime.

The whole thing had worked to his advantage, Prem decided as he idly flicked through a business magazine. After he'd risked slipping back through another entry, he'd had time to change his clothes and don a baseball cap in an attempt at camouflage, and phone the boss before boarding the flight. Even now, Prem wondered if the call had been a wise choice, but it was all he could think of to convince his boss he was back in form, back working for him as a trusted employee.

And hopefully save his own life.

He had been anxious to inform his boss that he'd fatally wounded Hinkley, and check if he was still required to watch the woman. The boss had ordered him to fly straight home. He had succeeded in sending a warning to Gray, ensuring he wouldn't dare consider a doublecross on the upcoming business deal; Prem was now needed elsewhere.

So he relaxed in his first class seat—he thought he deserved it now, after all—and perused the in-flight movie schedule. They weren't offering anything violent enough for his liking.

But Prem hoped that soon he would be inflicting some violence of his own, working for his boss in Bangkok, since he was now back to his old form.

If his boss would just let him live ...

Chapter 21

Bella wished she didn't feel so upset. Every time she thought of Jay falling to the ground, the ominous *click* of the silenced gunshot still piercing her ears and her heart, the tears would well up once more.

She was down to the last soggy tissue in her handbag. If only she knew Jay would be alright, then she could calm herself.

The ride in the ambulance had been terrifying. With one look at her stricken face, the paramedics had assumed she was Jay's partner, and so had let her travel in the back.

Bella had almost wished they hadn't. The screaming siren, the oxygen mask, drip, administration of pain relief, constant checks of Jay's heart rate and blood pressure ... She could almost feel the cold chill of death swooping in to take him away.

"Excuse me, ma'am?" A nurse stood before Bella in the cramped waiting room. Her white uniform, along with the antiseptic hospital smell, brought back a flood of unpleasant memories. Of watching her father fade away from the ravages of cancer; of visiting her mother during the rounds of countless tests, surgery, and radiation.

"You can go in and see your husband now."

Bella felt too drained to correct the nurse. She stood and numbly followed the woman down to the end of the stark corridor, before being ushered into a small room off to the left.

Jay was lying on a hospital bed, his face almost as white as the pillowcase. An IV line led into his arm, and a bandage and sling swathed his shoulder.

The white-coated doctor looked up from making his notes in Jay's medical chart.

"Hello, Mrs Hinkley."

Was omission really a lie? "How is he?" Bella asked, her voice hushed.

Jay's eyes snapped open at the sound of her voice.

The doctor smiled. "I'm happy to say he'll be just fine."

Bella felt herself go limp with relief. She sagged into the chair beside the bed, reaching out to grab Jay's hand.

"He's lost a bit of blood, but we've been pumping IV fluids into him."

"And the bullet?" For all Bella knew, it could still be lodged in his shoulder, requiring surgery to remove it. Jay could be in hospital for several days, and if she was to finish her feature, she would have to go without him.

No!

The realisation hit Bella hard in her stomach. Jay was more important to her than her work, than money, than recognition or success. She was prepared to put it all aside to be with him.

Was this what true love was like? Even with Andrew, she couldn't remember feeling the same intensity of emotion.

"... carved a small notch in the top of his deltoid," the doctor was saying, "but there's no nerve or major vessel damage, so when the stitches come out he should be as good as new."

"When will I be able to fly?" Jay's voice was quiet, yet steady.

The doctor studied his patient over the top of his glasses, as if trying to assess how determined Jay was to continue with his travel plans.

"Well ..." He scratched the back of his head. "Normally I'd advise waiting a couple of days, but it should be okay to fly within twenty-four hours."

Jay smiled weakly, relief and fatigue washing over his shadowed face.

Watching him, Bella wondered if he was pleased to be able to continue to Fiji on the next leg of their trip, or if he was now planning to return to Australia. She knew first-hand that traumatic events—not to mention a near-death experience such as being shot—could change a person's perspective.

Maybe Jay now felt an urgent need to return home to see his family. Or—her breath caught—he might even want to see Sasha, the woman he'd been about to propose to.

The doctor having left, Bella sat down and waited as Jay drifted back to sleep. It was hard to believe how special he had become to her in such a short time.

She just wished she could be sure he felt the same way about her ...

"Oh, that's so funny!"

Ethan regarded the giggling blonde seated across from him and secretly despised her—from her meticulously styled hair and skirt suit right down to the tips of her manicured fingernails.

He had finally convinced himself that holing up in his apartment and stewing every night wasn't good for his health—or his image. But neither was the pretty temp from the office he had invited out for a Friday evening drink at a nearby Fortitude Valley bar.

Work consumed him for at least 14 hours a day. Why did he then go and extend that by socialising with an employee?

Ethan frowned into his scotch, tuning out the woman's fawning chatter. When he thought about it, what else was there to focus on besides work? Except for this floundering deal on the side that was threatening to strangle the life out of him, of course ...

He sighed inwardly. Even when he was away from the brooding solitude of his apartment, he still couldn't escape the shadows.

"What do you think?" The blonde was looking at him

expectantly, her eyelashes fluttering in overt infatuation.

Taking a deep breath, Ethan looked up and smiled. Time to focus on something else.

"I think that's a great idea," he said, not having the faintest clue what she'd been talking about, "but I have an even better one."

He leaned closer across the bar table and looked her in the eyes, playing the charming role to perfection. "Why don't you join me for dinner, and then we can go out dancing." It had been years since he'd hit the clubs—saw it as beneath his hard-earned executive image—but tonight he felt the need to do something active, something young and crazy.

Anything to banish thoughts of everything that could go wrong during the next couple of weeks.

"I'd love to!" she gushed, and he winced. The woman was reminding him of his secretary, Susan, more each minute.

They were walking out of the central city bar when Ethan's mobile phone vibrated on his hip. He excused himself and took the call.

"Mr Gray."

Ethan's pulse stopped, then increased in anger—or was it dread? He'd given Sanouk strict instructions to phone him only at certain times, and this was not one of them.

Something had to be wrong.

Ethan walked away from the blonde and stopped at the entrance to an alleyway. He kept his voice low. "You have news for me?"

"Yes—good or bad, however you choose to interpret it."

This was not good.

Sanouk continued. "The photographer travelling with Bella—Hinkley—has been dealt with."

Ethan's heart froze in his chest. *Dealt* with? His contract photographer must have been killed. Things were getting way too deep, and he'd forgotten how to swim.

He could manage only one word. "How?"

Sanouk spoke slowly, as if explaining the obvious to a

child.

child. "I don't believe you need to know all the details. But consider this your warning. You will follow every detail, as previously planned." He paused. The silence was deafening. "The good news for you is that Ms Whitman was not also injured."

Ethan covered the phone receiver and exhaled quietly in relief. It would really ruin everything if Bella had also been hurt.

Sanouk continued. "Her future, however, depends entirely on you. We will talk again."

Ethan turned off his phone and sagged against the crumbling alley wall. All thoughts of dinner and dancing had vanished from his mind.

Krista let out a huge yawn as she slumped against the backseat of the taxi. "What's the plan now, missy?"

Bella looked at her quizzically, obviously trying to interpret the yawn-muffled words. "Oh—the plan! Well, I guess all we can do now is wait back at the hotel until Jay's released from hospital."

Despite the terror of the evening, Krista found herself smiling at her friend. Bella badly needed to look in a mirror. On second thoughts, she had better not—she'd probably die from shock. Her curls were frizzy and snarled, mascara-streaked eyes would have made a panda proud, and any sign of lipstick was barely a memory.

The main thing, though, was that Jay was on the mend.

"I can't believe how lucky he was to escape with little more than a graze," Krista marvelled. "He could have been killed!"

"*Should* have been, you mean. Jay told me in the hospital that he was pretty sure the guy who shot him was the same one who attacked him last night." Bella shook her head as if she was unable to comprehend the thought. "Do you think someone's hired a hit-man to get Jay?"

"Well ... we don't really know much about Jay, or his past. Maybe there's a reason." From the look on Bella's face, Krista instantly wished she could retract the words. She and her big mouth ...

"You can't really believe that!" Her friend's voice was incredulous, indignant.

Krista sighed. "No, I don't. I just wish we knew what was happening. Not that I mind the ex...tra time in Vila." She breathed an inward sigh of relief at having stopped herself from saying 'excitement' at the last moment. The whole situation *was* exciting, in a scary sort of way. And after all, Jay was going to be okay, and perhaps now Bella would be able to patch things up with him, get back to her normal self.

Krista looked out at the bright lights of the hotel as the taxi turned in to the circular driveway. "Do you think we could stay for two days instead of one? It'd be better for Jay, and we'd have a bit more time to relax after all this."

Bella frowned thoughtfully. "I guess that depends on my editor. I'll ring him first thing in the morning and explain the situation."

They climbed out of the car and walked into the lobby as the porter retrieved their bags. "It really would be best to wait a couple of days before Jay flies," Bella agreed. "I don't want him to overexert himself before he's properly healed." Her forehead crinkled in concern.

It seemed that Bella had forgiven Jay. Now there would be a chance for them to resolve their differences, maybe even pursue a relationship. Krista was truly happy for her friend.

But she found herself unusually quiet as they were allocated a room on the second floor and headed up in the elevator. Now she would be like a third wheel. While she had enjoyed this rollercoaster ride of a holiday, she didn't want to intrude too much.

As the elevator wheezed to a stop on their floor, Krista thought that perhaps it would be best if she cut her holiday short, returned to Ryan. And especially Samara. Her poor cat was probably in desperate need of a good feed and a cuddle.

"I'm sorry, sir, but Ms Whitman never checked in."

Ethan scowled into the phone. "What do you mean?

She was due to arrive in Lautoka last night." Where had that woman got to?

"Again, I'm sorry, but that is all our records show," the hotel receptionist soothed. "Perhaps her flight has been delayed. You could check with the airline."

"Thank you." Ethan's voice was curt, his expression grim. The last thing he needed now was another screw-up in his plans.

A twinge of apprehension invaded his thoughts. Bella's not being at the hotel wouldn't have anything to do with what happened to Hinkley, would it? But he'd been assured that she was unharmed ...

With a groan, Ethan leant back in his office chair and cursed himself for being a naive fool. Assurances meant nothing in this business.

He would have to locate Bella, and fast, to ensure that her vital role in his plan was protected. Much to his annoyance she wasn't answering her mobile phone, so he'd have to try other ways to reach her.

A call to the Vila airport proved fruitful. The flight had left over an hour late, but had arrived safely in Nadi, Fiji, prior to the transfer to Lautoka. Yes, Ms Whitman had a seat booked, but it had been cancelled just before take-off. No, they hadn't been informed of a reason for the cancellation, but suspected it may have had something to do with the shooting in the terminal shortly before.

Ethan's mouth went dry. *Shooting?* This was just getting better and better!

More determined than ever, Ethan phoned Vanuatu Royal Sands as a last resort, to see if Bella had rechecked into the hotel. He let out a long, pent-up breath as they connected him to her room. Now, if she would just work with him on this one, everything would be fine.

"Hello?" Bella's voice revealed caution, stress and fatigue all rolled into one.

Ethan smiled. This would be a pushover. "Bella, I heard the news. Are you alright?" Concern oozed from his voice.

"Mr Gray?"

"Ethan," he corrected.

"Yes, Ethan. Umm—I'm fine. A little shaken, I guess. But," her tone brightened slightly, "my notes on the feature are coming together pretty well. Except ..." she hesitated, "I guess you already know I'm not on schedule. I was planning to call you. But with Jay getting shot, and—"

Ethan nodded impatiently, even as Bella confirmed his suspicion that Hinkley was involved in the shooting at the airport terminal. "Yes, I understand. It must have been traumatic for you." But not half as traumatic as the situation would be for him if his plans went south.

"Actually, this might work out okay," he found himself saying, "as I was thinking of scrapping the next location anyway." Ethan paused, his mind going into overdrive. With the delay, and then an extra day in Phuket, things could still be right on schedule.

Bella's voice was shaken, yet determined. "Are you sure? I think the shorter itinerary should still work out, though, and Jay will be fine to travel in a couple of days." Her voice softened as she mentioned Hinkley's name, causing Ethan's temper to boil. Here he was, working his butt off to save himself from going down, and that guy was frolicking with Bella in the islands!

He shook his head as the realisation struck. Wasn't Hinkley supposed to have been killed? Something wasn't right here. Sanouk's sources must have been feeding him false information.

Bella continued. "The itinerary says you'll be in Bangkok. Since Jay and I will be in Phuket then, do you want us to meet with you and discuss any final changes or additions for the feature?"

Ethan's face lifted in a humourless smile. She was playing right into his hands. "I think that's an excellent idea. However, there's no need for Hinkley to come along, especially as he may still be recovering. I'll sort out a time for you to fly up and meet me, and we can spend the day together."

"Okay." Bella's voice was less than enthusiastic, but maybe it was just from fatigue.

"Well, I'll contact you at the resort in Phuket in a couple

of days.

of days." Ethan forced the words out with a jovial smile, his face dropping the moment he hung up the phone.

Through clenched teeth, he let out a hissing sigh. With some quick scrambling, he had managed to work things out.

For now …

Chapter 22

With a jaw-popping yawn, Bella stretched her arms up to the perfect azure sky, before turning back to her notes. "I should still be in bed," she grumbled to no one in particular.

Sprawled on the sunlounger next to Bella's, Krista didn't look up from her fashion magazine. "You could still be sleeping if you wanted to, Miss Workaholic. You have two days off—*relax*. And if you don't know how," she grinned, pausing to slap on a bit more sunscreen, "then just watch me and learn."

With cat-like agility borne of years of ballet training, Krista stood, unwrapped her sarong, and then performed a perfect backwards swan dive into the crystal lagoon swimming pool.

She resurfaced a moment later, her slicked-back blonde hair making her look like a Scandinavian mermaid. "How was that?" she sputtered.

Despite her concern over Jay, Bella had to smile. It was a pity the ballet lessons hadn't imparted more grace to Krista's everyday life. She was usually a klutz, with a capital K.

"You were a perfect '10'." Bella hoped Krista would be happy with her assessment and finally give her some peace to think. So much had happened in the past few days: her growing attraction, and then fight, with Jay; the intruder in his room; last night—she shuddered—when

Jay was shot ...

She desperately needed to process it all—but her usual method of coping was to throw herself into her work. Only this time, there was nothing left to do. She'd gone through and polished her article at least five times to date. That was a lot, even for a chronic perfectionist like her.

With a sigh, she dropped her notebook on the ground and closed her eyes. Now, what to think about first ...

"Hey, Bella!"

Bella jumped up from the sunlounger with a mini heart attack. A dripping Krista stood beside her with a goofy smile.

"Did I scare you? Sorry." Her grin was unapologetic. "Did you know this is a salt water pool? It won't even turn my hair green." She stopped to inspect the sodden strands.

Bella settled back on the lounger and shook her head. Just a moment ago, she had thought of asking Krista's opinion about something that was bothering her—but now she wasn't so sure. Still, there was no one else to talk to, and they weren't due to visit Jay until after lunch.

With a small intake of breath, Bella gathered her courage and verbalised what she'd been mentally examining for weeks.

"Krista, do you believe in God?"

Her friend dropped the lock of hair she was still scrutinising, and looked up at Bella with wide eyes. "Where did that come from?"

Bella coloured and turned away slightly. She should have known her friend wouldn't understand.

Krista flopped onto the lounger beside her and regarded Bella with a frank expression. "To be honest, I don't really know. It's not something I've thought about a lot." She let out a giggle, probably because she had correctly guessed Bella's assessment of her. Yes, Krista didn't think deeply about much of anything.

Her face grew serious. "I do believe there's something bigger than us, though. Someone has to be in control"—she circled her arms—"of all this."

Bella laid her head back in the chair, surprised at

her friend's insight. Despite her early years in Sunday School, she'd never truly believed God was in control of everything—particularly because she'd felt so abandoned during the two major tragedies in her life.

But still ... as she looked across the calm blue waters of the lagoon pool, she couldn't deny the various moments of feeling a certain *presence*, of somehow knowing that someone was looking out for her. A peace, like the other day in Noumea.

"What do you believe?" Krista probed.

"Well, probably the same as you do, but I've been giving it more thought lately. Maybe because Jay's been talking about God a bit."

"Really?" Krista seemed surprised, but interested. "Is he religious?"

"I wouldn't say *religious*." In Bella's mind, there was no comparison between his simple, living faith and the little she knew about traditional religion. Jay quite reminded her of her mother and Todd in that way. "But he is a Christian. And you know what," she smiled, "he's almost 'normal'!"

Krista nodded, but she appeared to be thinking awfully hard about something. Maybe their conversation had prompted even her to start thinking about eternity.

Bella grabbed Krista's magazine after her friend had dived back into the water. Mindlessly flipping through the pages, she couldn't help wishing she could plunge into cooling depths of peace and freedom—away from all her present uncertainty—just as easily.

He couldn't get out of there soon enough. Jay had been begging the nurses all morning to discharge him, and no doubt making a complete nuisance of himself.

"See, I can dress myself fine ... Yes, I know I've gotta keep the dressing dry ... Look, I can even lift my arm up this high." He'd had to turn away to hide the grimace of pain, but he must have fooled them.

The repeat glances of annoyance showed that the nurses were fed up with him, and if they had anything to do with it, he would be discharged as soon as possible.

Jay couldn't hide a grin as he slowly walked out of the ward towards the main entrance of the hospital. He'd pulled off a fine performance in there, as good as any actor on screen. Maybe he'd missed his true calling.

A fluttering of excitement niggled in his stomach as he took a taxi to their hotel. He couldn't deny that he was looking forward to seeing Bella. The girls were due to visit him at the hospital that afternoon, but he wanted to surprise them.

Now that he finally had a chance to think—without worrying about a nurse unexpectedly sticking a needle into him—Jay tried to remember the details of the shooting last night. He recalled seeing his attacker's face—the cold, hate-filled eyes were a dead give-away—and chasing him through the terminal.

Then, the bullet. Jay squeezed his eyes shut at the stabbing pain that coursed down his arm—despite the supportive sling and bandage—as the taxi careened around a corner. Yes, the shooting part he could definitely remember.

It was after that that everything got a bit fuzzy. He remembered lying on the ground, surrounded by faces. And Bella. But what was she doing, saying?

It was like struggling through a thick fog, not even being able to see his hand in front of his face. But for just a moment, the mist parted a little. Jay recalled the sensation of warm droplets hitting his face—tears. Bella's tears.

She was crying over him.

His heart leapt at the realisation that maybe she still had feelings for him, after all.

With a screech of worn brakes, the taxi pulled up to the Vanuatu Royal Sands entrance. Jay paid the driver, and wandered through the jungle-like foyer. Where would the girls be at this time of day?

Walking towards the lifts, he noticed the glittering pool through the full-length windows. The fresh air would do him good after being cooped up in the hospital, so Jay walked through the entrance to the lagoon-like pool and outdoor gardens. Maybe the girls were even there, enjoying the warmth of the bright September sun.

He strolled over to the water's edge and scanned the faces of those swimming, playing water volleyball, and sunbaking. A lithe brunette caught his eye, her mass of curls trailing over the back of her sunlounger.

Bella.

He headed straight over to her, seeing as he neared that her features were relaxed in sleep, a magazine lying open across her stomach.

Jay fought the urge to bend down and kiss her. The desire was so strong, he had to turn away.

He took a deep breath. *Slow down, mate.*

The last thing he wanted to do now was to further complicate things in their already-shaky relationship. Later, when they had worked things out between them, there would be plenty of time for affection. He would definitely see to that.

Krista climbed up out of the water, feeling refreshed after her swim. She was looking forward to a fun evening of dinner and then maybe going out dancing afterwards. That is, if Bella felt up to it.

Wiping her dripping hair with a towel, she looked over to where Bella had been taking a nap on her sunlounger. Was that Jay? She caught sight of his sun-bleached head through the palms on the other side of the pool. He was standing still, looking down at something.

But wasn't he supposed to still be in the hospital?

She sauntered around the pool, ignoring the appreciative glances from several occupants of the spa, and came up behind Jay.

He was still standing there, staring down at Bella. From the looks of things, he had definitely fallen hard for her.

"Jay! How are you feeling?" Krista touched him on the arm, managing to choose the uninjured one.

He spun around and flashed her a guilty grin. Nobody liked to be caught staring, especially when it laid bare their emotions.

"Krista! Yeah, I'm all stitched up and doped up on pain killers—never felt better!" His 'drugged-out zombie' impression was more comical than realistic. He was no doubt fishing for sympathy. Just like a man!

"You poor thing," Krista cooed. "Let me shout you a drink. But nothing alcoholic with those pain killers," she reminded as they stopped in front of the pool-side bar. Bella was still fast asleep on her lounger.

"I'd prefer a soft drink, anyway." Jay sat down slowly on a stool, favouring his left side.

"Oh, sorry!" Krista clamped her hand over her mouth. "Bella told me you were a Christian—so I guess you don't drink." Trust her to put her foot in it. Again.

Jay smiled. "Hey, I'm still a regular Aussie. I have been known to have an occasional light beer." He looked at her with frank eyes. "I do choose not to get drunk, and chance doing something I'd later regret."

Feeling uncomfortable, Krista turned away from his gaze. Luckily he couldn't see into her thoughts, or her past. Regrets—she'd definitely had her fair share.

She stared out over the groups of poolside holiday-makers, all pursuing fun like there was no tomorrow. Suddenly, it all seemed so futile, empty.

"How do you live with no regrets?" Where had that come from?

Jay looked up at her, a surprised expression in his eyes. He had probably never seen her so serious before. "Well ... to be honest, I don't think humans are capable of living a right life."

Krista's face fell. What hope was there, then? Was she doomed always to say and do stupid and futile things, to flit from one soulless relationship to the other—never feeling truly fulfilled?

"But that's with our own efforts," Jay continued, subconsciously rattling the ice in his half-empty glass. "We need help, someone bigger than ourselves. A relationship with our Creator God."

His eyes seemed to see into her soul. "What are your thoughts about it?"

This was the second religious discussion she'd had in an hour. That must be some kind of new record!

Krista struggled with her thoughts. No matter what

she'd heard, what people said, she couldn't help thinking that this whole God thing wasn't for her. She could see Bella following God—she was the more introspective one. But herself? She only lived for today and all its pleasures, could count on one hand the times she'd thought about the future, her destiny.

Jay was still waiting patiently for her reply, his glass now empty.

Krista tucked a damp strand of hair behind her ear. "Umm ... I just don't know if I'm ready to embrace this whole 'God thing' yet." She looked down at the bubbles rising in her mineral water, then deftly changed the subject to a discussion of their dinner plans.

Jay smiled wryly. It must have been obvious to him that she was generally closed-minded to spiritual things. But then, what was the vague ache that persisted inside her long after their conversation ended?

With a groan, Pat McKenzie pushed back from his desk and let out a sigh. He fumbled for a pack of aspirin hidden beneath a stack of paperwork. The tension of this past week had been unbearable.

At any moment, he was sure the game would be over. Every knock on the door was his secretary announcing that the police were here for him. Every letter was from one of the original passengers on that fateful diving trip, telling him they had informed the authorities of the cover-up. Every phone call was—

Ring, ring.

McKenzie made no attempt to search for the phone under the papers. His secretary would answer it. He reached for the water glass perched on a rare clutter-free corner, and swallowed two aspirins.

But what if the caller was that—he swore—Gray man? He didn't want anyone else to get wind of the situation, especially his secretary.

"I'll get it!" he yelled through the closed door to the reception area, and snatched the receiver up on the eighth ring.

"McKenzie," he barked, somehow knowing it would be

Grey.

Gray.

It was.

There were no polite preliminaries, no chatting about the weather. The man was blackmailing him, after all.

"Gray here. I want you on standby."

McKenzie felt the pressure rise in his chest, the veins in his neck begin to bulge. The fear he had initially experienced was rapidly giving way to white-hot rage. How dare this man order him around!

But McKenzie didn't express his fury over the phone, instead managing a mumbled, "When?"

"You'll be leaving early this Saturday," Gray continued, his voice steely. He relayed the rest of the details regarding the time and place of loading.

McKenzie nodded, not bothering to write anything down. He would remember every detail of this hated episode for the rest of his life.

"There is one more thing."

Dreading the worst, McKenzie waited. Another condition, another demand? If Gray pushed him just one millimetre further, that would be it. He'd rather give himself up to the authorities than pander to this blackmail.

"A woman will be accompanying you. She knows nothing about our little deal, but all the same, she's there to make sure you deliver."

Great. Now he had to play babysitter as well—or was it he who was being babysat?

"I'll contact you once you get to Indonesia."

McKenzie dropped the receiver into its cradle, feeling the anger rise once more. This time, he didn't try to contain it. If he was going down for this, then so help him, Gray would go down, too!

He grabbed the phone again and dialled the local police station.

For the first time in over two years, a thin ray of daylight penetrated the darkness, into black hole he had dug for himself.

Chapter 23

"It's great to have you back, Jay." Bella reached across the table and grabbed his hand, then found she didn't want to let go.

Jay just looked at her and smiled, his reply in the gentle squeeze of her fingers.

"Your arm must be healing quickly," she murmured, focussing more on the emotion in his eyes than the conversation.

"Yeah, lucky the bullet didn't hit you further to the right, or it would have gone straight through your heart," Krista remarked.

Bella sighed and gave her friend a glare.

"Sorry!" She flashed Bella an unrepentant grin. "I was just trying to get some conversation out of you."

Jay turned towards Krista, but Bella was glad he continued to hold her hand, needed the tangible evidence that he was still here with her.

"I'll have a conversation with you then," he teased. "What did you want to talk about?"

Krista rolled her eyes at his show of condescension. "I was wondering if the police have caught the guy who shot you?"

"Well, Miss Detective, I spoke with the chief investigator before I left the hospital this morning. He said they've done a preliminary search of the island, but haven't found him yet."

He paused and looked down at their intertwined fingers, an unreadable expression crossing his tanned face. Bella thought that it must have been incredibly frustrating—not to mention frightening—to know that a man trying to kill you was still out there.

"They seem to think that he might have escaped the island in all the commotion after I was shot."

Bella let out a sigh of relief. "Then you're safe. He's gone." She slumped against the back of her chair, only now realising how worried she'd been about a further attack.

"But didn't you say he looked Asian?" Krista piped up. "And we're flying to Thailand tomorrow." Her eyebrows rose to emphasise the significance.

"Thailand's a big place," Jay reminded.

"And Asia's even bigger." Bella refused to believe this whole thing might not yet be over. She had been on edge ever since the night of the intruder in Jay's room. The thought still nagged at her: *Why Jay. Why now?*

Why me?

She almost choked on her sip of water. Could all of this have something to do with her?

Suddenly, everything seemed to crystallise. The suspicious phone calls to Krista, the man watching Bella in Noumea, the attacks on Jay. Something very strange—and scary—was happening. But could it all be connected?

"And have the police worked out why this guy's targeting you?" Krista was asking Jay.

"They don't have any clues yet—and neither do I," Jay admitted. "But last night in the hospital—when they thought I was asleep—I heard two detectives talking about something big about to happen in Bangkok, and how there could maybe be a link."

Bangkok?

Bella's heart twisted in fear. Something criminal, perhaps connected to Jay's shooting, was expected to take place in Bangkok—and she was going there in two days.

Prem slunk through Bangkok's international airport,

his eyes darting everywhere. He couldn't shake the feeling of having a target on his back.

Despite the assurances that there was more work for him in Bangkok, the boss could feasibly have already ordered a hit on him for his perceived incompetence.

With this possibility shadowing his every move, Prem emerged into the cloying humidity of an afternoon shower and hailed a taxi. He directed the driver towards Bangkok's high-class residential district.

The boss would no doubt already be expecting him, having been informed by his 'eyes' at the airport. Prem shivered as he stared out at the rain. There seemed to be no escape, no way to leave it all and make a new life. Not that there would be much of a life for him away from this job, anyway. What transferable skills did a hit-man possess?

No, he sighed heavily, there was only one option for him now: to go and face the boss, and accept whatever punishment he meted out.

Demotion? Torture? Death? The boss was not known for his compassion, as Prem well knew. Being part of the 'inner circle', he had often been called on to exact reprisal on those who had disobeyed orders, or failed in some other way.

He'd just never thought he would ever be on the receiving end.

The taxi pulled up in front of a gated, high stone wall—the entrance to the boss's compound. Prem paid the driver the required number of baht, then approached the ornate iron gate.

Before a heavily armed guard could accost him, Prem barked out his code name and business. The entrance opened noiselessly, then slid shut behind him.

Prem stayed silent as he was searched, stripped of his ever-present weapons, and then led into the palatial mansion that dominated the compound. The boss had spared no expense when building the Victorian-style stone manor, living in comfort off the proceeds of countless broken lives.

But he obviously didn't care, and neither did Prem as

he nervously waited outside the boss's study. He had far more pressing things to worry about—like whether he would even be alive tomorrow.

Bella was just finishing her dessert when Krista's mobile phone beeped loudly. Smiling ruefully, Krista put down her spoon and grabbed her phone. "Probably Mum checking up on me."

"Best not to tell her about the shooting over the phone," Bella cautioned. "You know how she worries."

Krista nodded in agreement as she headed outside to the garden.

"Well, I think I'm done." Jay pushed his chair back from the table. "Would you like to go for a walk?"

Bella glanced over at him, trying to read the expression on his face. The last time they'd been for a walk after dinner, he'd dropped the bomb about Sasha.

"Okay," she said, silently chiding herself for being so suspicious. "I'll just send a quick text message to Krista to let her know we've gone."

It took only a few minutes to stroll through the balmy evening air to the beach. Jay took Bella's hand in his as they walked out onto the white sand.

"It's so beautiful out here," she breathed, giving his hand a squeeze.

"I agree. God sure does paint wonderful sunsets."

Jay waited to see if Bella would comment about his mention of God, and silently wondered then why he hadn't spoken more about his faith with her. He had to admit he'd sensed a certain resistance in her to Godly things and Christianity.

Well, he hoped there would be plenty of time to discuss spiritual things. Once he got everything sorted out.

He looked over at Bella, as a gentle breeze tugged at her curls. "God makes wonderful people, too," he observed tenderly. "Like you."

He stopped and looked down at Bella's upturned face. Her eyes were wide with surprise, but there was also a longing stirring in their depths. Was it a longing for him?

"I'm not so wonderful," Bella countered, her voice soft. "But you—" she touched his arm, making it tingle with warmth, "—if I'd lost you because of that bullet, I—I don't think I could ever recover."

Moisture began to pool in her eyes. "I was so worried, Jay. I didn't know how much I cared until—"

"Shhh." He gently wiped away the tears trailing down her cheeks. "It's okay now. I'm here—and I'm not going anywhere."

Unable to stop himself, Jay pulled Bella into his arms, pressed her against him. She was such a perfect fit—almost as if she was made for him.

His conscience pricked him, even as his pulse raced. As things now stood, they weren't made for each other, couldn't be together. He and Bella couldn't even see eye-to-eye on the most important issues, like his faith.

But how could he deny what he was feeling?

"You're so special," Bella murmured, reaching up to stroke Jay's face. He caught her hand and kissed the fingertips. With each kiss, he felt a little more of his resolve melt.

One, two, three, four ... he couldn't stop. Jay dipped his face towards Bella's, and found her lips in a passionate, almost desperate, kiss.

He knew that if nothing changed, it would be their last.

Bella seemed to melt into him, consuming all his senses. His heart hammered as he buried his fingers in her curls, inhaled the delicate fragrance of her hair. More ...

No! Jay pulled away abruptly, almost as if burnt. What was he doing?

Bella's face was still tipped up to his, her expression suddenly bereft. "What's wrong? Did I do something—?"

"No, it's nothing you did." Jay's voice was low, his breathing ragged. "It's me. I can't—I can't do this."

He ran a hand through his hair in frustration, then turned away. "I'm sorry."

"Is it Sasha?" she asked, her voice low.

"Yes—no. I don't know." Right now, it seemed as if

everything was conspiring to pull them apart.

Jay felt a sudden need to put some physical distance between them. "I'm sorry," he repeated quietly, not daring to look at Bella's face.

Then slowly, he began to trudge back up the beach, feeling his heart break.

But the worst thing was that now he had inflicted that same pain on Bella as well.

Chapter 24

Jay rubbed a hand over his face, feeling as if he'd been run over several times by a semi-trailer truck. It had not been a good night. Between alternating bouts of praying for Bella and for God's wisdom, and mentally kicking himself for not handling things better, he doubted he'd managed more than a few hours' sleep.

If it hadn't been quite so late when he'd returned to his room last night, he would have phoned Sasha straight away. Told her everything that had gone on the last couple of days, apologised for not having let her know sooner. And tell her he was sorry they had to end their relationship this way, over the phone.

But as he stood now, leaning against the door jamb to his bathroom and waiting for Sasha to answer his call, Jay's mind suddenly went blank. He'd never had to break up with a girl over the phone before, and certainly not someone whom he'd once considered as a potential life partner.

"Hello?" Sasha asked with an early-morning croak.

"Sasha—I'm sorry, did I wake you up?" In his desperation to call her, Jay realised he'd forgotten about the time difference.

"That's okay. It's just great to hear your voice again! How are you?"

Gulp. This wasn't going to be easy.

"I'm having a great time over here. The scenery is amazing!" He was careful to keep his tone upbeat, give no indication of the dramas that had recently occurred—like getting shot. "But I was mainly ringing to see how you were going, what you've been getting up to over the last couple of weeks."

"Oh, just the usual," she answered around a yawn. "I've been spending a fair bit of time with the young adults' group at church." Her voice brightened. "They're a great group of people, and I'm starting to make some good friends."

"That's great!" *Thank you, God.* Sasha would have to rely more on friendship and support from other Christians after he and she parted ways.

Unbidden, a picture of Bella looking up at him imploringly lit up the screen in his mind. Just like she'd gazed at him last night, her eyes darkened with sorrow.

And then there was the undeniable sense of God's peace at moving forward.

He had to follow through with this. Now. "Uh, Sasha—there was something else I wanted to talk to you about."

"Yes?" Was that a hint of suspicion in her voice, or was it just concern?

"Well, you know how things were progressing in our relationship before I left, and the expectations from everyone ..." Jay stopped, struggling for the right words to continue.

Sasha's voice was soft. "My parents asked me just after you left if you'd already proposed."

"I had to get away and think ... and pray." Jay knew his words sounded like a lame excuse.

"I know that."

Oh.

Sasha continued with a wry tone, "It was clear you were having some commitment issues, and I knew you needed some space."

Had it been that obvious?

"So," her voice turned sober, "what have you decided?"

Help, God. "I'm sorry, Sasha, but I don't think you and

I are meant to be together. I've prayed, and I don't have a peace about us. And—"

He stopped, just for a moment. Yes, he needed to tell Sasha about Bella. A Bible verse he'd read in his devotions just last night flashed through his mind: *The truth will set you free.* More than anything, he needed to be free. Not just from Sasha, but in his mind and heart, his conscience.

"And what?" she was prompting.

"And I've also met someone else over here. It's nothing serious yet, but I thought you should know."

There was silence on the other end of the line. Jay wished he could see Sasha's face, read the emotions he knew would be playing across her attractive features.

"Well, thank you for being honest with me." Her voice was subdued, yet resigned. "I've had a sense things were coming to this."

"You did?"

"Haven't you heard of women's intuition?" she asked, almost teasingly. "We're usually aware when something's not right in a relationship."

She seemed to be taking it surprisingly well. "You—you're sure you're okay with this?"

Sasha sighed. "Well, I'm not jumping for joy, if that's what you mean. But I'd prefer you didn't stay with me out of duty, when you don't feel right."

Jay stifled a sigh of relief. His stomach had been tied up in knots over how to handle this, and God had already prepared the way.

He thanked her for being so understanding before they said their goodbyes, the words heavy with finality. Jay had a lot of good memories of his time with Sasha, and now it felt like a chapter of his life was ending.

But a new one already beckoned, alive with possibilities.

"Ohhh," Bella groaned, closing her eyes tightly against the morning light. She'd just had the worst night of her life—tossing and turning for hours, before finally falling into snatches of restless sleep.

Each time she woke up, she'd forgotten about what had happened. Then suddenly, it all came flooding back: that short moment of intimacy, followed by Jay's cruel rejection.

Not wanting to alert Krista, Bella choked back a sob. If Jay knew he couldn't be with her—if this other woman was still an issue—then why had he allowed them to grow so close? One moment, he was kissing her with obvious desire, and the next he was pushing her away.

As much as she'd enjoyed it, it would have been far better if they'd never shared that one kiss.

Staring up towards the ceiling, Bella pulled the light coverlet up under her chin. Just thinking about last night gave her the shivers, so real was the sensation of being left cold and unprotected.

She had been so stupid, had dared to think it was safe to let her guard down ...

No, she shook her head, she actually hadn't *thought* at all. It was her heart that had guided her lately—and look where that had gotten her in life. A dead fiancé, and an 'almost-boyfriend' who didn't want her any more.

But they had seemed so right for each other! Bella almost smiled as she remembered the comforting warmth of Jay's arms around her, the passion he had stirred in her when they kissed. She'd dreamt of a lifetime of kisses like that—and the easy companionship they had shared, the mutual respect, the tenderness.

Bella rolled over restlessly, wondering how on earth she would face Jay at breakfast. Maybe it would be better to skip it. Just looking at his face would evoke such conflicting emotions of confusion, anger, and growing affection, that she wouldn't be able to think straight. And she certainly wouldn't be able to eat, so breakfast would be a complete waste of time.

"Bella?" Krista murmured sleepily. "You awake?"

Bella held her breath, wondering if she could fool her friend into thinking she was still deeply dreaming. Unfortunately, she never was a very good actor, and she would have to face Krista eventually.

The matching twin bed creaked as Krista sat up, her

hair in its usual morning tangle. "Where were you and Jay last night? I waited up 'til late, but must have fallen asleep before you got in."

Bella propped herself up on an elbow, wondering if she should tell her room-mate everything or keep the painful truth to herself. Maybe she could just answer one or two questions and leave out the difficult details.

"Well," she yawned, "we left dinner early because we thought you'd be in for a long conversation with your mum, and we wanted to walk on the beach before it got too dark." She laid back down, hiding her face from her friend. "So, that's what we did."

"It sounds like someone's trying to hide something here," Krista admonished playfully. "I saw the way you were both looking at each other."

The thin string of Bella's patience snapped. "Look, I'm really tired, 'cause I couldn't sleep last night, so I don't really feel like going over the details of my *private* life," she emphasised. "Now, can you *please* go down to breakfast so I can get some more sleep—in peace?"

Krista was as always unphased by Bella's occasional morning grumpiness. "Okay—so things obviously didn't go that well for you last night." She threw off the bed cover and stood up with a stretch. "I'll leave you 'in peace' if you want," she called from halfway inside the wardrobe as she gathered her clothes. "But what I really think you need to do is talk this thing out—and who better to pour out your troubles to than the Queen of Talk and Love—" wearing a ridiculous floral hat she'd bought at a market stand, she presented herself to Bella with a flourish—*"moi?"*

"Okay, okay!" Bella laughed in spite of herself. "Maybe later. Now, will you just go?"

It was not long after her room-mate left that Bella's despairing mood returned. More tears slipped down her cheeks, adding to the growing wet patch on her pillow.

For some reason—whether God hated her, or she was simply cursed—she was obviously not meant to find lasting love on this earth.

"I'll have a Scotch, thanks. On the rocks." Ethan smiled tightly at the air hostess, noting her slender figure as she bent to get a glass from her cart. *Hmm, nice.*

Ethan could barely remember the last time he'd had a serious relationship with a woman. His personal life lately had consisted of a series of short-lived flings with pretty twenty-somethings, or career-climbing business women who were only looking for a little 'no strings' fun.

Ethan sighed as he sipped his drink. There was no room in his life for anything—or anyone—else. Running *Healthy Lifestyle*, plus organising these extra deals on the side, didn't leave him with any remaining resources for a permanent relationship.

Maybe once this was over, things would change. Or—he grinned to himself—maybe there would even be a chance for a little fun on this trip.

The image of Bella, as he had last seen her in the restaurant, filled his mind. She was hardly his type—a little too conservative—but there was no denying the fact that she was attractive. Now, if he could just win her over when they met in Bangkok ...

On second thoughts, it might be a better idea to head to Phuket first, squeeze a little fun into his tight schedule. There would be time to spend an evening with Bella before returning to his business dealings in Bangkok.

With a smile of anticipation lifting the corners of his mouth, Ethan drained the last of his drink, the fiery liquid scorching down his throat.

Jay felt a twinge of apprehension as he watched Krista enter the dining room alone and take a seat at their table. "Where's Bella?'

"She said she didn't sleep well, so she's still in bed," Krista answered with a touch of concern. "Just what happened between you two last night? I suspect that's got something to do with her frame of mind this morning."

Jay subconsciously crossed his arms over his chest at the thought of reopening last night's wounds. Then again, it would be good to talk to someone.

"Things started really well—too well," he admitted

wryly. "I guess I took it too fast before—well, before sorting out if it would work between us." He stared moodily into his orange juice. He'd really messed things up this time.

Krista gave a sympathetic smile. "Isn't a cup of tea what you should be looking into? I'm not sure if juice is as effective as tea leaves in predicting your future."

Jay shook his head in frustration. "Somehow, I doubt that'd help."

"Well, perhaps if I put my counselling hat on," she offered, pantomiming the action. "Now, Mr Hinkley, I believe you've already hit the nail on the head." She wagged her index finger in emphasis. "You need to look at the pros and cons objectively. There's no point in jumping into this relationship without first contemplating the consequences."

Looking past the comedy, Jay knew there was a kernel of truth in Krista's words. Once again, he'd followed his own path, instead of first asking God to mould and direct his desires. Would he ever learn?

Laying aside his introspective brooding, Jay decided to play along. "Dr Krista, you're right again. How do you do it?"

"Years of training in the School of Life," she answered sagely.

"Seriously, Kris, how is Bella? I've blown it again, but I hate to see her suffer for it."

Krista arched her eyebrows. "She hasn't told me anything, only that she was tired. But how am I supposed to dispense helpful advice if I don't have all the details?"

"Don't you ever stop?" Jay asked in (mostly) mock irritation. "The main problem with Bella and I having a relationship is that I don't see how it could work."

"But—"

"No *buts*. Just hear me out. Bella and I are completely different. I believe in God—she doesn't. I'm trying to trust Him to guide my life—she believes in making her own destiny. I'm even praying for Him to send me the right marriage partner—but she's just relying on her own choices."

Finally serious, Krista sat in thought for a moment. "I

don't know if this helps, but Bella told me yesterday that she's been thinking about God a lot lately. She's not quite the complete opposite to you as you may think, Jay."

He stirred his cereal in puzzled surprise. Maybe God was working in her life, was using his comments to get through to Bella. Perhaps they *could* have a future together, after all ... Especially now that things were sorted out with Sasha.

"Why hasn't she told me about this?" he wondered aloud.

"Well, maybe you haven't given her a chance!" Krista exclaimed, then asked pointedly: "So, what are you going to do now? Anything I can do to help?"

"No!"

Jay sighed, then continued in a calmer tone, "I won't have you meddling, Krista," he warned. "I've got enough problems with Bella without you making more. Why don't you use that creative talent of yours and plan a fun distraction for this morning before we leave?"

"Okay," Krista exhaled an injured sigh. "Hey," she suddenly brightened, "what about golf? I've heard there's a great course near here—and a bit of fun might be just what you two need."

"Point taken," Jay laughed. He looked down at his injured shoulder. "I should be okay—I heal quickly. I'll just take it easy." Seeing Krista's horrified expression at her forgetfulness, he hurried on, "I'll book the course and organise three sets of clubs. Your job is to get Bella down here in"—he checked his watch—"three-quarters of an hour."

"Okay, I'm on it!" Krista got up and hurried from the dining room, apparently completely forgetting her breakfast.

Also suddenly losing his appetite, Jay pushed his full cereal bowl aside and sent up a quick prayer.

If he guessed correctly, he was going to need plenty of divine help today.

"I can't believe I'm doing this," Bella groaned as she made her fourth attempt to sink the putt on the seventh hole at the Port Vila Golf and Country Club. She was exhausted from lack of sleep last night, and from countless futile air swings on the golf course.

But mostly from trying to avoid Jay. Just feeling him sitting beside her in the motorised golf cart sent Bella's emotions into a combined frenzy of despair and delight. If something didn't change soon, she felt she would crumple on the inside—and maybe on the outside, as well.

Her golf ball finally dropped into the hole with a mocking *clunk*. Bella started to walk over to retrieve it, but Jay stopped her.

"I'll get it," he said as he bent down. Still crouching, he looked up at her with a concerned expression in his eyes. "You look awful."

Hey, thanks.

"Is there anything I can do to make it up to you?" he asked in a low voice, below earshot of Krista, who was already sitting in the buggy. "Apart from having a long discussion about where we're at, and ... and trying to explain my actions."

"Well, that would be a good start." Embarrassed to feel her eyes filling with angry tears, Bella dropped her putter to swipe at the moisture on her cheeks. As much as she hated being a cry-baby, she couldn't seem to stem her emotions where Jay was concerned.

With a comforting hand on her arm, he assured, "We'll sort it all out tonight—"

"Come on, guys!" Krista interrupted from the cart. "Let's head to the next hole!"

"—without your meddling friend," Jay finished with a wry smile.

Bella felt herself begin to relax as they played the final two holes, even allowing herself to enjoy the beautiful views out to Mele Bay on the ninth hole. She was still bone-tired, and increasingly frustrated at her lack of golfing skills. But she felt some small comfort in knowing that she would get an explanation from Jay tonight. While she was still very uncertain about what lay in their future, some open and honest communication would definitely help.

As she attempted to extricate her ball from a sand bunker, Bella decided that once and for all, she needed to know where Jay stood, to understand his feelings as clearly as the ones she was desperately trying to deny within herself.

"Hey, Bella," Krista barged into her thoughts, "when did you say you were going to Bangkok?"

"Oh—umm, Thursday, I think."

Jay looked surprised. "I didn't know that was on the itinerary. Did you want some company on the trip?" His voice betrayed an undercurrent of hope.

"No, it's just a meeting with Ethan—but he said you didn't need to be there," Bella said, refusing to look up and view the effect of her rebuttal on Jay's face. "We'll just be discussing any final requirements for the feature—I can let you know if any last-minute photos are required."

"Why don't I come along to check out the shopping in Bangkok?" Krista piped up as they drove back to the clubhouse. "And then I can also get a chance to meet this handsome editor of yours."

Bella shook her head and frowned. "It's just a quick meeting. And trust me, you wouldn't be interested in him," she emphasised. "He's got an ego the size of Australia—but then," she grinned cheekily, "it just might be large enough to match yours."

"You're in trouble, now!" Krista leapt out of the slowing buggy, but she wasn't fast enough to catch her sprinting friend.

Bella had gained the safety of the clubhouse and was demurely sipping a soft drink at the polished wooden bar when Krista and Jay entered a few minutes later. "You're a pretty slow runner, Kris," she smirked.

"For your information," Krista huffed, "I stopped to help unload the golf clubs."

"Come on, girls." Jay looked at his watch. "We've got time for a quick drink before we head to the hotel. I hope you're already packed?"

"Sort of," Bella and Krista answered simultaneously.

Jay shook his head. "Okay, we've only got five minutes, then. Drink up!"

"Why the rush?" Bella asked with a small smile. She thought it was funny when Jay pretended to take charge. Instead of coming across as a competent leader, he always ended up looking like a harried parent.

"Well, I've got to phone the police again before we leave—I may even have to provide further information if they've found anything new."

"What more could you give them?!" Krista exclaimed. "They've already interviewed you—and us—for hours!"

"What are the chances they'll find the shooter?" Bella asked doubtfully.

"Pretty slim, I'm afraid. When I phoned them yesterday they'd almost exhausted all their avenues." He drained the last of his drink. "The detective mentioned they would now be working with Interpol—so I guess they think he's left the country."

"Will this never end?" Bella sighed. "I worry about you, Jay."

He gave her a small, hopeful smile, but she looked away, pretending to be focussed on finishing her soft drink.

It was one thing to be worried about a guy, but it was another thing entirely to give him her heart.

Chapter 25

"Okay, so I'll take some extra shots of the resort's pool and grounds tomorrow while you're at Bangkok, and that should be it for this section," Jay said as he finished jotting down some notes.

"Yes—thanks." Bella sipped her cola and looked around at the lush tropical greenery and palms clustered around the outdoor bar of Phuket Paradise. While she was glad for the distraction of work, she knew that the knot in her stomach would persist until she and Jay took the time to discuss what went wrong last night.

She sighed. Even if things didn't work out between them, just being friends would be better than being in this limbo of not knowing.

"Are you alright?" he asked, reaching out to touch her arm.

Bella resisted the urge to jerk away. She would say her piece calmly, and then give him—and herself—some space to think about it.

"Jay, I just really need you to tell me what happened last night." She was surprised at how composed she sounded.

"Umm—" Jay stared into his drink, obviously forming his words carefully.

Bella braced herself for the inevitable. Her friends had described these situations, uncomfortable "break up" speeches followed by accusations, anger, and hurt. Not that she and Jay were even a couple, really—but the final closure to further 'what ifs' would still be painful.

Well, she'd gone through a lot in her life. This would just be another thing she'd have to handle ...

"You're a very special person, Bella," Jay began, "and I really didn't mean to hurt you."

Well, you've done a great job, regardless.

He sought out her eyes, waiting for eye contact before continuing. "You've done nothing wrong—you've been a wonderful friend, someone I've enjoyed spending time with."

Bella swallowed hard, forcing herself to stay seated. The rejection was coming next, and all she wanted to do was leap up and run—or lash out.

"The problem was with me," Jay continued softly. "I let myself grow close to you before I told you more about my life—my values, the things that matter to me most. And before I'd ended things with Sasha"—Bella stiffened—"which is all finished and sorted out now, by the way."

He paused, seeming to weigh his next words. "But even more important to me than finding a partner to commit to, is my commitment to God."

Bella frowned. What was he saying? Was this a matter of choosing God over her?

"Bella, we're following two different paths. I'm walking in the way God's got for me, and you're following your own road map. Sure, we might be together here physically, but inside we're poles apart. Do you see?" he asked, his normally laughing eyes now shadowed with sorrow.

Bella sat back further in her seat and crossed her arms. She was desperately trying to understand—her mind could even grasp on some level that Jay's viewpoint was logical—but her heart was screaming at the betrayal. Why couldn't he have told her sooner—about his girlfriend, about God?

Jay sighed deeply in the silence. His voice was low, strained. "I didn't expect you to forgive me. But I hoped ... maybe we could work something out ..."

She looked up just as he slid his chair back and stood to leave. "I'll see you at dinner," he mumbled, then was gone.

Wishing for the privacy of her bedroom back home, Bella also got up, and started walking in the other direction. Krista would be back from her workout and taking a shower in their room by now, and there was nowhere else to go to have a good cry—to rail at God—in peace.

Peace! What she would give for just one day filled with it—where she knew who she was, and where she truly belonged.

"Ohhh!" Prem groaned loudly as he tried to open his eyes. A shooting pain ricocheted through his head, echoed in the throbbing of every inch of his body. Cautiously, he opened his eyes again, despite the splitting headache. He needed to find out where he was, work out what had happened. Remember.

His swollen eyes swept the room in recognition, then dismay. While he was unconscious, some of the boss's men must have transported him back to his apartment.

By the far wall stood what used to be a six-piece dining setting. Now all that remained was a pile of hacked pieces of wood and ripped-open cushions.

Looking through to the kitchen, Prem saw that every drawer and cupboard had been opened, its contents smashed on the floor.

So, they'd ransacked his apartment. He'd expected as much.

At least he was still alive. Battered, bruised, bound, and probably left with several broken ribs—but alive.

However, something didn't seem quite right. What he had done—or not done—was punishable by death in the boss's books.

Had he missed something in his quick perusal of his living area? Perhaps there was a trip wire linked to a bomb. Or a hit-man lying in wait in the bedroom.

Prem's swollen face creased into a half-smile at the irony of it all. He was the one who was used to 'lying in wait', not the other way around.

Well, he sighed heavily, there was always a first time. He had better get up—or at least try to—and search through his apartment. It was preferable to know what he was up against, than to slump here worrying all night.

But wait—what was that strange smell?

Scanning the room, he noticed a grey haze hovering just below the ceiling, and an increasingly acrid odour.

Smoke!

With frantic movements, Prem struggled with his bonds, but they were too tight.

The smoke was growing thicker now, and he was sure that was a sound of crackling coming from behind the closed bedroom door.

Prem slumped back against the living room wall, realising that he was facing a painful death.

True to his cruel form, the boss had shown that there were worse ways of dying than being killed by a bullet.

Krista vigorously dried her hair with a towel, humming a nameless tune. She felt refreshed and full of energy after her workout. Now it was time for a seriously big dinner, and then a seriously good time exploring Phuket's nightlife.

She wrapped a towel around herself and opened the bathroom door through to the room she shared with Bella.

Her friend was lying face down on her bed, motionless. Either Bella was in a really deep sleep, or she was just too exhausted to move.

"Bella!" Krista gently shook her friend by the shoulders, almost losing her towel in the process.

"What?" Bella rolled over and looked up, an irritated expression on her blotchy face. She looked awful.

"Are you alright? Is it Jay?"

Bella sat up stiffly and sighed. "Unfortunately, yes, although I'm still not sure he's worth it." She grabbed a tissue from the bedside stand and wiped her face.

From the looks of things, reflected Krista, Bella definitely thought Jay was worth it.

"Can you believe," her stricken friend complained, "that he actually thinks it's a choice between God and me? Like, he can't have both?"

Feeling suddenly uncomfortable, Krista shifted her weight from one bare foot to the other. She'd known this was coming, yet she hadn't thought to give Bella any warning.

Well, Jay *had* ordered her not to meddle.

"I can see he really likes you," she began tentatively, "but it must just be a matter of different priorities. If you want to be happy for the long term, doesn't it make sense to get the right guy from the start?" *Like, I really know what I'm talking about.*

"I was sure he *was* the right one—even though we've only known each other for two weeks and already had a few fights, and even though he wasn't totally honest with me from the start ..." Her voice trailed off as she stared up at the ceiling.

Krista hid a smile. She'd always known talking was great therapy. Maybe that was why she indulged in it so much herself.

"Hmm," Bella mused. "Jay doesn't sound so much like the 'right guy' now, does he?"

Krista padded over to the wardrobe to select an outfit for dinner. "Well, he's either not the one for you, or you—and maybe he, too—may have to make some changes, re-look at what you want." Hey, this was sounding good. Maybe she should consider a career in psychology ...

Bella's voice was thoughtful. "You've got a point there, Kris. I never thought about what I really want, assessing my values. But remember," she sat up straight, a hint of playfulness colouring her tone, "I still haven't worked out if he's worth it yet."

Krista stopped mid-stride as she returned to the bathroom. "You don't really mean that," she chided. In her opinion, Jay was definitely 'worth it'.

"No, I guess I don't," Bella sighed, picking at a speck of lint on the coverlet. "I just wish things in life could be a little less complicated."

"I'm with you on that one," Krista agreed, sliding the *en suite* door shut. She'd certainly had her fair share of complications in her twenty-four years.

What was it Bella had said a moment ago about assessing values? Her own values could do with a spot of reassessment, as well.

Krista stared at her reflection as she brushed her hair. Despite her blasé attitude towards spiritual things during her recent conversation with Jay, she had found herself thinking more about God lately.

And watching the subtle change in Bella over the last couple of days had made her even more curious about the One behind her friend's gradual metamorphosis.

"Kris?" Bella's voice was slightly muffled through the door. "Are you okay?"

"I'm fine." Krista put down her brush and turned to get dressed. "Why are you asking?"

"I've never heard you this quiet for so long," Bella answered with a teasing giggle, "so I automatically thought something must be wrong."

"For your information," Krista answered with a mock huff as she poked her head around the door, "I was *thinking.*"

Too late, she realised she'd played right into her flatmate's hands.

"Well, something must be *seriously* wrong then."

Krista put her arm back to reach for her hairbrush, just as Bella pretended to cower. She brandished the brush and adopted her best stern voice. "Maybe you should leave the thinking up to me, and instead—" she paused, trying to recall what she'd heard Jay say that time "—try trusting God for help. Not relying on your own strength."

Wow—maybe she had taken in more than she'd thought!

Bella's face sobered. "I never thought I'd be agreeing with you about spiritual things, but you're right, Kris." She stood up and walked over to the wardrobe. "Thanks for the reminder."

"No problem." Krista hid a small smile as her friend quickly got ready for dinner. Without even realising, the constant restlessness within her had begun to abate.

"Can you hurry it up a bit?" Ethan couldn't contain his

irritation at being stuck behind a lumbering produce truck. He had been travelling for hours—first from Brisbane to Bangkok, and then another connecting flight to Phuket. He desperately needed a long shower and a meal. And perhaps an evening rendezvous with Bella.

Which was why he was anxious to get to the hotel where she was staying.

Thank God! As the truck turned off into a side street, the Thai taxi driver accelerated quickly, after a frustrated glance back at Ethan in his rearview mirror.

Okay—he was acting like an arrogant, impatient tourist. But surely they had to be used to that in this tourist mecca? He might even pay the driver a little extra for the trouble.

Now that they were on their way again at a faster pace, Ethan allowed himself the luxury of leaning back in the seat and closing his eyes. But, as so often in the last few months—ever since he'd initiated this accursed deal—rest eluded him.

Instead, he began to mentally rehearse each step in the plan, towards its culmination in less than a week. Everything was in order—everything except Bella's role, that is. Again, he silently berated himself for having to rely on another person, and a temperamental female at that.

Her role would be not only to accompany the shipment, but to notify him if the boat was stopped by customs or border security officials. That would give him enough time to make his escape, leave his current life of stress behind and disappear somewhere. But as tantalising as it sounded to leave everything and start over, he wouldn't attempt anything that drastic until absolutely necessary.

With a squeal of ageing brakes, the taxi pulled up in front of Phuket Paradise. Ethan got out, grudgingly paid the driver the fare plus a small tip, and entered the tropical foyer. He noted the luxurious décor with a smile. This place was perfect for indulging in a little fun and relaxation. Now, he just had to find Bella ...

Overnight bag and briefcase in hand, he strolled

towards the check-in desk. Bella would probably be out for dinner, so he would just leave a message before checking in for the night.

Buzzing conversation, mingled with traditional Thai music, drifted across the foyer from the hotel's open restaurant doors, attracting his attention. The large room was already almost filled with diners, mostly foreign businessmen and tourists.

A young couple was seated just inside the door, laughing with a blonde woman. The man was resting his arm on the chair back of the woman next to him, her chestnut curls tumbling down her back.

Bella.

Ethan looked at the relaxed scene with new eyes. So, that must be his contract photographer, Hinkley, hovering over Bella.

Feeling slightly threatened, Ethan strode into the restaurant, determined to break up the cosy little gathering.

Chapter 26

Jay watched Bella smiling as Krista recounted one of their adventures back home in Brisbane, and felt himself relax. He couldn't believe how unburdened he felt since talking with Bella this afternoon—even though he'd hated to see her so confused and hurt.

But no matter how hard he'd tried to convince himself otherwise, it had to be done. He'd had to tell Bella what was blocking them, even if it meant an end for their relationship.

After their talk earlier, he'd prayed that God would open Bella's eyes, show her the truth in his words. Draw her to Himself.

To be honest, he didn't expect anything to change. But just before they sat down for dinner, Bella had pulled him aside, said she'd been thinking about his comments. She wanted to talk about it some more, after dinner.

Jay was quietly optimistic. As a Christian, he believed in miracles. And maybe there was one just around the corner.

Bella's voice now rose with surprise as she stood to greet a man. "Mr Gray—Ethan. I thought you were in Bangkok?"

"I decided to pop down here and say hello, spend a night in Phuket." His voice was warm, as though greeting an old friend.

Jay lifted his head to study Gray. Despite the humidity, he was dressed in a dark business suit. Everything about him, from his expensive watch and tie to his impeccably groomed dark hair, spoke of power and wealth.

Jay took an immediate dislike to him.

"Oh, excuse my manners," Bella giggled nervously. "This is my housemate from Brisbane, Krista Spence. She's come over for a bit of a holiday."

"Pleased to meet you." Ethan took her hand and smiled, all oily charm. Krista blushed prettily. Jay felt slightly nauseated, but still put out his hand in greeting—although he didn't bother to stand up.

"Jay Hinkley." Ethan's grip was steely, like his eyes. Sure, he was smiling, but the pleasant façade failed to hide the underlying scrutiny. Jay felt himself being sized up—and found wanting.

"Good to meet you face-to-face, instead of just over the phone." Gray cleared his throat and turned back to the girls. "Anyway, I must apologise for interrupting you like this," he said, without a hint of apology in his voice. "Have you ordered yet? No? Then I *must* take you to my favourite restaurant in Phuket. They serve authentic Thai—nothing like this Westernised slop."

Bella stammered to explain. "We—we were going to go to a local restaurant, but we only arrived late this afternoon, and—"

"Well, I'd be happy to show you around." Ethan smiled benevolently.

To Jay, Gray's move appeared to be merely a ploy to assert his power, to take control of the situation. Even now, he was pulling out the ladies' chairs, taking them each by an arm.

Jay's anger began to simmer. But he didn't want to cause a scene, so he followed them out of the hotel and into the warm night air.

Ethan turned back towards Jay as they walked. "So, how have you found working with Bella?" The question was casual, but voiced without a smile. Now that Bella and Krista were up ahead, there was obviously no need for further pretence.

Jay struggled to keep his tone civil, sent up a quick prayer for help. "It's been great, no problems at all. She tells me her angle for each resort, and I use her input to take relevant photos, plus some more of the tourism hotspots."

Ethan nodded, slowed his pace a little so that they dropped even further back behind the girls. "How well do you know Bella?"

Jay stopped and stared at the editor. "What are you getting at?"

"She's an attractive woman, I'll admit," he confided in a low voice, "but she has the tendency to get entirely too clingy, manipulative. Tries to take over your life. Trust me—I know from experience."

Jay rubbed a hand over his face as he tried to recover from the bomb just dropped on him. "Y—you had a relationship with Bella?" he asked, his mind curious while his heart dreaded the reply.

"Yes, just before she left. Short but intense." Ethan smiled, presumably at the memories of his time with Bella. "She's a bit of a tiger, if you know what I mean. But she manages to hide it beneath a demure exterior."

Jay sat down heavily on some nearby steps, his head reeling. Had he been so totally wrong about Bella? How could he have been so blind?

"But then, like I said, things got a little too close for comfort," Ethan continued, "so I sent her away on this assignment." He clapped Jay on the back. "Just trying to help you out, mate. Forewarned is forearmed, so they say." He paused and looked up ahead. "Hey, we'd better catch up to Bella and her friend. I told them the restaurant was just around the next left, but being women, they've probably got themselves lost." He laughed at his own joke, the harsh noise grating on Jay's nerves.

Blindly, he stood and stumbled after Ethan, his illusions about Bella, his own ability to judge character—even his confidence in God's guidance—tumbling down around his ears.

The first chance he got—right after dinner—he would confront Bella and ask her for the truth. Find out if their relationship was over before it had really begun.

"Dinner was nice, wasn't it?" Krista called out to Bella from her bed.

"Uh—gah," Bella managed around her toothbrush.

"I'll take that as a *yes*." Krista let out a tired, contented sigh as she stared up at the ceiling. "We may never have even seen the more authentic side of Phuket if Ethan hadn't taken us to that restaurant."

Bella stuck her head around the bathroom door, arched her eyebrows and looked down her nose in mock superiority. With toothpaste around her mouth, she failed to appear even slightly haughty. "That's *Mr Gray* to you," was her garbled reply.

"I don't think so," Krista scoffed good-naturedly. "You introduced him as Ethan. Come to think of it, you two looked pretty friendly when he put his arm around you during dessert."

Bella rinsed her mouth loudly. "Don't blame me!" she glowered, wiping her face with a towel as she stepped out of the bathroom. "I can't stand the guy."

"Neither can Jay, judging by the look on his face all through dinner. He looked like he was ready to punch Ethan's lights out!"

"Maybe he's feeling jealous." Bella smiled. "Maybe that's a good thing." Her expression grew serious. "But I didn't get a chance to talk to him, since it got so late."

"Now that you mention it, Jay *did* look like he was trying to get your attention after dinner," Krista observed.

Bella flopped onto her bed, letting out a disgusted sigh as she turned off the lamp. "How dim of me! Why didn't I notice?"

Krista smiled wryly in the darkness. "Well, it was pretty difficult with Ethan monopolising the conversation. He may be handsome, but you're right—he definitely is a bit over-bearing."

She realised with a start that she would once have been attracted to such a man. Now—well, now things seemed to be different. She was even beginning to think that it was time she headed home, gave things with Ryan a chance to work out. Thought about settling down a bit; focussed on her future.

Krista suspected her changing outlook may have had something to do with her talks with Jay and Bella about God. Who knew—maybe even she would consider looking into this 'God thing' further down the track.

"Penny for your thoughts," Bella whispered from her bed across the room.

Feigning sleep, Krista stifled a sigh. Her friend would never believe the path her musings had been taking lately.

As she let sleep claim her, her last thought was that if she could really have a relationship with God, as Jay had said—instead of merely viewing Him as some remote, distant being—then perhaps this was something she would be interested in.

Jay leaned against the shower wall and sighed heavily. Now that he was finally alone, he could feel the anger begin to drain from him with the hot water blast, leaving behind confusion—and frustration.

It couldn't be true what Ethan had said about Bella—could it? He wished he'd asked her about it tonight, but there'd been no chance to. Bella had said nothing about Ethan previously, except on that last day in Fiji, when they were playing golf. Something about him having a huge ego. It certainly didn't sound as if she cared for him at all.

It didn't make sense.

But then, nothing had made sense since Jay had met Bella.

His instincts told him that Ethan had to be lying. From what he had seen so far, there was no reason for him to trust the editor's words.

Jay couldn't quite put his finger on it—was it Gray's overt arrogance, his insincere charm, or the too-familiar way with Bella? All he knew was, he detested the man.

Detested? His conscience pricked. Okay, maybe that was too strong a word. There certainly wasn't any room there for 'Love thy neighbour'. And as a true follower of

Christ, he needed to let God's love flow through him to others.

Even to people he hated.

Jay sighed again, prayed silently for heavenly help. He obviously hadn't been relying on God's strength lately—why else would he feel jealous about Ethan and Bella, when he shouldn't even have been actively pursuing a relationship with her?

If what Ethan said was true, then maybe he had to put it behind him, lay the whole situation with Bella to rest. For good.

Sure, he could still pray that she would come to know God, but until that miracle happened, there was no point in getting his hopes up. It could be next week, or in the next decade or two. The Bible was clear about Christians not becoming involved with non-believers, and Jay could see why. There was no point being joined to someone who didn't share your same values and core beliefs, who hadn't yet accepted the gift of God's love for them.

So, as beautiful and friendly and desirable as Bella was, he wasn't going to mess up his emotions by chasing after the unattainable.

With a heavy heart and resolute mind, Jay finished his shower and dressed for bed. He knew he was wasting his time—there was no way he would sleep after making such a potentially life-altering decision—but he could only try.

Tossing and turning throughout the night, Ethan's strange behaviour kept returning to Jay's mind. The editor had acted pretty weird all through dinner. It wasn't too noticeable, but enough to make Jay feel distinctly uncomfortable.

Everything Jay had said—which wasn't a lot, considering his foul mood—seemed to be taken the wrong way by Gray, every movement and glance was analysed. It was more than just another male sizing up the competition. This was decidedly hostile.

But why? Jay had never even met the man, or at least he didn't think so. There was no past history, no reason for Gray's attitude.

In an attempt to quieten his churning thoughts, Jay

resolved to check into Gray's background tomorrow.

Especially if Bella was going to have any future contact with the editor—quite likely, considering she was still working for *Healthy Lifestyle.*

As for himself, Jay hoped he would never have to see Gray again.

Chapter 27

"Isn't this beautiful?" Bella gazed through a fringe of palm leaves to Patong Beach and sighed contentedly. "I wish we could have this view every day while having breakfast."

"Well, if you're feeling wealthy, there's a beach-side apartment back home at Noosa that I've had my eye on," Krista teased. "I'd be happy to keep you company."

Bella wrinkled her nose. "It would take over an hour to travel to any work meetings in Brisbane. Otherwise, I'd consider it."

She grinned, knowing it would be years before she could afford an apartment on the beach. For now, she would have to be content with having breakfast outside a little Thai café, just across from rolling breakers and white sand.

"I think I like Thailand the best," she declared, pulling a wisp of wind-blown hair from her face.

Krista gave a cynical snort. "Why? Phuket's just as touristy as all the other places."

"I guess ... but it still seems exotic, alluring."

"You always did have a way with words, 'Miss Writer'. Me, I'm ready to go home."

Bella studied Krista's face, certain this was another of her jokes. "Oh, sure!" she laughed. "You'd leave this—" she spread her arms wide "—for good ol' Brisbane. I bet you've even booked your flight."

"I have." Krista's voice was serious—a very rare event.

"B-but there's only a few days to go. You can't leave now!" Bella wondered about her friend's state of mind. Fun-loving Krista, going home early?

"I really should get back, mainly to try and make things work with Ryan, reconnect in our relationship. I've been doing a bit of thinking the past couple of—"

"Thinking's highly overrated," Bella interrupted, feeling a little lonely just imagining Krista gone. Despite their differences, Krista was a good friend. And Bella needed a friend now more than ever. "Besides," she whined, trying a new angle, "who will keep me company?"

Krista gave a lopsided grin and shook her head. "If you hadn't already noticed, we're travelling with a very handsome man who, I have it on good authority, is very attracted to you. I just know you guys can work it out—you've just gotta try harder. Hey, speaking of Jay ..." Frowning, she checked her watch. "Where is he? And where's our food?" She twisted in her seat to get a better view into the café.

Bella's appetite had suddenly deserted her, along with her carefree mood. She couldn't get over what Krista had just said. *Try harder?*

But that would mean giving up her way of life, her view of the world, and following another Way. She didn't think she was ready yet to make such a life-changing commitment, even if she had been going to talk to Jay about it last night.

Unfortunately, he'd left straight after dessert, looking pretty upset. Which was just how she was beginning to feel ...

Krista turned back around towards Bella and gave her a curious stare. "You don't look too happy all of a sudden," she observed. "Was it something I—? Oh, here comes Jay with the food, thank goodness. I was beginning to shrivel with hunger!"

Bella sighed with relief at the diversion. The last thing she wanted right now was another rehashing with Krista about her relationship with Jay, or her views on God. Right now, she just wanted to relax—or try to, at least.

"Sorry about the wait," Jay apologised, flashing them both a grin.

Bella quickly looked away. When would she learn to be comfortable around him, knowing that he would never be hers?

He placed a heavy tray on their table, laden with bowls of tropical fruits, juice, and bread rolls. "Continental breakfast, Thai-style. Dig in."

"Too late—I already am," Krista managed around a mouthful of bread roll. "This may have to last me until dinner on the flight to Australia, so I'm making the most of it."

Jay frowned. "Flight to Australia? When?"

"Krista's leaving us," Bella explained as she picked at her fruit salad.

"But we're near the end of the trip."

"I tried to tell her that, too, but apparently she feels the need to get back to Ryan, her boyfriend."

"Ahem." Krista put down her spoon with a bang. "Has anyone thought of consulting *me* about this, since I am the subject of conversation here? I'll admit I was a bit hasty booking my flight. Last night, I just felt I really needed to get home, so I phoned the airline first thing this morning." She paused, a sly grin crossing her face. "I *could* be persuaded to delay the flight, maybe even cancel it altogether."

Bella and Jay looked at each other, sharing a conspiratorial—and rare—smile. "We can't break up the 'Three Amigos'! So, what do you want?" Bella asked. "Your own drinks waiter, twice-daily massages, a chauffeur—"

"Hey, hold on!" Jay laughingly protested. "We'll be spending all our time serving her!"

"Hmm." Krista appeared to be considering the offer. "I *do* like the sound of all that, particularly the twice-daily massages. And yes, I think a drinks waiter—for when I'm lounging beside the pool—would be excellent. You've got a deal."

Bella and Jay gave each other a playful high-five. She pulled her hand away quickly, not willing to touch him for a second longer than necessary. Memories—like the feeling of his arms around her as they shared that passionate kiss on the beach—were best left dead and buried.

"Unfortunately, I'm afraid I'll have to pass today's 'Krista-servant' shift over to Bella," Jay said suddenly, as if he'd just remembered something. "I've got to get to Bangkok to pick up some urgent photographic supplies."

Bella noticed he looked decidedly uncomfortable.

Krista, too, was sceptical. "Didn't you bring everything you need with you?"

"Uh—yeah, mostly. But I'd like an extra lens for some of the more creative shots." He stood up and looked at his watch. "My plane leaves in an hour, so I'd better go. I'll be back sometime after dinner. Oh, and Bella—we need to talk. See you both later."

Yes, they definitely needed to talk, Bella thought.

It almost looked as if Jay was hiding something from them as he quickly walked over to the adjacent road and hailed a taxi. Shrugging his shoulders by way of apology as he got into the vehicle, he left without a backward glance.

"What's with him?" she wondered aloud, her forehead creased with concern.

"I'm not sure," said Krista airily, "but does it really matter? I've got a slave for the day!" She smiled triumphantly, obviously plotting a long list of jobs for her 'servant'.

Bella sighed. Perhaps she'd been a bit hasty in trying to convince Krista to stay—although her flatmate *did* provide a distraction from her issues with Jay.

At any rate, this was going to be a very long day.

With a frustrated frown, Ethan forced himself to turn away from his hotel window overlooking the street. He had only just checked in to the Grand Siam—after an early flight to Bangkok—but was already imagining that people knew where he was. Had he been followed from the airport? Could his Thai contact have people planted in his hotel? Was checking in under a different name precaution enough?

"Get a grip!" he cursed himself, sitting heavily on the queen bed. He'd done everything he could—even picking up a handgun from a dealer on the way to his hotel—so now he would just have to leave everything else up to fate.

Ethan Gray didn't believe in divine intervention, had never seen the need for it. He charted his own course in life, made his own choices.

And what choices they were ...

Even a year ago, he never could have imagined himself sitting in a Bangkok hotel, a gun on the bed beside him, waiting for a lunchtime meeting with one of Asia's most notorious felons.

What had he done?

Ethan picked up the gun with a mirthless laugh, and turned it over in his hands. The Beretta PX4 Storm—its ammunition clip already in place—was a semi-automatic 9mm pistol, deadly in its power. As importantly, the compact design made it easy to conceal. Ethan doubted he would ever use the weapon, but felt better having it as a backup.

He was in a different world now.

Here, there were no stressful deadlines, petty office gossip, flirting temps. The most stressful thing he had to think about now was how to deal with hardened criminals—and come out alive.

Slipping the gun into the waistband of his trousers, Ethan stood and strolled over to the window again. He felt himself drawn to the bustling normality of the motorbike- and car-clogged street. What he would give to be leading his regular life ...

His downward spiral had begun just a year ago, when he'd set the plans in motion for Australia's newest magazine, *Healthy Lifestyle*. The reception had been overwhelmingly positive, from investors, the public, and others in the industry.

He was riding high, dreams of power, influence and wealth clouding his vision—and common sense.

First, there was just the occasional weekend session at the casino to wind down. Soon, it was every night after work. And before he could stop himself, there came the horses, and sports betting, and Internet gambling. So convenient, rewarding. The rush!

The debt.

Once was never enough. And now he was paying.

Perhaps if this deal—his biggest to date of this nature—went well, this too would become just another gamble. More lucrative, but with infinitely higher risk.

Ethan checked his watch: eleven o'clock, and he still hadn't had breakfast. Food was the last thing on his mind right now, but he needed the energy. Who knew what stamina he would need for the day ahead?

Slipping into his suit jacket—primarily to conceal the gun in his trousers—he left the room.

But not before checking that the door was securely locked and that no one was loitering in the hall, ready to follow him.

Sometimes you couldn't be careful enough, especially when it concerned your life.

"But you're supposed to be my slave!" Krista pretended to pout, crossing her arms in a feigned 'sulking' stance.

Joking aside, Bella was already beginning to feel the first twinges of a headache. "Like I said," she explained again, "this is my main day to review the resort." She pushed the elevator button impatiently, anxious to get into her work. "Tomorrow, I'm meeting Ethan in Bangkok, and then we fly out on Friday."

"Ethan said you could stay an extra couple of days," Krista reminded. "You could do it then."

Bella's voice was firm—but she couldn't resist a patronising tease. "Thanks for the reminder, Kris, but I really need to do it now. Why don't you go and amuse yourself by the pool? Unfortunately, some of us have to work."

With perfect timing, the elevator opened, and Bella stalked out into the lobby.

She had waited until they'd arrived back at the hotel, after breakfast, to break the news to Krista. While she expected her friend to put up some good-natured resistance—who wouldn't, when they were losing their drinks waiter/masseuse?—Bella still found herself losing patience.

She was now looking forward to some time in the day spa, not merely to review the service, but to finally relax and be alone. The combination of her friend's chatter and the drain of unresolved issues with Jay left Bella feeling in definite need of some 'time out'.

She had already decided to try the Vichy shower first—a calming experience of lying down while being gently sprayed all along the body with multiple jets of water.

Bliss ...

A few minutes later, Bella felt the stress trickling from her. The only sound was that of sprinkling water, amid a sensation of utter relaxation and calm.

She once again found herself wondering if this feeling of serenity would be the same as trusting in something—Someone—bigger than herself, of giving control to Someone who had her best interests in mind: God.

For some reason, the idea didn't seem as scary any more. She certainly knew *she* didn't have the answers, had stumbled through life for years. So what would it hurt to try another direction?

Looking back, Bella realised that she had known all along, had seen the evidence in the lives of people around her. Mum, Todd and Carly, Jay ... they each possessed a quiet assurance, a peace, even when things didn't go their way.

They had what she lacked, and now wanted more than anything.

All thoughts of reviewing the Vichy shower gone, Bella whispered to her Creator, telling Him of her need to hand over her hurt, pain—her life—to Him. Asking Him to be her guide, to take control. For Jesus to wash her completely clean on the inside.

Until the shower stopped, Bella poured out her heart to God, her tears mingling with the water spray.

For the first time in her life, she felt completely at peace.

"We will be descending to Bangkok shortly. Please fasten your seatbelt and return your seat to the upright position."

Jay only half listened to the announcement made in Thai and English. All during the short flight he'd been berating himself for his impulsiveness, even stupidity. Here he was, flying to Bangkok, to sit outside a hotel he didn't know where to find, to watch a man he barely knew, for a reason he didn't understand.

Smart thinking, Hinkley.

On top of all that, he was also feeling guilty. He'd tried to reassure himself that he hadn't actually lied, that he *would* pick up an extra lens and memory card or two in Bangkok. But he didn't really need them.

And now Bella and Krista were suspicious.

There was no way he was telling them the real reason for this trip, Jay decided as the jet descended rapidly. If the girls knew about his sceptical—okay, jealous—motivation, they'd never let him live it down.

It could also be the final seal on the end of his and Bella's fledgling relationship. But Jay still couldn't escape his nagging feeling of distrust about Ethan Gray and his motives. He needed to know the truth.

The airliner landed smoothly, its wheels hitting the tarmac with a roar. Jay remained seated until the passengers behind him had walked down the aisle, then grabbed his backpack and camera bag.

His telephoto lens would prove its worth today, particularly as he wanted to observe Gray from as far away as possible. And if that slimy editor so much as twitched his nose in a suspicious way, Jay would be there to capture it.

As he disembarked and entered the air-conditioned chaos of Bangkok's Suvarnabhumi Airport, Jay hoped that he wasn't here on a wild goose chase; that he would uncover something underhanded.

Still, he almost couldn't help praying that he wouldn't find anything—for Bella's sake.

Chapter 28

Breakfast had been a bad idea. Ethan's insides were now churning like a washing machine, making the task of forcing down a croissant and coffee nigh impossible.

Wasn't coffee supposed to help with focus and concentration? He ordered another cup as insurance. It would take a caffeine infusion to quell the uncomfortable fluttering, the sweaty palms.

Starting on the second cup of coffee, Ethan bolstered himself with the thought of the money that would soon be his. Millions! The mental picture grew each time he turned it over in his mind, now amassing piles of notes and several coin mountains.

Once he paid off his debts, the piles would be slightly diminished, but still enough to last him for a lifetime.

If he managed to live that long.

He nervously checked his watch for the tenth time. It was half-past eleven, leaving an hour before he needed to make his way to the meeting point.

What would he do with the time? He had no desire to explore Bangkok's renowned markets or stores, was too jumpy to relax in his hotel room.

There was nothing left to do but sit in the Western-style café, slurping coffee, until the time arrived.

Silently, he rehearsed how he hoped the meeting would unfold. First, they would discuss the location and time

for the pick-up,

for the pick-up, and then go over details of the transportation.

Finally—but most importantly—they would talk money. They already had a verbal agreement, but Ethan had a sneaking suspicion it wouldn't stand.

In any case, he was going to try his luck at haggling. Which was why he needed the Beretta.

He checked his watch again, drained the last of his coffee, and reached for his planner.

Normally an extension of his arm, it was gone.

A chill slithered down his spine. All the details for the deal were in that notebook, the reason he never let it out of his sight.

The hotel room—in his anxiousness over the gun, and being followed, he must have accidentally left it there.

Not even bothering to say *khob-kun*—thank you—to the Thai waitress, he paid for his breakfast and almost jogged the block to his hotel.

The city's sights and sounds rushed by unnoticed. The heat, however, was inescapable, unbearable.

Loosening his tie, he strode into the Grand Siam's imposing lobby and straight to the elevators. Naturally, they took an eternity to reach the ground floor, just when he was in a hurry.

A man was sitting on a couch opposite the check-in desk, holding a newspaper up to his face. A man in dark glasses.

Ethan halted his pacing mid-stride. He was either being followed, or that guy had a thing for spy movies.

He wasn't about to wait around to find out. The end elevator's door wheezed open with a chime, and he launched himself inside, punching the button for his floor.

Just as the doors closed, Ethan caught a last glimpse of the man, his newspaper now fully lowered.

He could have sworn he'd met him before.

After she had finished reviewing the resort's day spa, Bella drifted outside and over to the pool. She felt deliriously happy, but at the same time, peaceful. If there weren't so many people in and around the pool, she would shout out just for the joy of it.

An impish giggle rose in her throat. Maybe she *would* shout out, just to see people's reactions.

Deciding to restrain herself—at least for the moment—Bella plopped down on a vacant sunlounger to revise her notes. There were pages of scribblings from the last three resorts, plus printed notes from before her laptop was stolen in Noumea.

In spite of her buoyant mood, she sighed at the amount of work left to do. She had hoped to be able to enjoy these last couple of days, do some holiday-type things with Krista.

And Jay, her mind silently added, before she could squelch the thought.

She doubted that Jay would want to do anything with her, judging by their conversation last night before dinner. Although he had seemed okay at breakfast this morning—before he bolted to Bangkok for an apparently lame reason.

Without conscious thought, Bella breathed a prayer, handing the whole situation over to God. "I'm Yours now," she whispered, her face hidden behind her curls. "I'll follow You, whatever happens between Jay and I."

The comparison of just a day ago—when she struggled with worry over everything—stunned Bella. Like suddenly moving from the dead of winter to a bright summer's day, her outlook had completely changed.

Thanks, God.

She stared contemplatively across the pool, forcing her mind to return to her notes. A flash of pink bikini and a blonde ponytail caught her eye—Krista, diving to make a save in a game of pool volleyball.

Bella grinned as Krista's laughter wafted over on the warm breeze. Her friend deserved some fun on this trip, after having to endure Bella's days of work, and nights of moaning about Jay.

No more whinging, she decided. It was up to God now.

Phew! That was a close one!

Jay was sure Gray had been about to talk to him, had maybe even seen through the disguise.

He smiled wryly as he walked out of the Grand Siam's lobby, ready to follow Gray when he left the hotel. Who was he kidding? With the newspaper and sunglasses, Jay looked like someone trying to appear *incognito*—and failing miserably. But so long as he was able to follow Gray from a distance, escaping detection, then it would be alright.

He was still amazed at how easily he'd managed to discover where the editor was staying. One quick call to the receptionist at *Healthy Lifestyle*, posing as an old college friend of Gray's, and he was given all the details. Jay almost felt like a real sleuth.

Now, as he waited around the corner from the hotel's entrance, he remembered the conversation he'd overhead in the Port Vila Hospital. Two detectives had said something was about to happen in Bangkok—could it be possible that Gray was involved?

Not a chance, Jay thought as he adjusted the camera strap around his neck. Ethan may be sleazy, overbearing, and entirely too arrogant—but he doubted the editor would flush his life down the toilet by stooping to something illegal.

But then, why had Jay followed the guy to Bangkok, hoping to discredit him? There had to be *something* going on.

A flash of charcoal suit jacket and dark hair alerted him that Ethan was on the move. He stayed out of sight around the corner until Gray crossed the road half a block down, and then stepped into the crowded sidewalk.

The editor's height made him appear like a giraffe amongst zebras in comparison to the shorter Thais. Jay had no problems following him for two more blocks, then around a corner into a wide, restaurant-lined street.

Gray had certainly chosen a very public place for whatever he was up to. In his suit and tie, he looked like any other Westerner come to Bangkok on business.

But what exactly did that business involve?

Hesitating for just a moment, Gray turned into the entry of a traditional-looking establishment. Both Thai and English writing on the window advertised the special of the day, Gang Gai.

Jay groaned. So the editor was hungry. That didn't make him a criminal.

Still, he kept watching the restaurant from his position across the road and behind a sidewalk sign. His eyes followed the dark suit's progress past the front counter and to an end table—right beside the window.

Gray sat down across from a Thai man and began to talk earnestly.

Jay didn't have a clue who Gray's Thai dinner partner was, but he definitely knew he wouldn't want to run into him in a dark alley.

Every feature was clear through the telephoto lens: cropped dark hair, deep-set frowning eyes. A thin moustache emphasised the hardness of his mouth.

Though Jay didn't know what he would do with them, he took a few shots—a couple of Gray and the Thai man talking, and then individual close-ups of them both.

Once he got back to Phuket, maybe he would download and email the images to Marcus Fletcher, a friend in the Australian Federal Police. Asking his friend to check for any criminal background of the men he'd photographed was no ordinary request, but Marcus owed him.

A climbing expedition two years ago—to take photos of the elusive condor in South America's Andes Mountains—had turned potentially fatal. A spring-loaded camming device had given way, leaving Jay to hold on while Marcus dangled two hundred feet above a ravine.

Yes, Marcus definitely owed him.

And hopefully, he would find something to explain the strange tightness in Jay's stomach ever since he'd first set eyes on Ethan Gray.

Chapter 29

Ethan gripped the coffee cup until his knuckles turned white, willing his nerves to settle. He would have taken in some deep breaths, except for the cloud of cigarette smoke hovering around the head of Sanouk's deputy, Lek—a small man with hard eyes that meant business.

"You're late," was all Lek had said since Ethan sat down.

Ethan supposed there was no time—or need—for politeness here. He launched into his pre-memorised list of questions. "Do you have the goods?" He kept his voice low. You never knew who could be listening.

"Of course," Lek replied tersely. "When do you want them?" Except for his mouth, the man didn't move a muscle.

Ethan clutched the coffee cup tighter. "Friday. I'm transporting them out early Saturday morning."

He paused, wondering how much he should reveal, but then decided to go ahead anyway. "I've strong-armed a charter-boat operator into shipping them for me. We should be able to avoid detection using such a small boat. And I'm getting a woman to travel with the shipment to alert me if there are any problems."

Ethan looked into Lek's face, checking for any acknowledgement of the ingenuity of his plan. He hadn't even blinked.

Coughing nervously, Ethan opened his planner, flipping through for the slip of paper on which he'd recorded the address of the dockside warehouse—yet another precaution against eavesdroppers. He admitted to himself that an electronic planner would have looked more professional, more fitting for a magazine editor. But perhaps because he *was* in the magazine business, he much preferred the feel of pen and paper.

The Thai man sat silently, taking another drag on his cigarette.

Ethan handed over the slip of paper, wishing that he too had brought his cigarettes. He needed something to calm his nerves, give his shaking fingers something to hold onto.

"Sanouk will personally see to the delivery," Lek said, folding the note and slipping it inside the pocket of his dark shirt.

He leaned over the table and fixed Ethan with an unblinking stare. Ethan felt as if he was looking into the darkest corner of hell.

Lek's voice was quiet, deadly. "I assume you have something for us in return. You know the account details." He paused, patting his jacket pocket almost imperceptibly.

Ethan got the message. "Yes, of course. The payment. The agreed amount?"

Coward.

"Yes—not a bit less. Or you won't enjoy the consequences."

Ethan almost choked on the last sip of lukewarm coffee.

What had he gotten himself into?

He set his cup down and looked up, ready to assure Lek that the deal would go ahead as arranged, that there was no need for threats.

But he was already gone.

The flight back to Phuket seemed to take twice as long. Jay was anxious to download his photos, send them to Marcus, and find out the identity of the Thai man Gray had met.

But most of all, he wanted to warn Bella to stay away from Ethan Gray.

Had she somehow become tangled up in something—maybe underhanded, even illegal—that the editor was doing? Jay worried about her all the way through the flight and landing, the terminal in Phuket, and the taxi ride to their hotel.

He tried to relax, think objectively—pray—but nothing could erase the image of the man's cruel face, those cold eyes.

Of course, it was possible that he could be a business contact for Gray's magazine, maybe even a friend. But Jay wasn't buying either explanation. He was sure the editor was up to no good.

The taxi had barely stopped before he leaped out, paid the driver, and raced into the lobby of Phuket Paradise.

Part of him wanted to see Bella first—but what would he say? Besides, she thought he'd gone to Bangkok for reasons other than watching her editor.

Jay groaned silently, realising that he had forgotten to pick up supplies. So now he was a liar, as well as a stalker! This day was getting better all the time, he thought sarcastically.

Feeling guilty, he decided to send the photos before facing Bella. He couldn't help it if he wanted to protect her, he rationalised as he rode the lift and headed towards his room. Any decent man would do the same thing. At times, she seemed so vulnerable, fragile even—traits that practically confirmed for him that Ethan had lied about Bella being a 'tiger'.

Jay sighed. He was leaving it all in God's hands now—He was the only One who could truly take care of Bella, meet her needs.

Up in his room, Jay drummed his fingertips on the table as he waited for the photos to download. He tapped out a quick message to Marcus—slipping in a reference to the climbing accident as leverage—and attached the saved images.

A click of a button, and they were whizzing through cyberspace.

Jay sat back in his chair, suddenly feeling drained. He decided that he was either close to turning into a nutcase ... or just trying to save a woman he cared about from potential danger.

"Ahhh, smell that fresh sea air," Bella sighed, pretending not to notice Jay's side-long glance. He had looked at her guardedly, too, when she had asked him to go for a walk.

She couldn't blame him. Even though they were now on speaking terms, it wasn't as if they were best friends.

Certainly not 'kissing friends', like before.

"How was your day?" she asked politely as they scuffed through the soft sand towards the water line. "Did you pick up your supplies?"

Jay took a long time to answer. He stared down at his feet while they walked, his hands jammed in his pockets.

Bella frowned. Maybe things were worse between them than she had thought.

"I sort of forgot," Jay finally answered, his voice quiet. "When I got to Bangkok, I was thinking about so many things, that the main reason I was there just slipped my mind," he finished lamely.

Bella decided right then that Jay was a terrible liar. But at least she could easily tell when he wasn't being entirely truthful—not like some people she'd encountered.

Uninvited, her thoughts suddenly flitted back to two years earlier, on another beach. Only this time, she was confronting the owner of a local charter boat company. And he was lying through his teeth ...

"What happened?" Bella had demanded, struggling to keep tears of worry at bay. "Why hasn't my fiancé returned? He was supposed to be back four hours ago!"

The man took a step back, blustering. "That's odd. The operator didn't mention anything when he came in."

Bella could have sworn he was lying. As owner and manager of the company, he would surely have been told if a diver was missing. "You don't know Andrew," she

insisted,

insisted, brushing wind-blown curls from her face. "He's always on time. We had a dinner date."

She pushed down a sob, as old fears arose. Andrew's love of diving had always concerned her, its element of danger and the unknown, threatening.

But Andrew was so competent, never took unnecessary risks. So where was he?

"Okay, lady, I'll look into it. We always check off a list when the divers return to the boat." He rubbed a hand over his balding head in a nervous gesture. "I'm sure your fiancé's somewhere close—he may even be back at your hotel room already," he reassured.

Bella turned away, a glimmer of hope burning as she walked back to their beach-side hotel. Andrew had probably just gone off to do something else—maybe even to organise a surprise for her, as he often did—and would now be back in their room.

But he wasn't there, and Bella never saw him again.

Despite the findings of the ensuing investigation and signed statements from all those involved, deep down she knew that somehow Andrew had been tragically left behind at sea.

And after being lied to so blatantly on the day he disappeared, she vowed never to trust another man—until Jay.

But now he was doing the same thing.

Inhaling a calming breath of salty air, Bella pushed the hurtful memories away. Surely there was a reasonable explanation? Anyway, her new faith required her to forgive others.

"I'm flying to Bangkok tomorrow morning to meet Ethan. I could get your things for you." She felt good making the forgiving gesture—until she saw Jay's face.

"Bella, I don't think you should meet with him," he cautioned, eyebrows drawn in a frown.

"Why?"

"I just don't think it's a good idea. I've heard some things about him." He paused, then rushed on. "He's even said some unprofessional things about you, and—"

"About me?!" Bella interjected. "I barely even know him."

"—and I don't like him personally, either."

Bella stopped walking, one hand on her hip. "I'm guessing that's the *real* reason why you don't want me to see Ethan," she snapped, her frayed emotions wearing thin. "Could it be that Jay Hinkley is jealous?"

"Yes—I mean, no!" Frustrated, Jay ran a hand through his hair. "It's true I don't like him, but I'm mainly concerned for your safety. I checked out some things today, and I'm waiting to hear back if my suspicions are right. And if they are," he looked down at her with troubled eyes, "then Gray's an extremely dangerous man. You should stay away. Email your notes, tell him you can't make it."

Bella shook her head in disbelief. The lengths to which men would go to edge out another rival!

"I can't believe this! Ethan's only treated me well. Oh, I'll admit he gets a bit touchy-feely sometimes, but other than that, he's mostly very businesslike."

Both hands on hips now, she lifted her chin and fixed Jay with a defiant stare.

"He's an editor, for goodness sake, not a terrorist! *You're* even working for him. I have to do what I have to do as a professional writer. I'm meeting him tomorrow to discuss the feature, and that's final."

She turned and stomped up the beach, having a distinct sense of *déjà vu* from their last argument.

Just thirty seconds later, she stopped, breathed out a deep sigh. She had just been going to tell Jay about her new faith, and now she'd really blown it.

Turning back around, she saw him standing at the water's edge, staring out at the moon as it rose out of the ocean. A feeling of tenderness swept over her—confirming that despite their differences, she did truly care for Jay.

But there would be time later to focus on that. Right now, they probably both needed some time alone.

Bella slipped back along the path to the hotel, her thoughts turning into a prayer as she gave her life and relationships over to God.

True, she had messed up in her first day as a follower

of Christ, but there was always tomorrow.

Thankfully, His grace was new every morning.

I read the first part of this chapter twice! Thought I'd lost it first time. I think my second reading is better

Chapter 30

Gray's an extremely dangerous man. Bella tightly squeezed her eyes shut, trying to banish Jay's warning from her mind.

He can't be *that* dangerous, she reasoned, absent-mindedly twisting a curl around her finger. Jay had said he'd only had suspicions, none of them proven. And, she thought grimly, his doubts were probably motivated more by jealousy than real evidence.

With a sigh, she rested her head back on the airline seat. Her life was becoming terribly complicated, with so many problems and choices. Nothing was clear-cut, black-and-white.

So why didn't she feel the familiar, gut-squeezing worry?

Thank goodness I've got God to help me now.

And perhaps *because* she was trusting His help, she'd felt the need to go ahead with her trip to Bangkok today, to meet Ethan.

"Excuse me, ma'am. Would you like some tea?"

Bella looked up in surprise at the hostess's voice, suddenly remembering where she was. Her first instinct was to refuse—normally she didn't feel hungry while she was mentally working through issues—but her stomach rumbled in protest. It had been a long time since breakfast.

"Yes, please."

Bella remembered she had rushed through her meal, the silence of Jay's disapproval almost palpable.

Of course, Krista hadn't noticed a thing. "What's everyone doing today?" she chirped. "If you're free for lunch, you'll have to come and meet some of my new friends. We're playing another game of pool volleyball afterwards."

Jay didn't look up from his meal. "I'll be busy working today," he said quietly, a hint of fatigue beneath his words.

Bella ignored the twinge of guilt. She wasn't doing anything wrong, so she had nothing to worry about—right?

"I'm meeting Ethan in Bangkok today," she reminded Krista. Seeing her friend's smile deflate just a little, she quickly added, "Why don't you book us a table somewhere for dinner tonight, at around seven? Invite a few of your new friends, too."

Bella noticed Jay's head pop up then. More jealousy?

I really should go a bit easier on him, she decided as she placed her empty tea cup on the tray table. He'd had a difficult time lately, too—being attacked by an intruder in his room, the shooting, being lumped with her emotional baggage ...

Ex-emotional baggage, she silently chided herself. As long as she continued to give her burdens to God, she wouldn't have to lug them around herself—or dump them onto others.

As the plane winged towards Bangkok, Bella unloaded one more burden—her niggling feeling of unease at her meeting with a potentially dangerous editor.

Jay felt unusually restless after breakfast. He had planned to hire a boat and travel up the coast for some jungle shots. Ever since arriving in Thailand, the sheer abundance and diversity of its wildlife had cried out to his creative instincts.

But the chance that Marcus had already sent through the information about the photos sent Jay heading to his room to check his emails instead. Would there be a confirmation of his suspicions about Ethan? And was he warranted in his concern about Bella meeting with the editor today?

He was too anxious about Bella to think about anything else. He opened the door to his room and went straight over to his laptop, wondering as he did what Bella was doing right now. Was she worried after his warnings yesterday, or naively at ease?

There was no email from Marcus, so Jay opened up the photo files from yesterday to have another look at the images.

Just then, the phone in his room began to ring. It was Marcus. "Hi, mate—what have you got?" Jay demanded, his worry precluding small talk.

The voice on the other end of the line was both approving and tense. "You've hit the jackpot this time, Jay. I should put you on as an undercover detective."

Jay's heart plummeted into his shoes. "So there *is* something going on?"

"You'd better believe it. Those shots you sent were of Ethan Gray, editor of Brisbane-based *Healthy Lifestyle* magazine—"

"Yeah, I know that bit."

"Okay. But the other guy ... His name is Niwat Kunchai, nicknamed Lek, a notorious organised crime figure. He's the deputy to the head of Thailand's major underworld drug operation, Sanouk Panjaphan."

His mind reeling, Jay sucked in a gulp of air. Could this get any worse?

Only if Bella gets hurt.

His mind slammed into overdrive. "Marcus, Bella Whitman, a friend of mine, is meeting with Gray today in Bangkok. Could she be in danger?"

"There is a small chance," Marcus said soberly, "but the Thai police have already been alerted, and would have someone watching Gray by now."

Jay should have felt relieved, but couldn't quite manage it.

"I probably shouldn't be telling you this," Marcus lowered his voice, "but I've heard that they were planning a raid on Sanouk's operation anyway. If Gray's involved, he'll be brought down."

"Good," Jay couldn't help saying. "As long as Bella's okay."

"You know, it wouldn't hurt for you to phone the Bangkok police yourself and tell them about your friend. I wouldn't want someone *I* knew spending time with anyone involved with Lek or Sanouk. They're ruthless. Apparently, their head hit-man was found burnt to death a couple of days ago—a typical MO for Sanouk."

Jay squeezed his eyes shut, breathed a prayer for Bella's protection. "Thanks for your help, Marcus. I owe you one."

"We're not even square yet, mate," Marcus chuckled. "You saved my life, remember? Be careful with this," he added seriously, "and make sure your girl doesn't hang around with Gray anymore."

Jay thanked his friend again, ended the call, and then tapped out the number for call information. He had to call the police, alert them to the danger Bella was in, demand protection for her. He had to do something, *anything* to assuage the growing sense of helplessness.

Bella was possibly right now walking into a police raid, and all he could do was wait and pray.

Ethan checked his wristwatch for what seemed like the twentieth time and wondered what could be keeping Bella. He had arranged for her to meet him at half past eleven in the lobby of the Grand Siam, but she was almost forty minutes late.

He frowned, and compulsively looked at his watch again. If he'd thought it through more beforehand, he would have planned to meet with Bella at the airport, talk to her in one of the restaurants there.

But he wanted to meet her on his own turf—on his terms—and the Grand Siam fit the bill nicely.

Now, if he could just contain his frustration over the lateness of this hussy writer ...

He lifted impatient eyes towards the entrance, and there she was. Dressed to impress, Bella was the epitome of businesslike professionalism—or eye-candy on legs, whichever way you chose to look at it.

Ethan suppressed a leer, recalling a similar situation when she had walked towards him in the restaurant in Brisbane. He preferred that red dress over today's suit.

Hopefully, she would be more willing to do his bidding today than she was that night. Standing to meet her, he decided he would just have to bide his time.

"Bella Whitman—punctual as always."

She flushed, obviously noticing his mild undertone of sarcasm. He mentally kicked himself—getting her offside could cause problems later on.

"Sorry I'm late. Traffic was horrendous from the airport."

He smiled, putting on the charm. "Tell me about it. Sometimes it would be quicker to walk."

He stared at her while she put her satchel on the floor beside his single-seat couch, wondering what sort of mood she was in, if she would be willing to play her part in the plan. He had never been able to understand women, almost felt it was useless to try.

However, this particular woman appeared to relax a little at his light banter. Perfect.

He stood suddenly, motioning towards the chair. "Forgive my lack of manners." Bella smiled just as he caught a whiff of her perfume—the combined effect was highly alluring.

"I'm sure you must be starving," he continued smoothly, looking down at her as she settled in the chair, "especially with nothing but airline food since breakfast."

"I *am* a little hungry," she admitted, wrinkling her nose.

Ethan reached out a hand. "Allow me to take you out for lunch. There's an excellent restaurant just a short walk from here."

As he described the delicious menu, he quickly stifled any miniscule shred of concern he may have had over placing her in danger.

If it came down to him going to jail or her taking the fall, he would choose Bella every time.

Sanouk leaned back in his leather office chair, exhaled a cloud of cigar smoke, and smiled. Business was good—better than ever. Revenue was high, problems were low, with new opportunities constantly arising. Organised crime in Thailand was big business, and he was King.

His dark brows suddenly lowered in a frown. There was just one niggling irritation marring his perfect outlook: Ethan Gray, and his small-time deal.

Normally, Sanouk wouldn't bother getting personally involved with something of this nature, but he occasionally liked to keep in touch with the grass-roots of his business, deal directly with his clients.

And in this transaction, he had decided that what Gray was offering—the 'agreed price' they had settled on—was too low. Gray was purchasing a specialty, not to mention contraband, product; not candy.

No, the money was definitely not enough. But Sanouk was prepared to negotiate—his way.

He'd gone through the same scenario countless times before. The buyer would hand over the cash, Sanouk—or more usually, one of his employees—would demand more, and so on. It usually ended with one of two outcomes: he got his asking price, or the buyer got a bullet.

So clean, so simple. Hopefully, dealing with Gray would be just as easy.

Sanouk took a sip of brandy from an ever-present glass, and realised he wasn't so sure. Beneath Gray's professional veneer was ruthless ambition, verging on desperation. Built on a foundation of greed.

It took one to know one, and Sanouk was intimately acquainted with all of the vices.

The best plan would be to surprise Gray, get the upper hand. Waiting until the hand-over would be too risky.

Putting down his glass, Sanouk decided that something needed to be done now, today. He leaned towards his intercom to summon a few of his most competent employees.

The corners of his mouth lifted in a grim smile as he pictured the fate awaiting Gray. If the snivelling Australian editor thought he could play hardball with the pros, then he would have to be prepared for the consequences.

Ethan Gray was heading for a lesson he would never forget.

Chapter 31

The loud knock startled Krista. Towel and sunscreen in hand, she moved towards the door. She was supposed to meet Sophie, one of her new friends, by the pool in ten minutes, but she had probably grown impatient.

"Sophie?" She swung the door open. "Jay! Are you okay?"

His tanned face was pale, his hair sticking up as though he'd been pulling at it. He barged past her, then quickly shut the door as she turned back into the room.

'Bella's in trouble!" he blurted.

"Wha—?"

"I'm flying to Bangkok."

"Whe—?"

"It seems her editor is mixed up with an underworld drug lord."

"Thank you for finally explaining!" she exclaimed, hands up in frustration. Then his words registered. "Oh, no! I hope she's alright. What can I do?"

Jay was already halfway out the door, but now he stopped and turned, fixing her with a desperate stare. "Pray. I don't care if you've never prayed before, but I need you to do it now. For Bella's sake."

In her shocked state, it took Krista half a minute to realise he was gone. She slowly shut the door then crossed to the bed, wringing her hands. Poor Bella! She desperately hoped Jay—and the police—would find her before anything terrible happened.

Krista tried not to dwell on the worst possible outcomes. Instead, she reassured herself that Bella was a smart girl—had always been smarter than she herself was—and Ethan didn't seem that dangerous, either. Perhaps Jay was just being overprotective.

All her rationalising, however, couldn't stop her active imagination from going into overdrive. The mental picture of Bella, bound and gagged and being interrogated by criminals, brought tears to her eyes.

What could she do? Here she was, stuck at a resort in Phuket, with nothing to do but pray. But how?

A memory of Jennifer Whitman, Bella's mother, sprang to her mind. Last year, Jennifer had come up from Victoria for a visit. At dinner that first evening, she had prayed over the food, talking to God as if He was her friend, was right there at the table. This recollection, combined with the sense of peace Krista felt whenever she spoke with Bella's mum, prompted her to pick up her phone and call her.

Jennifer answered on the second ring, her calming voice bringing more tears to Krista's eyes. "Hi, Jennifer," she managed to choke out. "It's Krista."

"Krista—what's wrong, honey?" she asked, concern evident in her voice.

"It's Bella," Krista sobbed. "She's in trouble in Bangkok, and I—I can't even pray!"

"Bella! What's wrong? Is she okay?" Jennifer asked in alarm

Grabbing a tissue, Krista managed to calm herself a little. "She's gone to visit her editor, but Jay—a friend—has just found out he's involved with someone who sells drugs." She struggled to remember Jay's frantic words. "An underworld drug lord, or something like that. Sorry, that's all I know."

She stopped, wondering—too late—at the wisdom of blurting this out to her friend's mum. She was bound to be frantic with worry.

But although Jennifer did sound concerned, that

unshakeable peace remained.

"There's only one thing we can do, Krista—and that's pray. I'm certain that God is watching over Bella right now."

Krista clutched her sodden tissue and felt just a bit foolish. "Yes—Jay asked me to pray for Bella," she said with a sniff, "but I don't know how. Can you teach me?"

Despite her obvious strain, it almost sounded as if there was a smile in Jennifer's voice. "Of course. The most important thing with prayer is that you believe—the Bible calls it faith."

"I believe." The simple words, spoken in a moment of desperation, swept aside all of Krista's preconceptions and cynicism. For the moment, at least, she truly believed.

"Dear God," Jennifer began softly, "we thank You that You hear our prayer. We ask You to protect Bella, to keep her from any harm, and to give her strength. Surround her with Your angels, Lord. And please also help Krista through this difficult time. Amen."

"Amen," Krista echoed in a whisper, wondering at the quiet peace that had just stolen into her heart.

Speaking with Jennifer for just a short while longer, she hung up the phone with a sigh. Somehow, she knew that everything would be alright.

God was in control. Bella would be safe.

"How have you found your time in the islands?" Ethan asked, turning on a full wattage smile over their lunch of Thai green curry with chicken and rice.

Bella began to relax a little. Ethan was just being polite, not trying to chat her up, or involve her in some sort of illegal activity.

"It's been lovely—when we haven't been terrorised by room intruders, or hit men with poor aim," she answered truthfully. She omitted to mention that she had almost fallen to her death in the mountains above Noumea. There was no sense in alarming her editor further, informing him that his feature was almost cancelled before it really began.

But he didn't even seem to hear her, instead continuing on with his own questions. "And Jay"—he spoke as though he had just found a fly in the curry—"you two have worked well together?"

"Yes—he's an excellent photographer, and he's even given me some useful suggestions for the articles." Bella hoped Ethan didn't automatically assume she and Jay were together, because they weren't—not yet, anyway.

The last thing she wanted was a jealous, 'extremely dangerous' editor on her hands.

If he was feeling possessive—though he had no right to be—Ethan didn't show it. "I hope he didn't distract you from your writing too much," he remarked drily, wiping his fingers on a napkin.

Bella chose to ignore the comment. Editor or not, he had no business digging into her private life.

She glanced at her watch, feeling that their earlier discussion about the feature, while waiting for their meal, had been sufficient.

Ethan must have noticed the gesture. "I realise you're probably in a hurry to catch your flight back, but there's just one more detail we have to discuss."

He paused for so long that Bella began to worry that he might be about to propose they cross the boundaries of professionalism.

"It's not exactly to do with the feature, but more as a personal favour—"

She narrowed her eyes in suspicion.

"—for which you'll be fully compensated."

Bella crossed her arms defensively, despite an undeniable feeling of curiosity. What was he suggesting?

Ethan rushed on. "I've got a shipment of sample products to be included with future issues of the magazine, products that are quite valuable over here. I'd hate for them to be stolen and disappear in the black market, so I'll need someone to accompany them on the trip back to Brisbane."

Bella nodded, relieved that her earlier fears were unfounded, but wondering why he was telling her about this. What sort of 'products' were these, anyway? Precious jewels?

"I was hoping you'd do it for me," he said, tugging nervously at his collar.

"Why?" She blurted out the first thing in her mind.

"Well, I—I trust you, and ... you're here," he blustered, his earlier composure slipping. "Unfortunately, I have other business to attend to, and won't be able to do it myself. I'll pay you well," he reminded, the self-satisfied expression now back in place.

"I don't know," Bella hesitated, Jay's words ringing in her ears. Maybe what he had said about Ethan was correct, that the editor really was a criminal. Maybe she should have listened.

Then Ethan gave her another, half-pleading smile, and she dismissed her doubts with a wave of her hand. "I'll think about it."

"Don't think too long—the products will be shipped out this Saturday."

"Shipped? Does that mean they'll be on a boat?"

"Yes—it's cheaper than by air. It should only take a few days." He smiled, as if he was doing her a favour. "Just think of it as a short extension of your trip—a holiday."

Bella frowned to herself as she wondered, shoving the remaining curry around on her plate. Ethan's words, despite his assurances, didn't ring true.

He certainly sounded as if he had something to hide.

Oh God, help!

Jay found himself on a flight to Bangkok for the second time in as many days. This trip, however, was much more tension-filled than the last. In between snatches of praying and fidgeting in the cramped seat, a mist of hopelessness surged forward, threatening to envelop him. What could he do? How could he help?

Apart from the obvious—and he'd already prayed more today than probably in his entire life—Jay felt at a loss when it came to protecting Bella. He'd done a lousy job so far. Since they had met, she'd fallen over a cliff, been dangerously close when he was shot, and was right now meeting with a suspected drug smuggler.

Frustrated, he ran a hand through his hair, knowing it

was a tangled mess but not caring. The only thing he did care about right now was finding Bella, making sure she was alright—and then pulling her into an embrace.

If she let him, that is. But he had noticed a definite softening in her the last day or so. A peace, even.

Could she have—? Frowning, he dismissed the thought. Surely she would have told him about something as amazing and life-changing as becoming a follower of Christ.

Maybe she had tried. He mentally rifled through the last twenty-four hours, their fight on the beach standing out like an angry wound.

You idiot!

She *had* been going to tell him something last night, had organised the walk on the beach. Said she wanted to talk.

And now he might never know what she wanted to say.

No! Refusing to believe the worst, Jay drew on every shred of faith he possessed. *Trust in the Lord with all your heart ... The Lord is a shield, a very present help in trouble ... Be anxious for nothing ...*

Scriptures came thick and fast now, bringing with them a reassuring peace.

Thanks, God. I needed that.

A flight attendant's voice sounded over the speakers, jerking Jay back to the moment: "We'll be descending to Bangkok shortly, and are due to arrive in fifteen minutes. We ask that all passengers return to their seats and refasten their seatbelts."

Jay raised his tray table and started to grab his things. He wanted to be first off the plane as soon as they landed. Bangkok was a huge city, and other than heading to the Grand Siam, he didn't have any idea where to start looking for Bella. One thing was certain—he had to find her and get her away from possible danger. And Ethan Gray.

Ethan pretended to concentrate on spearing the remaining piece of chicken on his plate. The woman was asking too many questions! And more than anything, questions were something he wanted to avoid.

It was time to wrap up this lunch date. "I'm sorry, Bella, but I don't have all the details here. I left them in my hotel room." Standing, he put down his fork and napkin. "Shall we go? I'll need you to look things over, so you can make a decision."

He didn't miss the fact that Bella's eyes narrowed at the mention of going with him to his room. Her expression remained guarded during the short, silent walk back to the Grand Siam.

Ethan knew convincing her wasn't going to be easy, but had been stupidly hoping for a miracle. Now it was crunch time, and all he had was some fast-talking, his wits, and charm to win her over. Hopefully.

Outside his room, Bella stood back as he unlocked the door, anxiously twisting a stray curl around her finger. He strode into the room, smiling to himself. Her nervousness could work to his advantage. Maybe she would be so intent on escaping that she would agree to his plan.

He studied her out of the corner of his eye as he rifled through some papers. She was facing the wall-length window, arms crossed defensively. If he didn't know better, he could have sworn she looked scared.

But why would she be afraid of him? Other than the obvious—that he might make a move on her?

At any other time, Ethan would have considered acting on the thoughts that had been lurking for weeks, but right now he was focussed on convincing Bella to do his bidding in an entirely different area.

She turned towards him now, impatience obviously overcoming her fear. "Do you have it yet?"

Nodding, he handed her the single-sided typed page, prepared expressly for her. Only the essential details were included—and most of them weren't the complete truth.

No matter. It would all be over by the end of next week, and he would be insanely rich.

Bella spun around suddenly and thrust the piece of paper at him, taking him by surprise. Her face was blanched, blue eyes shooting sparks.

"Is this some sort of cruel joke?!"

Chapter 32

Khun Sanouk, can we go through it one more time?"

Sanouk sighed. Luk, son of a close friend, was the largest of the three enforcers riding with him in the dark Mercedes. Unfortunately, he was far from the brightest. However, what he lacked in intelligence he made up for in fighting and weaponry skills. Sanouk had decided to keep him on—for the moment, at least.

"Gray is staying on the fifth floor, room 512. Our man tailing him informed me that a woman—Bella Whitman, from his description—entered the room ten minutes ago. There's no exit other than the door to the main corridor.

He paused, looking each man in the eye. They were all good at what they did, which was just as well. He couldn't afford to have this little 'visit' messed up.

"Annan will stop at the front entrance and let me out. He'll then take you round to the back, where you'll enter an unlocked emergency door. I'll meet you on the fifth floor landing of the stairs."

Luk nodded seriously, his brows drawn in concentration. If he did well this time, Sanouk may even consider promoting him. If not ... there would be time to worry about that later.

The Grand Siam came into view on the left. As Annan, the chauffeur-cum-bodyguard, guided the car into the circular driveway, Sanouk checked his weapons: a Steyr

TMP automatic machine pistol resting in a shoulder holster, a tiny Kel-Tec P-3AT sub-compact handgun inside his breast pocket, and a knife strapped to his ankle.

Normally, he didn't bother about being so heavily armed, but he wasn't taking any chances lately. Pressure from the local and international police was increasing, and Sanouk had felt the heat, even right at top level.

The car slowed to a stop. "Annan, you know what to do. Wait by the car round the back, and notify me of any trouble down here."

Without a backward glance, Sanouk grasped the handle of his briefcase—ensuring he looked the part of a man visiting the hotel for a business meeting—and exited the open car door. He almost smiled as Annan touched his cap in a mock salute. The man had been well-trained in the role of a chauffeur—no one would even suspect his criminal ties.

As he entered the imposing entrance the doorman and receptionist both smiled, the porter standing to attention. Sanouk nodded briefly at them all, perfectly playing the part of a preoccupied businessman.

He had actually started in business, manufacturing cheap goods for the West. But a series of personal and professional disasters had forced him to turn to more profitable ventures.

Years later, he was now head of a huge underworld empire, and one of the leading drug lords in Asia. Still, he liked to keep his hand in now and then, by his presence at the occasional hit. It was ... cathartic.

Sanouk smiled as he rode the elevator to the fifth floor. He'd done well for a poor village boy. Everything he ever wanted was now his.

Which was why, if a nobody like Gray even thought about getting in the way, he would be removed—permanently.

Exiting onto the fifth floor, Sanouk gripped the pistol in his hand, his face a grim mask of hate.

Bella struggled for composure, struggled to stop herself from shouting and screaming. If only the room would stop spinning for just a moment!

"What's wrong?" Ethan asked with a frown, reaching out a hand to her.

"Don't touch me!" she bit out between clenched teeth. She wanted to run and run and not stop until there were a million miles between her and the editor.

But first she had to know why he would do such a terrible thing to hurt her. "Why are you doing this to me?" she addressed the carpet, unable to look up at him.

"Wh—what do you mean?" He sounded genuinely confused. "Is there a problem? Maybe a misunderstanding?"

"No, I think *you* misunderstand what's happening here." Bella took a deep breath, steeling herself to recount the past. She'd thought she had worked through it all, but deep wounds heal slowly—this one would need years. And she was about to rip it open again.

"You want me to travel on a vessel from McKenzie Charter Boats," she said in a monotone, distancing herself from the conversation, the room. Her life.

Ethan moved to stand in front of her, hand on hip. "They're a reputable company, good boats and competitive pricing." He cleared his throat and began to pace in front of the side table. Bella followed the path of his feet, her eyes still downcast. Ethan was acting nervous, contrary to the innocent image he presented.

He knows.

He stopped suddenly, threw up his hands in frustration. "I don't know why you're acting so silly, Bella. This is a simple business transaction. And you're turning down some good money," he added, as if to demonstrate her foolishness.

"I don't care about the money!" Bella cried, angry tears threatening to overflow. She turned on her heel and made for the door. How dare this man overturn her emotions—her world—without a scrap of compassion?

She stopped with her hand on the doorknob. Ethan had to be made to understand what he had done to her. She didn't want to give him the pleasure of seeing how much he'd hurt her, but shock him into realising he'd hugely overstepped the line.

"Two years ago, my fiancé was killed on a diving trip with McKenzie Charter Boats."

There. She'd said it. Now she could go somewhere and cry.

"Wait a second!" Ethan's voice sounded truly shocked. "Are you trying to say that you're connected with that diving accident, that it was actually *your fiancé?"*

Bella turned to see him sit down heavily onto the couch, his head shaking in amazement. "So you knew about the accident, then?" Her heart felt as wooden as her voice.

"Yes. An ex-girlfriend of mine—just a short-term fling, really—was on the dive boat when it happened. But I had no idea you were somehow involved. Of all the rotten luck ..."

Bella had no time for his incredulous self-pity. Summoning every last ounce of strength, she turned back to the door and said, "Well, we've both had a bit of bad luck lately. The difference between you and me, though, is that I'm trying not to wallow in mine. Oh, and your answer is no!"

She started to open the door, but the handle twisted beneath her fingers.

An Asian man pushed his way in, the force shoving her aside.

Bella peered out from behind the opened door. She looked from Ethan—whose face was suddenly white as a ghost—to the three men who now filled the room with a menacing presence.

Something was terribly wrong here, Bella decided as she sent up a silent plea for help.

"Come on, come on! Can't you go faster?" Jay demanded, drumming his fingers on his knees.

"I'm trying, sir. Traffic can get pretty bad in the afternoon."

Jay clamped his mouth shut against a terse reply. The traffic *was* awful, backed up for hundreds of feet in each direction.

The problem was, he couldn't do anything about

it—and for Jay, that was the worst thing imaginable.

Especially when Bella's life could be at stake.

He swiped away a trickle of sweat from his forehead. The humid air was thick despite the air-conditioned cab interior, and his tension seemed to increase the temperature by several degrees.

If someone had told him that instead of taking wildlife photos in the Pacific he would be evading criminals and rescuing a damsel in distress, he would have laughed in their face—or cancelled the trip.

But Bella needed him now, and he couldn't let her down, couldn't leave her in the company of Ethan Gray and possible danger.

Nothing could ever have prepared him for an experience like this. Nothing except faith in God and trust in His protection. Because, in the situation he was about to burst into, he'd need every bit of divine protection he could get.

As the sluggish line of vehicles started to move again, Jay realised that in some strange way, he was glad to be in this mess, wouldn't want to be anywhere else.

Who knew, maybe—like Esther—he was brought here 'for such a time as this'?

All he did know was that this had been one crazy assignment—rescuing Bella from a cliff face, having his room broken into, grappling with an intruder, getting shot, spying on criminals ...

Despite the stress, Jay couldn't stop a wry smile from lifting the corners of his mouth. Maybe he would take Marcus up on his teasing job offer.

"The Grand Siam is just two blocks up ahead," the cab driver warned, "so we should be there in—"

"Thanks!" Jay opened his door and shoved a handful of *baht* at the startled driver. "Keep the change."

He started jogging along the sidewalk, dodging through the crowd of pedestrians. Getting there on foot had to be faster than crawling through the traffic snarl, and speed was his priority now.

Jay refused to worry about what he'd do if Bella and Gray weren't at the hotel. He didn't have a clue where else to look. They just *had* to be at the Grand Siam.

Nearing the entrance, he saw that it was blocked off by a barricade and several Thai policemen.

Oh, no!

"Excuse me, sir." He struggled to catch his breath. "I need to visit someone in the hotel. What's happened?"

The officer raised his palm in a "stop" gesture, shook his head. "No," he ordered in accented English. "We are not allowing anyone through."

Jay's fists were clenched so tightly they hurt. He wanted to yell, or punch something.

Instead, he took a few deep breaths, asking, "Can you at least tell me what's happening?"

The policeman would not bend. "No, this is police business. Move on."

"Look, I may know something about what's going on here. Can you please take me to your superior officer?"

If this tactic didn't work, Jay would have to try and push his way through. Part of him hardly cared if he was arrested, or got shot again—so long as it wasn't fatal.

He wouldn't stop until he knew Bella was safe.

Ethan's first thought was wondering if he could make a run for it, maybe push Bella towards them as a diversion, then slip out the door.

But there were three of them, all heavily armed. Each man had murder in his eyes.

Ethan swallowed convulsively around his fear. If ever there was a need for fast-talking and negotiation, this was it.

But how do you negotiate with several guns trained on your head?

He held up his hands in a—hopefully—placatory gesture. "Gentlemen, please. That's not necessary." His voice sounded like a timid squeak in his ears, mirroring his quivering insides.

He sneaked a glance at Bella. She was standing still as a statue next to the now-closed door, her eyes wide in horror.

One of the men, obviously the leader, nodded to the

other two. They lowered their weapons before proceeding to roughly frisk him and Bella. "I assure you, it's merely a precaution," the leader said. *Sanouk!* Ethan would recognise that voice anywhere. "You can't be too careful in this business."

Straightening his jacket with trembling fingers, Ethan seized on the word like a lifeline. "Business. So that's what you're here to discuss?" If only he could somehow return the situation to some normality, steer the conversation towards the parameters of the deal, then everything would be alright. He hoped.

Sanouk crossed his arms, his hard eyes flicking around the room. "I've come to renegotiate. Things have changed."

Ethan's hands balled into fists, a wave of anger rushing up and almost blinding him. No! He'd done everything right so far, planned every detail.

This wasn't supposed to happen.

Externally, he played dumb. "I—I don't understand. We agreed on a price months ago. And yesterday, I thought Lek said—"

"You thought wrong. Besides, a lot can happen in three months. Market value changes, overheads increase. The agreed price has risen—by thirty per cent."

Ethan watched in dismay as the two enforcers raised their guns a little to emphasise the futility of argument. He felt like he was falling into an ever-darkening nightmare, where all his worst fears were suddenly coming true.

He needed to do something. Fast. "Well—this is a surprise," he stammered. "I'm afraid, with such a large price increase, you'll need to give me time to reconsider, try and scrape more finance together." He looked at each of the granite faces in turn, not a relenting expression or flicker of mercy among them.

It was then that Ethan realised there would be no leniency, no chance to back down.

This was it, their final offer.

Sanouk confirmed his fears. "Normally, I would give you a chance to 'reconsider', as you say—after all, I'm a reasonable man." He smiled, his face almost appearing human.

But the next second, his expression reverted to its hard, impersonal mask, hatred once more shuttering his eyes.

Ethan shivered.

"However, I'm afraid that I'm a little short of time right now. The authorities have been snooping around, asking questions." Sanouk glared over at Bella, his dark eyes narrow slits of accusation. "I don't suppose anyone has spoken to them in a moment of weakness?"

Bella's face turned even paler, her eyes sliding shut. Ethan thought she was going to faint.

Instead, she looked across at him, her expression a mixture of confusion, fright, and a peculiar resolution. "What's this about, Ethan?"

He opened his mouth, but was quickly silenced by a cold metal jab in the ribs.

"I don't believe Miss Whitman needs to know all the details," Sanouk announced with menacing calm. "Particularly since she may not be with us for long." He stuck out a hand towards one of his henchmen, who passed him a deadly-looking revolver.

The room was deathly silent as Sanouk inserted one hollow-tipped bullet into a chamber, then spun the cartridge around with a metallic *whir*.

Surely he wasn't planning to ... Ethan's growing sense of dread felt like it was about to strangle him.

"I hear you're a gambling man, Mr Gray," Sanouk mocked. "How would you like to play a game of roulette with the lady's life?"

"You can't be serious!" Ethan blurted out.

Bella's face was now completely blanched, and she had begun to wobble a little on her feet.

"Would I joke with you?" Sanouk's voice was deadly calm. "Either you tell me now that you'll find a way to pay the higher price—I'll need it within twenty-four hours, of course—or your friend here will have to pay the *ultimate* price."

His mirthless chuckle ran up Ethan's spine, chilling

him to the core. For one futile second, his mind raced wildly with plans to escape, before succumbing to frozen terror.

Sanouk raised the gun at Bella.

Ethan closed his eyes and waited.

Chapter 33

Krista, please stop pacing. Let's go out to the pool—have a swim and take your mind off this—you'll feel much better."

Krista looked up at the sound of Sophie's gentle urging. "You're probably right," she sighed, "but I don't think I can relax right now. My best friend's in danger—and I can't do anything to help!" Pushing down a sob, she flopped back onto the bed. "Do you think God really hears us? Does He actually answer our prayers?"

Sophie sat down on the bed next to Krista. "I believe He does," she said, tucking some stray copper-coloured strands behind her ear. "I was raised in the Catholic church, and my mother taught me to pray. I still often do." She smiled. "I remember that it says somewhere in the Bible that if you believe, nothing is impossible. It even says that you could tell a mountain to move into the sea—and if you truly believed, it would."

"You're not teasing me, are you?" Krista frowned. She'd heard that passage somewhere before, but had dismissed it as a fable, an old wives' tale.

"I'm serious," Sophie said. "That's what it says, and I believe it."

"Well, I don't think I'd start with mountains right away," Krista grinned in spite of herself. "Maybe something a little smaller." Her voice sobered. "Like having an angel fly down and pluck Bella out of wherever she is now, away from that horrible Ethan."

"You've got to have faith, remember," Sophie said with a gentle smile.

Krista stood and walked over to the window. "*Knowing* and *doing* are two completely different things."

A strong wind had whipped up the waves into choppy peaks, mirroring the turmoil in her heart. Would she ever be able to handle situations like Jennifer, and even Sophie? Face them head-on with calm faith?

Krista sighed, resolving to ask Bella's mum about it after this was all over, and her friend was back safely.

If she ever would be.

She set her jaw resolutely. She had to believe.

Jay was just about to push his way through the barricade, risking arrest—or worse—when the police officer relented.

"Alright," he said with a clipped tone. "You can speak to the captain of our Special Operations Unit. Come with me."

Thanks, God, Jay breathed silently as he followed the officer past the barricade and up to a distinguished Thai man in uniform.

The Special Operations captain, although in conversation with a worried-looking man, gave Jay an appraising stare.

Jay straightened up a little, trying to appear more credible—anything to grant him an audience with the captain. And get him through the closed glass hotel doors.

The captain raised his hand, cutting off the anxious speaker mid-sentence, and exchanged some rapid words with the first officer.

Jay didn't have a clue what they were saying, but could detect overt annoyance in the officer's tone.

Great! I'm about to be thrown out on my ear.

But then the captain motioned him closer, and addressed him in perfect English. "My officer told me you insisted on seeing me. How can you assist our operation?" His expression was serious, a small frown line between his dark eyes.

"Thank you for your time, sir. The officer wouldn't tell me what was happening here"—Jay glanced at the man to his left, resisting the urge to glare—"but I do know that an Australian drug dealer is staying at this hotel, and he could be involved."

The Special Operations captain rubbed his chin, his eyes darkening. "What is this man's name? And how do you know him?"

"Ethan Gray," Jay blurted, not surprised to hear the sharp intake of breath from the officer, or see the chief's jaw tense.

"He's the editor of an Australian magazine. I have a police detective friend in Australia who identified Gray as a drug dealer from some photos I sent him."

"And your connection with Gray?"

"I'm a contract photographer for his magazine, and my colleague, Bella Whitman was writing an article for him, but"—he paused, swallowing past the tension in his throat—"but I think she may be in danger. She was meeting him here for lunch."

His revelation initiated a brisk interchange between the men, the captain barking orders into a radio.

Jay's heart pounded harder. The two situations were obviously connected. They may even have been preparing to go after Gray.

He continued to pray silently—desperately—as he was led through the hotel entrance and over to where the members of the Special Operations Unit were gathered, their faces determined, weapons drawn.

They seemed to be taking huge precautions to capture one man, Jay wondered. Maybe the situation was worse than—

He cut off the thought. There was probably no sense worrying about everything that could go wrong until he found out the facts. Which, he hoped, would be any time now.

The unit filed quickly through the door to the stairwell. Several other officers, along with Jay, waited behind in the lobby. It was now devoid of all guests, who had either been already evacuated where possible, or shut safely in their rooms.

Jay's task—once the Special Operations Unit secured the room and the danger was past—was to identify Bella and verify her story.

Jay thanked God for the tenth time that he'd made it here before the raid, alerted the police to the presence of an innocent bystander. Otherwise, Bella could have been arrested and hauled off to prison with Ethan.

Jay was determined not to let that happen—or allow any other harm to come to the woman he now knew he couldn't live without.

He stood off to the side a little as the other officers listened to a radio receiver. All was quiet for a short moment, and Jay even felt himself begin to relax a little.

Then the officers suddenly came to life, as the radio transmitted the unmistakeable sounds of silenced gunfire, a loud pounding on a door, and shouting in Thai—*"Dtam rùat! Police!"*

Jay's heart thumped wildly. He couldn't quite believe this was actually real, a living nightmare! It was easy to trust in God when life was going fine. Even when stress built and things went wrong, he could believe that God was faithful, still in control.

But this ...

Jay was now standing in the huddle of policemen around the receiver, ears straining for any indication of what was happening upstairs. Part of him wished he was up there in the middle of it all, to perhaps catch a glimpse of Bella as they burst into the room, see if she was safe.

If he did, though, he'd just be in the way. The siege unfolding was totally out of the league of a photographer. It was nothing like tackling an intruder or chasing a hit-man—even if he did get shot in the process.

If he tried to venture anywhere near Ethan's room upstairs, Jay realised he probably would be shot again, either by the criminals or police. They distrusted Jay as much as he was wary of them.

Yet he was trusting them to rescue Bella from the clutches of a drug lord.

It wasn't enough. Jay suddenly knew—with a clarity

that surprised and terrified him—that he would have to be involved somehow. He had to make the police understand that if they barged into the room and started firing at everything that moved, Bella would be killed.

She was already in enough danger just meeting with Ethan, now that the police raid was in full swing.

Jay's eyes slid shut at the overwhelming hopelessness of the situation, then breathed a desperate prayer for courage.

He wouldn't—couldn't—allow the woman he loved to go through this alone.

Somehow, he had to get up there.

Zzipp! Zzipp! Sanouk heard the muffled sound of a silenced bullet, and tensed. Either Yai, their look-out, had just disposed of someone, or—

Thump! Thump!

He turned, startled, at a pounding on the door. Yai must be alerting them to an intrusion.

Sanouk stopped with his hand on the doorknob, eyes narrowed. Yai had an access card. There was no need for him to knock.

Something was wrong.

There was more pounding, then a shouted command. The police!

Sanouk bolted away from the door, furious that there'd been no warning from downstairs. Annan must have been captured! And he'd bet on his life that those silenced shots he just heard had been aimed at Yai.

Mind racing, he considered the options: he could grab Gray and Bella, use them as hostages—or save them as bargaining collateral for later, after a shoot-out with the authorities.

Sanouk was feeling unusually confident today. He made a split-second decision to try his luck. "Shut them in the bathroom," he shouted at his men as he reached for his weapons, "the police are here!"

Luk shoved Gray and the woman through the *en suite* doorway and slammed it shut, while Tong joined Sanouk on the floor beside the bed, which would act as a shield between them and the doorway.

Breathing hard, Sanouk studied his men. "There's bound to be a whole team of them outside," he whispered harshly, as Luk squatted down beside him. "You got plenty of firepower?"

His men both nodded—Tong with apparent anticipation, and Luk with thinly-veiled fear of the unknown.

Sanouk went on, feeling a strange sense of detachment. Things had never been this close—so threatening—before, but he was well prepared. Including being ready to make sacrifices.

"They probably know we have hostages, so that should slow them up a bit. In any case," he paused, emphasising the gravity of the words, "you know what you have to do."

They both nodded again. All his men were well-trained, to the point of dying for their master.

Which was what Sanouk was asking of them now.

He looked back at the closed door, wondering at the silence. There was no other entrance to the room, so the assault would have to come through there.

And hopefully it would be soon. The tension was fraying his nerves.

Slam!

The door hurtled open, followed by a barrage of gunfire. Sanouk barely had time to get off a few shots, before blackness claimed him.

Chapter 34

Jay's heart hammered wildly in his chest as he began to inch towards the stairwell, eyes fixed intently on the closed door. He couldn't quite believe he was actually attempting to disobey police orders and walk upstairs into the middle of a raid.

But if it meant he could somehow protect Bella—even catch a glimpse of her and make sure she was alright—then he was willing to do something crazy.

The police officers were still gathered in the lobby around the radio receiver. They didn't even notice as Jay left the group and began creeping silently towards his goal. Twenty feet to go, now fifteen, ten, five ...

He was reaching his hand out to grab the door handle, ready to push the door open slowly so that the hinges wouldn't squeak, when—

"Sir! Stop!"

Oops. He was sprung.

One of the policemen touched Jay on the shoulder. He turned slowly, half-expecting the officer to slap him in handcuffs.

Instead, he said, "Please wait for me. The room has now been secured, and I'll escort you upstairs to identify Ms Whitman."

Jay's heart missed a beat. He hoped the officer meant that Jay would be introducing Bella as Ethan's employee, corroborating her version of events—and not identifying a body.

"Help, God!" he whispered, praying more fervently for His protection with each step they climbed.

Bella squeezed her eyes shut in terror, trying in vain to block out the sound of guns blazing, men shouting and falling to the floor. And now, after daring to open the bathroom door when all was finally quiet, she could see blood. So much blood!

Strangely, she felt like an extra in a horror movie—on the edge of the action, yet part of it.

But even with her heart racing as she quickly scanned the room, a quiet calm seemed to envelop her heart. Somehow, she knew that this wasn't the end. God was in control.

Ethan was slumped beside her on the tiles, staring straight ahead in shock. She thought of shaking him out of it and telling him it was all over. But maybe it would be good for him to take it all in, realise what he'd set in motion.

"Police!"

Suddenly, the room was filled with uniformed officers, guns raised in readiness. Bella's first instinct was to lift her arms in surrender, even though she was innocent and unarmed.

"Please, get me out of here!" Her voice sounded unnaturally high-pitched, almost hysterical. Now that the prospect of rescue was here, she felt herself unravelling from shock.

Two Thai officers headed straight over to her. "Bella Whitman?" one asked in accented English.

"Yes," she managed to choke out.

Steadying her with strong arms, the men led her out of the room, where she promptly collapsed against the hallway wall.

The officers made sure she was comfortable, before disappearing into the room once more. Other Special Forces personnel milled around the doorway, speaking into radios, or talking to each other in rapid Thai.

Bella inhaled a shuddering breath in an attempt to

calm herself

calm herself. She couldn't quite believe that the nightmare was over. Still, she was extremely glad they'd be heading back home to Australia soon, away from intruders, attackers, people putting guns to her head.

Away from everything here. Except ...

She raised her head then, and saw him coming towards her down the hall.

"Jay!"

In an instant he was crouching down beside her, crushing her in an embrace. "Bella! Thank God! Are you okay?" His eyes were shadowed with a mix of concern and relief.

"I was so scared!" she felt herself say against his chest, all her strength suddenly deserting her. "There were these three men with guns, and I'm sure they were going to kill Ethan and me if the police hadn't come when they did. I still can't believe it's all over, and that you're here!"

Bella knew she was verging on hysteria, or shock—or a combination of both. So she was glad for the distraction of Jay's kiss, drawing on the strength of his arms around her. For just a brief moment, she was transported back to the beach at Vila, feeling all her senses consumed by Jay. Except now, unlike that night, he was holding nothing back.

When she finally pulled away reluctantly, Bella smiled up at him in spite of herself. "I feel better already."

Jay's voice was tender. "There's plenty more where that came from. But for now I'm just glad you're safe, that God rescued you out of this mess Ethan got you into."

He looked around at the crowd of policemen filling the hallway, then back at Bella. "Speaking of the devil—where is he?"

Bella shrugged her shoulders and frowned. "I don't know. The last time I saw him was just before two policemen helped me out of the room, after the shoot-out."

She hadn't given Ethan a second thought—(and if it wasn't for her newfound faith in Christ, and His teachings of forgiveness and loving others, she doubted she'd be bothered with him ever again.)

(Sorry, please delete the first time

Ethan could feel himself descending into shock as he sat slumped against the cold bathroom tiles. He had some awareness that Bella had called out for help and was now gone, and that a Thai Special Ops officer had come to escort him out also. Ethan had asked for a minute to calm himself, so the officer had left to stand outside the bathroom door—no doubt guarding one of their chief suspects, Ethan thought glumly.

So here he sat, shuffling on the cold floor, an idea borne of desperation beginning to percolate. With all the flurry of activity in the room beyond the bathroom, perhaps he could manage to slip out unnoticed, make his escape.

But how would a tall, suit-clad Westerner blend into his surroundings? Especially since he would surely be a 'person of interest' in any subsequent police investigations.

But it appeared luck was on his side. One of the Thai officers had been struck down in the gunfight, just outside the bathroom door. The paramedics had checked for any signs of life, before covering him with a sheet.

Now, if he could just manage to distract the guard outside his door and drag the body into the bathroom without anyone noticing ...

Ethan shuffled towards the doorway, ready to speak to the officer, but the man had left, was talking to a paramedic across the room. Perfect.

Just over a minute later, Ethan quickly surveyed himself in the bathroom mirror. With the Special Ops uniform and headgear on, he thought he could just about fool them enough to escape. Too bad about his fair skin, though. Or the fact that the trousers were at least two inches too short, revealing a wide band of black socks at the bottom. For once, his height was a definite liability.

With a quick intake of breath, he cautiously peered out into his hotel room. A group of paramedics was wheeling an unconscious Sanouk out into the hall, while more were working on someone lying on the bed. Other paramedics and police officers were checking the dead men on the floor.

Everyone looked busy. Now was his chance.

SLIGHTLY FARFETCHED!!

SANDRA PEUT

He walked into the room with purpose, trying to appear as if he belonged there, was merely popping out the door for a moment. Past the paramedics, past the police officers, past—

"Ja bpai nai?"

Ethan swore silently. He kept his head down, motioning with one hand towards the door, as if he had urgent business outside.

And then by some cosmic coincidence, a paramedic called on the police officer for assistance in lifting a loaded stretcher. The man turned away.

Two steps later, and Ethan was free. He disappeared down the hallway, leaving a career and life in tatters, his heart full of bitterness and hate.

"I can't believe this is all over!" Bella sighed as she rested her head back on the seat in the airport lounge, and closed her eyes. It had been a whirlwind couple of days. She'd given statements to seemingly scores of Thai policemen and investigators, from several different departments.

She felt her forehead crease in a frown, a build-up of tension in her neck and shoulders. The whole ordeal seemed like a lifetime ago—someone else's lifetime. She wouldn't have believed just a month ago that she—a mere freelance writer—would be travelling through exotic islands, tangling with a hit-man, and being taken hostage by a Thai drug lord!

And Jay ... Meeting him was the best part of her adventure. *Apart from finding God, of course.* Just the thought of His constant peace prompted Bella to offer a short prayer of thanks—for His protection, His blessings, His love. She smiled at the irony of it all. Here she was, just coming through the most stressful situation of her life, and yet she felt this foreign, God-given calm.

"What are you so happy about?" a voice next to her asked.

Bella opened her eyes and grinned as Jay squeezed her hand. "Caught me napping again, huh?"

"I thought you were too young for a 'nanna nap'," he teased, then narrowed his eyes in feigned suspicion. "Just how old did you say you were again?"

Bella swatted him playfully, feeling much more awake now. "Cheeky thing. I'm glad to see you've still got your sense of humour, even after all that's happened." She glanced down at her watch. "Speaking of joking around, where's your partner-in-crime, Krista? Our plane leaves in half-an-hour."

"I'm guessing she should be back any minute. She just went to get a juice."

Bella was glad for the chance to be alone together. It had seemed like ages since she and Jay had had a decent conversation, just the two of them. She hadn't even had a chance to tell him that she'd finally found God.

Now seemed like the perfect opportunity. "Jay," she began seriously, "I've been meaning to tell you something important."

He looked over at her, blue eyes expectant.

"I've met Someone."

A shadow crossed his face. Oops, bad choice of words.

"Not another man," she hurried on. "Well, not on this earth, anyway. I've met Jesus, Jay. I finally understand now what it's like to have a personal relationship with God, to know that He's wiped my past clean. That I can have a better future, a hope."

"Thank the Lord!" Jay almost whooped, his face beaming. "I've been praying—I just didn't expect God to answer so soon. Great faith, hey?" he chuckled, squeezing her hand tighter.

"You weren't the only one praying," Bella reminded him. "My mum's been after me for years, and my brother. I guess I didn't have a chance!"

"You know, this is great news, for more than one reason. Now maybe *we've* got a chance," Jay said softly, his gaze unwavering.

Bella felt her cheeks grow warm. She'd been hoping—praying—for things to work out between them. And now maybe they would.

Jay cleared his throat, a little nervously, she thought. "I've got something to tell you, too, Bella." He stroked her hand gently, starting a tiny shudder up her back. "I've been thinking and praying a lot about you, about our relationship. I know we've had our ups and downs over the past few weeks. But when you were taken hostage everything became clearer to me."

He grabbed her other hand then, enveloping it with his warm fingers. Bella felt that same warmth spread right through her as she waited for Jay to continue. Just what was he about to say?

"I know now that I couldn't imagine going through life without you, couldn't bear to lose you." His gaze was tender, a slight smile playing on his lips. Bella felt her chest tighten.

"I guess what I'm trying to say is—Bella, will you marry me?"

Bella took in a quick breath of surprise. She thought he was going to discuss *some*thing about their future together, but a marriage proposal was more than she'd expected—or dared hope for!

Jay was looking at her, a question in those bright blue eyes. Bella started laughing, sure she sounded almost delirious. "I guess you want an answer, then."

"That'd be nice," he chuckled. "I'm hoping it's good news."

"Well, that depends," she teased. "If you're talking about 'for richer or poorer, in sickness and in health' sort of stuff, including seeing me with my hair all fuzzy every morning—" he squeezed her hand, seeming to indicate that he'd like that very much—"well then, this *is* good news."

Jay pulled her closer to him then, his eyes never leaving her face. "Even in fifty years' time, I'll still be looking forward to waking up next to you," he whispered.

Bella surrendered herself to the moment, the nearness of him, the touch of his lips on hers. It almost felt like a little piece of heaven on earth.

"You still haven't said 'yes', yet," Jay reminded, tenderly reaching out to tug one of her curls.

Bella managed to get out just one word before he claimed her lips—and her heart—once more. "Yes!"

Epilogue

Two months later

"Mmm ..." Bella wriggled her toes in the warm sand and sighed contentedly. Along with Jay, Krista, and Ryan, she'd spent the perfect day: a long, lazy lunch by the ocean at Wellington Point, followed by an afternoon swimming in the waves.

Now she was happy to sit back and watch Jay and Ryan try their hand at kite-surfing, and wait for Krista to return from getting another towel from the car. The guys were spending more time *in* the water—trying to get their kites up—than surfing *on* it. They still seemed to be having fun, though.

She gave Jay a wave as he glanced over momentarily. Just the sight of him—his hair and bare torso glistening with water droplets—almost made her heart skip a beat.

And now he had moved here to Brisbane to live. Jay was only too happy to leave the congestion and crowds of Sydney behind, had assured her that being in Queensland would give him better opportunities for his photography.

Bella couldn't be happier.

Thankfully, everything had fallen into place for her during the past couple of months. After doing such a great job on the day spa feature, she'd been offered a position as a staff writer for *Healthy Lifestyle* by the new editor—a no-nonsense woman in her fifties who'd been appointed by the magazine's new publishing company, and who was poles apart from Ethan Gray.

Ethan had disappeared, and despite an extensive search across several countries, the authorities hadn't been able to locate him. Bella found herself praying for him occasionally, especially that he would come to know God just as she had. Surely, if anything could bring him to the point of recognising his need for God, a life of running from the law as a fugitive would.

Along with work, Bella had been busy making wedding plans. Jay and she had chosen Valentine's Day as the date for the big day, which also happened to be her father's birthday. Bella smiled sadly. He would have loved to have walked her down the aisle.

But she knew she would see her dad again someday, in heaven. And as she gazed out at the summer sun's late afternoon rays glittering on the water, Bella imagined that heaven must be something like this. A beautiful place, full of freedom—the fullness of which she was just beginning to get a taste.

If freedom was a colour, Bella decided as she tipped her face up to the sky, it would be blue. As blue as Jay's eyes looking at her lovingly, as blue as the cornflowers in her grandmother's garden.

And freedom, just like the sparkling Pacific Ocean before her, had no end.

The Author

Sandra Findlay Peut began writing stories for her school friends when she was a young girl. Growing up, she was a voracious reader, with friends and family describing her as always having her face buried in a book! A trained dietitian, Sandra has worked in the fields of both nutrition and women's health promotion. Through her writing and speaking to women's groups about nutrition and life-balance, she desires to encourage women to reach their full potential in life.

Her scribing background includes writing articles on health and fitness and parenting for several magazines, as well as being a sub-editor for an Australian girls' magazine. In addition, her job in public relations requires her to produce media releases on an on-going basis. Sandra is also a member of both Faith Writers and Omega Writers online groups.

She and her husband have four small children, and are blessed to live in regional Queensland, Australia, in a house with views of the ocean.

Blue Freedom is Sandra's first novel, and won third place in the Rose & Crown New Novels Competition 2009. She is currently working on another romance, this time for the Young Adults genre. Watch her web site for more details:

www.sandrapeut.com

PREVIEW SAMPLE CHAPTER:

A FLIGHT DELAYED

by

KC LEMMER

Rose & Crown
A Flight Delayed
KC LEMMER

A Flight Delayed is a quirky, exotic tale you'll love! When career-focused Amanda McCree discovers that her controlling Great Aunt, as a last request, has especially asked that Amanda carry her Aunt's remains to Cape Town, Amanda is furious. The last thing she wants is to be forced to visit her parents there, after so many years of bitterness over their rejection. To top it all, she finds herself stranded at her stopover in Bulawayo due to fuel shortages! But through the love of a family that takes her into their game reserve home, the economic crisis of Zimbabwe, and a man who daily lives with his own guilt and heartbreak, Amanda realises that God is more interested in her than she had ever thought. In the heart of the African bush, as she is let into the hurting world of the handsome Caleb Jacobs and his family, Amanda is forced to face her own family divisions and to depend upon the God she thought had failed her.

"A delightful read which incorporates intrigue and romance and holds a forthright Christian message. The author writes knowledgeably about Zimbabwe and provides convincing glimpses of the country's natural beauty."
— Diana Valerie Clark, Ordained Pastor

"Fascinating story! Follow Amanda McCree as her life takes some unexpected, unplanned twists and turns on an unwanted journey to Africa. Through these, she learns the truth about her family and regains her faith in God, who shows her He is a Father of the fatherless, a defender of the widow, is holy in His habitation, and that He sets the solitary in families (Ps. 68:5)."
— Dr. Karen Joy King , Christian Leadership University professor, journalist, Counselor, Musician

A FLIGHT DELAYED

by KC LEMMER

Chapter 1.

She presided over the fireplace in death, just as she had presided over whatever room she had occupied in her life. The fact that she was incapable of speaking did little to lighten their despondent hearts. Even in the dim light, Amanda could see her sister's shoulders slumped forward wearily. Great Aunt Marie had always had that effect on those who'd been in her company for longer than an hour.

The sole light in the room came from a fine china lamp on the mantelpiece. It illuminated the green alabaster jar in an eerie way, especially as its shadow fell across the portrait behind it—Aunt Marie's portrait.

The whole effect was sinister.

Just like Aunt Marie!

Amanda shuddered, rubbing her upper arms briskly to rid herself of the sudden chill. She glanced over at Polly, so still and pale, with dark rings under her eyes. Polly wasn't handling this well—or was it the pregnancy? Aunt Marie and a pregnancy were a super-bad combination, Amanda thought, pitying her sister's misfortunes.

"So what are we going to do?" she asked, moving slowly over to the window. It was such a clear day that the Ochils looked like they were just minutes away, rather than all the way across the Firth of Forth. On a day like today, Amanda would have happily driven across the bridge and gone jogging up one of the mountain paths. Anything but this.

She turned back to the dim room. All she could see was a dark huddle in the chair, until her eyes re-adjusted to the lighting.

As Polly stood, she could make out the familiar pointy chin, fluffy pink slippers, and bulging stomach. It was impossible to know what was going through her sister's mind as she crossed over to the mantelpiece and touched the alabaster jar gingerly.

The stomach turned to face her, exchanging the distorted shape for a slim one. From this aspect, one might never know Polly was almost eight months pregnant. It was amazing how shadows and angles could hide the truth.

Once again, Amanda gratefully rejoiced that it wasn't herself. She frowned as she watched her sister gently rub the round bulge, her focus once again on Aunt Marie's ashes.

Amanda flopped into the rocking chair that her sister had just vacated. It was still warm.

Polly tapped the jar. "What choice do we have?"

Was she checking to see that Aunt Marie really was dead?

"Great Aunt Marie was a tough nut, Pol, but I think she is well and truly gone," Amanda remarked dryly. "We no longer have to live under her wrath and dictatorship. We are finally free."

"Oh, Mandy!" Polly scolded with a shaky laugh, "she wasn't all that bad..."

"Says you!" Amanda exclaimed. "You didn't have her stalking you at every possible chance, waiting to pounce, or start an argument. She could never pass up an opportunity to begin some hullabaloo with me!"

Polly didn't argue. She smiled sweetly and tapped the jar with a little more confidence. "Well, it doesn't change the fact that we have to come to some decision about what to do with her. It's a pity Dad and Mum aren't here to sort this out."

Rolling her eyes, Amanda bit back her sharp retort. She wouldn't upset Polly further, not tonight.

"Well, they're not, and that's all there is to it." The words still came out in a snap, despite her resolve.

Sighing, Amanda pushed out of the chair and paced restlessly to the window again. The little china lamp made Aunt Marie too much of a focus. Growing more and more angry, Amanda crossed the room and with an open hand slapped the main switch on. The room was flooded with sweet light; the china lamp was just a dim glow now.

Glaring balefully at the jar, she shook a finger at Polly in warning: "This won't be the last request from Aunt Marie; there's *always* something more when it comes to her!"

Polly began to shake her head in defence of Aunt Marie, but stopped as she met Amanda's quelling gaze. The two sisters stared at each other, green eyes sharp as they bored down into the softer blue ones. They had the same curling black hair and big eyes, but beyond that the similarities ended.

Polly was slightly shorter than Amanda, and more rounded, thanks to the pregnancy. Amanda, at five foot seven, was her senior by two years. Some of the older church folks said Amanda took after her father and Polly after their mother... *But what would she know of that?* she thought bitterly, reflecting on their years of separation.

Polly was gentle and thought too well of people. Amanda considered that it was just as well she'd had a big sister who tended to become more cynical than anything else when in doubt. There were countless memories of times when she had stood up for Polly, defended Polly, protected Polly. She'd needed to be tough. So had they all, what with Dad and Mum never at home. And as far as Amanda was concerned, those two years between their ages had made all the difference in the shaping of their characters. Polly friendly and warm, Amanda reserved and suspicious. Polly positive and enthusiastic, Amanda driven and independent. And here they were, once again, the two of them trying to make decisions that should never have been their responsibility. And, once again, Polly was looking to her for leadership.

Heart heavy, Amanda rubbed her right cheekbone. If she had her way she would smash the jar out in the backyard, or toss it over some cliff. Maybe a holiday to the White Cliffs of Dover...? What a joy that experience would be! If nothing else, at least some of her own tension would be released.

Scrutinising the tired features before her, Amanda bitterly pushed aside thoughts of her parents. They hadn't been around physically in times of need, and she certainly wasn't going to let them occupy any space in her mind either. It was her time to make the call on what to do.

She tried to be gentle as she said, "Polly, there is no way we can get Aunt Marie's ashes back to Africa. It is an impossible request, and she knew it was too, the old crone. I can tell you this – I'm not going!"

Polly said nothing, her eyes on the red patterned carpet.

"It's true!" Amanda insisted, striding back to the window to glare out at the frosted grass. "The woman won't let us rest and get on with our lives. She planned this to rile us all up." An image of Polly's peaceful eyes sprang into mind. Giving a half-hearted laugh, Amanda corrected herself. "Or rather, to rile *me* up."

The bird tray under the spruce tree had one lone pigeon on it. There wasn't room for any others, judging by the size of the fat bird.

"Greedy thing."

A door banged just then, and the quick step in the hallway caused both women to turn as a slim man, just an inch taller than Amanda, pushed open the lounge door and grinned at them both.

"Hello hello, ladies!" His lively eyes were warm as he bent to give Polly a quick kiss. "You're both looking very subdued." He glanced over at Amanda, noting the fire in her eyes. "Or perhaps subdued isn't the best word to use?"

"We *are* a little put out," Polly admitted, leaning against her husband for support.

"Put out!" Amanda exploded. "I am *more* than put out." She turned on Sam. "Tell me you agree this is a ridiculous request. Great Aunt Marie wants her ashes taken back to Africa! For goodness sake, the woman was only there for the first three years of her life. And what's more, she had the nerve to go as far as to quote some Scripture about Joseph asking for his bones to be taken back to Israel when the Israelites returned there from Egypt."

Sam's face twitched, and then, unable to hold it in, he chuckled, and was promptly rewarded with a firm warning nudge in his ribs.

"I'm sorry—" his smile broadened, "—but look at it from my point of view. Aunt Marie up to her usual pranks of winding up Amanda—and she can always do it. Why, Amanda is fairly bursting..."

"Sam," Polly hissed, "hush up!" She glanced cautiously at the scorching eyes of her sister and tried to be diplomatic. "I'm sure we can work this out sensibly. I'll get in touch with the family and tell them about the will, and then we will calmly come to a decision, alright?"

Hands on her expanding waist, Polly dared Amanda to argue—and for once, she won.

Ramming the car keys into the ignition five minutes later, Amanda laughed bitterly. "The family! Poor little Polly. Beats me how you're going to find Cobs' address, never mind get hold of the parents! And if you get Ruth to co-operate, that *will* be a miracle."

She twisted the key and felt the car shudder and then splutter into life. Shaking her dark curls, Amanda reached for the black gloves on the passenger seat and absently pulled them on, her thoughts clouded with Great Aunt Marie's request.

She just knew what was going to happen. Ruth and Cobs, if Polly located him at all, would both have some *very* valid excuse as to why they were not the right choice for Aunt Marie's mission. And Polly couldn't go, what with her being so near to delivering her baby. No one wanted their smooth little lives to be disrupted by one difficult old woman's request.

Would Polly tell Ruth and Cobs the truth – that Great Aunt Marie had actually asked for Amanda to go?

"Maybe we can just post the ashes and pay someone to bury them somewhere," Amanda mused, smiling thinly. "That'd get you hopping, Aunt Marie. Tit for tat! Or even better, let's just wait for Polly's children to grow up and we'll pass your message on to them. After all, it was generations later when Joseph's bones were finally carried to his homeland!"

Her shoulders sagged as the fight slowly slid out of her. Clutching the steering wheel, Amanda laid her forehead against its cold leather and groaned. "Oh God, why did this have to happen? You know it'll be me who has to go. They'll all think: 'Single Amanda with the good-natured boss she can wrap around her finger—*she'll* be available.' But please, God, I *really* don't want to go trekking across Africa. I have my job to do, deadlines to meet, a career to think about. I'm happy!"

Sighing heavily, she released the handbrake and pulled onto the road, guiding her car through the neat residential area. Her sister's neighbour looked up, from where she was pulling shopping bags out of the boot of her car, and waved. Flashing up a hand in response, Amanda glanced down at the Bible and the thick green folder on the passenger seat. It was five-fifteen. There was at least half an hour in which to run into the office before evening church.

And no Aunt Marie to whip me afterwards. Some of the heaviness lifted. *It's just a pity the office is right next door to the church.* Amanda felt faintly uncomfortable as she heard her thoughts. "Well, it *is* a little awkward if anyone sees me going into the office on a Sunday," she argued aloud, "even though this is crucial work that needs to be done."

When she reached Almond Avenue Amanda hesitated at the intersection, then steered the Fiesta into the back parking of the church. This would leave more parking spaces at the front for the elderly, she reasoned. It was much easier for them to go into the church from that entrance, wasn't it? Nothing furtive about it; she was being considerate.

A quick glance around showed the car park was deserted. Grabbing her office keys from the cubby-hole, Amanda picked up the green folder and slid cautiously out of her car, glad of the wintery darkness of the evening. The street lights gave a pretty orange glow that created a cosy effect, rather than an exposing light as in some more suspect districts.

Head held high, Amanda hopped the stairs up to the office block two at a time and punched in the door code to the office. Just half an hour in the office would relieve some of the pressure of work tomorrow.

"Amanda?" Her sister's voice was tinny across the telephone line.

Amanda silently groaned and shifted the phone to her other ear. Forcing a brightness into her voice she answered, "Polly, is that you? What's up?"

"I never saw you at church. I thought you were coming tonight?"

The disappointment in her sister's voice made

Amanda feel like a convicted sinner. "Oh Pol..." Amanda wriggled in her seat uncomfortably. "I did mean to come, I just got caught up." Her gaze flicked over the neat piles of paper, the desk lamp focussed on the single sheet in front of her, and the black laptop pushed over to the right of the paper.

Trying to sound open and interested she asked, "How was church? What was the sermon about?" She regretted the questions the moment they were out of her mouth.

"I was a wee bit distracted," she heard Polly admit.

Amanda fidgeted while she waited for Polly to ask Sam about the sermon. She heard his deep rumbled answer: "Jonah". Just great!

Lord, this had better not be You talking to me. This is not the same as Jonah's situation. Great Aunt Marie's ashes have nothing to do with warning a city of Your anger and impending destruction.

"Amanda, are you still there?"

Clearing her throat, Amanda nodded, before realising Polly wouldn't see her response, "Yeah, I'm here."

"Look, I managed to speak to Ruth, but I couldn't track down Cobs."

"No surprise there," Amanda muttered under her breath.

"Ruth is committed to her school until July holidays, but she said she really wants to be involved so she's willing to pay for the flight."

Amanda rolled her eyes. Ruth couldn't care two pence about Aunt Marie and her ashes and who went, except to clear her conscience and feel she was doing something. And Polly was swallowing the story hook, line, and sinker.

"Good news, though—I also got through to Dad. He and Mum agree we need to honour Aunt Marie's request."

Amanda's heart sank at her sister's soft words. It was all very well for Dad to talk; he was too far away to have to worry about it. As usual.

Scooting the lap top over, Amanda opened up a Spider Solitaire game. There was no way she was going to disrupt the smooth flow of her research work for even a few days. There would be jet lag, lost time...

"—So I've tentatively booked the first available flight."

What! Amanda froze, her knuckles whitening around the phone. "Look Polly, that's out of the question, in your condi—" She stopped short as her sister's words sank in.

There was silence on the other end of the phone. Amanda gulped nervously. She just *couldn't* go instead of Polly! Hand pressed over her mouth, Amanda closed her eyes—waiting.

"Sam's agreed." Polly's voice was small, small and scared. "I'm leaving the day after tomorrow—on Tuesday."

"Amanda McCree!" The triumphant bellow had Amanda clinging to a lamp post in fright. A diminutive figure emerged from the shadows of Amanda's car, her cane knocking against the sidewalk as she approached.

"Mrs May!" Amanda gasped, squinting through the darkness as she recognised the familiar shape.

"That's right, hen." The little woman reached up and caught Amanda's jaw firmly in her small wrinkled hand. "When I saw your car, and the light on up in your office, I just knew you were bunking church."

Flushing, Amanda tried not to shift under the scrutinising gaze of her former teacher. She opened her mouth with some excuse but was instantly shut down.

"Don't argue with me; we both know who always won the war in the end." Mrs May clucked her tongue, as though the memories were fond ones. Amanda could only remember nightmarish fights with this strong-willed teacher who refused to budge one way or another. She had dreaded Biology lessons, which was probably why she had been more difficult than usual in them. The fact that Mrs May and Great Aunt Marie had been great pals had not helped raise Amanda's regard for the woman.

Amanda backed out of the firm grip and circled cautiously around Mrs May, to her car. "What are you doing out so late?" she queried, unlocking the back door of her car to lay down the green folder, which was now joined by a matching blue one—her current research on children suffering from depression. The fact that Mrs May was stalking around in the dark near her car, waiting for her, was possibly worse than a car-jacker hiding there, Amanda thought, slamming the door shut.

She turned back to the little eyes and sagging cheeks, wearily wondering what the persistent woman wanted this time. She had long since wondered if Aunt Marie and Mrs May were part of a conspiracy, with the sole goal of imbuing her with their opinions and concerns—usually on spiritual matters.

"I just wanted to give you this," Mrs May said, peering up at Amanda and leaning heavily on her cane as she held out a slim white envelope. "Open this when you have time."

Insides churning, Amanda suspiciously accepted the letter.

"God will get you, my lassie." Mrs May reached up in a loving gesture to touch Amanda's cheek.

Amanda jerked back before she realised what was happening. The hurt that filled Mrs May's eyes was awful to see.

"Mrs May!" Amanda was horrified at her own response. "I—I'm so sorry. I don't know..." She stared at the pile of grey curls below her, trying to find something to say—anything that might explain her appalling response.

"It's alright Amanda." Mrs May shook her head,

and then glanced up. Her eyes were watery. “You are in my prayers, Amanda...” She hesitated, as though suddenly unsure what to say, and then catching Amanda’s hand briefly she whispered, voice breaking: “I truly care about what happens to you.”

Hugely disturbed, Amanda watched the little frame shuffle along the dark car park and head up the lane behind the church. She watched until Mrs May was out of sight, and then slid slowly into the driver’s seat. Out of the corner of her eyes she could see her still-zipped up Bible lying where she had left it.

# # #

TITLE: A Flight Delayed
AUTHOR: KC Lemmer
PAGES: 256

ISBN: 978-0-9555283-8-5
(9780955528385)

MORE FROM ROSE & CROWN INSPIRATIONAL ROMANCE:

EMBRACING CHANGE: Sarah and Luke were about to move from South Africa to an exciting new life in New Zealand when Luke was brutally murdered. Sarah takes his ashes to NZ and starts afresh, but can her bitterness and hatred be overcome by the love of a new man? She finds she must return to her home country and face her demons, before facing her future. Brilliantly written by Debbie Roome, an emotional high-ride.

A FLIGHT DELAYED: *En route* to South Africa, Amanda finds herself stranded in present-day Zimbabwe and suddenly taken under the wing of an eccentric family on a safari game park. Finding out about the realities of life under Mugabe's regime, she is faced with challenges which change her heart and soul before she reaches her final destination. KC Lemmer has captured the essence of current-day Zimbabwe in this lovely bush setting.

BLUE FREEDOM: Bella thinks her life is taking a turn for the better when she lands a writing assignment that takes her on a journey across tropical islands, with two new men on her tail—if you don't count the contract killer, that is! A hair-raising thriller that chases our lovers across the South Pacific as rapidly as the professional assassin who is following them. Sandra Peut's love of exotic locations will light up your world, adding intrigue and drama too.

REDEMPTION ON THE RED RIVER: Cheryl Riley Cain offers an historical adventure romance set in 1800's America. Anna, a young teacher, takes a steamer downriver to Indian country, to teach pupils who barely understand schooling, with a war raging around them and an Indian vendetta that threatens her life. In the end she must choose between the man she almost married, and the man who has become her protector.

MORE FROM SUNPENNY PUBLISHING:

DANCE OF EAGLES: Explosive adventure set in 14th-century Africa, and in the 1970's bush war of Rhodesia-Zimbabwe. Tcana, daughter of a cattleherd, wife of a prince, high priestess of a new religion that rips apart her world; journalist Rebecca Rawlings, caught up centuries later in the remnants of Tcana's faith and a violent war of attrition; Peter Kennedy, commander of the famed Selous Scouts; his friend and right-hand man, Kuru—and Kuru's brother, trained as a top flight freedom fighter: the Mamba.

MY SEA IS WIDE: One man's journey, in his 70th year, to rediscover his purpose. In this beautifully lyrical work, with great depth of insight, internationally renowned missionary, trainer and speaker Rowland Evans takes us on a journey from Wales to the scatterlings of China and Tibet, and our lives are changed forever. Wondrously written, and lush with his love for the people and landscapes of all these lands. Thoughtful, thought-provoking, heart-searching, and definitely not to be missed!

THE MOUNTAINS BETWEEN: Blaenavon and Abergavenny surge to life in this vibrant, haunting, joyful masterpiece by Julie McGowan; a celebration of the Welsh people in the 1920s to '40s—a saga of two families and their communities, in a smorgasbord that keeps the pages in perpetual motion. It's a war story; a love story; a hate story; about the people of Wales, the people of the mountains and the valleys who formed the beating heart of that country in this chunk of Wales' lifetime.

GOING ASTRAY: At what precise moment does a church become a cult? Christine Moore writes a tense, gripping story of a family whose new community, meant to bring them into a life closer to that of the early church, becomes more and more of a jail. Their struggle to escape rips the family apart as the story builds to a terrifying climax. Told with empathy, insight, and great moments of humour, this book will get you thinking!

Lightning Source UK Ltd.
Milton Keynes UK
14 October 2010

161264UK00001B/13/P

9 780955 528354